# Death by Design

# Death by Design

## BARBARA NADEL

headline

First published in 2010 by
HEADLINE PUBLISHING GROUP

1

Cataloguing in Publication Data is available from the British Library

ISBN 978 0 7553 3567 1 (Hardback)
ISBN 978 0 7553 3568 8 (Trade paperback)

Typeset in Times New Roman by Palimpsest Book Production Limited,
Grangemouth, Stirlingshire

Printed and bound in Great Britain by
Clays Ltd, St Ives plc

Headline's policy is to use papers that are natural, renewable and recyclable
products and made from wood grown in sustainable forests. The logging and
manufacturing processes are expected to conform to the environmental
regulations of the country of origin.

HEADLINE PUBLISHING GROUP
An Hachette UK Company
338 Euston Road
London NW1 3BH

www.headline.co.uk
www.hachette.co.uk

To my son Alex and all his friends from John Cass – explorers of old Mark Lane and witnesses to its secrets. Also to Mike Wilkinson, one of the Mark Lane Two.

# Cast of Characters

*İstanbul*

**Çetin İkmen** – middle aged İstanbul police inspector

**Mehmet Suleyman** – İstanbul police inspector – İkmen's protégé

**Sergeant Ayşe Farsakoğlu** – İkmen's deputy

**Sergeant İzzet Melik** – Suleyman's deputy

**Dr Arto Sarkissian** – İstanbul police pathologist

**Commissioner Ardiç** – İkmen and Suleyman's boss

**Fatma İkmen** – Çetin İkmen's wife

**Tariq** – an Afghan boy working illegally in İstanbul

**Abdurrahman Iqbal** – a Pakistani migrant passing through the city


*Berlin*

**Wolfgang** – a German people trafficker


*London*

**Ahmet Ulker** – a businessman

**Maxine Ulker** – his wife

**Derek Harrison** – Ahmet Ulker's right hand man

**Ali Reza Hajizadeh** – an Iranian, Ahmet Ulker's driver

**Mustafa Kermani** – security guard at Ahmet Ulker's Hackney Wick factory

**Hadi Nourazar** – an Iranian cleric

**Abdullah Yigit** – owner of the Rize Guest House, Stoke Newington

**Wesley Simpson** – getaway driver

**Haluk Uner** – Mayor of London

**Acting Commissioner Dee** – of the Metropolitan Police

**Superintendent Wyre Williams** – Metropolitan Police

**Detective Inspector Patrick Riley** – Metropolitan Police

**Inspector Carla Fratelli** – Metropolitan Police

**Detective Inspector Roman** – Metropolitan Police

**Detective Inspector Hogarth** – Metropolitan Police

**Detective Constable Ball** – Metropolitan Police

**Sergeant Terry Springer** – İkmen's undercover handler

**Sergeant Ayşe Kudu** – Greater Manchester Police, seconded to the Metropolitan Police

**John Richards** – London Underground employee

**Fatima Khan** – young pregnant mother

**Sınan İkmen** – Çetin's eldest son, a GP in London\

**Fasika** – an Ethiopian illegal immigrant

# *Prelude*

---

*Tarlabaşı District, İstanbul*

'Don't!'

Inspector Çetin İkmen fixed the trembling figure in front of him with the most penetrating stare that he could muster and then, calmly, he repeated himself. 'Don't.'

The figure, a male not much older than a boy, clutched the hand grenade he was holding to his chest and began to cry. Tears, heated up by the adrenaline raging inside his thin, spotty cheeks, fell down into the wispy beard that was just about noticeable on his chin.

'Son, there's no need for anyone to die for the sake of a few fake Prada handbags,' İkmen said as he stepped just slightly forward towards the boy.

'You don't understand!'

'Counterfeit designer goods are big business,' İkmen said. 'I know that. Where are you from, son? You're a long way from home. What accent is that?'

He wasn't dressed like a Turk. Not even the country people dressed like this boy. A long white shirt over thin white trousers trimmed with gold thread at the ankles. He looked, to Çetin İkmen, rather more like a Pakistani or an Afghan than a local person. There was also his weird grammar and his accent which was clearly not that of a citizen of the Republic.

Noticing now that the policeman had moved forward slightly the boy shouted, 'Go back!'

İkmen, raising his hands in a gesture of submission, moved one pace backwards. 'Whatever you say.'

The crying continued. The shaking, if anything, became even more intense. İkmen noticed that behind the boy, on the wall of what appeared to be the office for this illegal factory, was a map of some sort. At the time he didn't register what it was, just as he didn't really take in anything else about the scene before him apart from the trembling boy.

'Son,' İkmen continued, 'don't harm yourself. There's no need. We can—'

'I will end in the hell!' The weeping eyes snapped open and he looked into the policeman's face with what could only be described as raw hatred. 'I must be rid of you or my soul is damned!'

Surrounded by fake Prada, Gucci and Louis Vuitton handbags, religious fundamentalism was not something İkmen had expected. But then he supposed that the slave labour that was used to make these things included all sorts of individuals.

'I—'

'Allahu Akbar!'

İkmen saw the boy's left hand remove the pin. He flung himself backwards just before the boy, and the little office he had been in, exploded.

# Chapter 1

Everyone in İstanbul had a fake something or other. Inspector
Çetin İkmen himself had been given a counterfeit Rolex watch
by his youngest son for his last, his fifty-seventh, birthday. The
child, Kemal, had purchased it from one of the many scruffy-
looking vendors of such things who plied their trade underneath
the Galata Bridge. As was typical of such purchases, the watch
had worked for a week, died and then been put into the drawer
of İkmen's office desk. There it would probably languish until
the policeman either retired or the watch itself met with some
sort of accident. At the other end of the scale, his daughters paid
not inconsiderable amounts of money for their fake Prada handbags and his son Bülent felt himself very dashing in his almost
perfect replica Police sunglasses. Forgeries, not least because the
tourists loved them, were a fact of life. Many young men and
women from the poorer suburbs of all the major cities, including
İstanbul, worked in the 'knock off' trade. They did so of their
own volition.

But in recent years things had changed. Not only in Turkey,
but across the world, the trade in forged goods had become a
multibillion-dollar industry. Controlled largely by criminal gangs
known loosely as 'mafias' (some could indeed be traced back to
the original Sicilian Cosa Nostra), these counterfeit businesses
were known to run sidelines in prostitution, money laundering,

drug dealing and contract killing. Many had dispensed with local cheap-ish labour in favour of slaves from poor former Warsaw Pact countries, South-east Asia or Africa. Illegal immigrants, desperate to escape the poverty of their own countries, would readily agree to work for nothing in return for a route into a country, like Turkey, on the doorstep of the European Union. What these people rarely knew was how long and hard they would be forced to work in order to pay off their 'debt'.

It had been an unseasonably stifling day in April when the İstanbul Police Department, via one of İkmen's colleagues, Inspector Mehmet Süleyman, had been tipped off about a possible slave factory in the rundown district of Tarlabaşı. Just seconds from the bright lights of the fashionable district of Beyoğlu, Tarlabaşı was a rabbit warren of tenements, illegal brothels and small-time drug dealing operations. It was also home to many, many migrants from the country as well as people from places very far from Turkey. Süleyman who, like İkmen, was principally concerned with the crime of murder, had met with his informant, as arranged, aboard one of the commuter ferries that shuttled people back and forth between the European and Asian sides of the city. The informant, a man known only as 'George', told the handsome policeman that the Tarlabaşı factory had been operating for some time. It produced mainly handbags and, although George didn't actually own up to having any sort of personal connection with the place, it was obvious to Süleyman that he had at some time worked there. Why George was talking to the police about the Tarlabaşı factory was because people were, he claimed, dying in there now. Mention was made of a young African girl who had died from exhaustion. Her body had apparently been disposed of in a fire up in the equally dodgy district of Edirnekapı. The bosses,

4

Turkish mafiosi, George reckoned, were bringing people into the country to work for them in record numbers.

'Like tissues, they use them to do one job and then they throw them away,' George said as the ferry passed beneath the pointed roofs and green gardens of the Topkapı Palace. 'I make things, Mr Süleyman. I make things that are not real or honest, but I do not kill people. I won't have anything to do with that. Not now, not ever.'

Süleyman nodded gravely, put his hand inside his elegant jacket pocket, took out his mobile phone and called Police Headquarters. By six o'clock that evening Süleyman, together with İkmen and a team of rather more junior officers, listened intently as their superior, Commissioner Ardiç, outlined how the operation against the illegal factory in Tarlabaşı was going to work.

It was just after dawn the following morning when they went in.

'Stay where you are and put your hands in the air!'

Even a cursory glance around the hot, seething factory floor was enough to convince İkmen that very few of those he was addressing could actually understand him. African, South-east Asian and what appeared to be Indian or Pakistani faces looked up at the squad of armed police officers who had just burst in upon them with confused and fearful expressions. Only two men, standing up between a couple of the rows of now silent sewing machines, looked as if they might be local. Clean, by the look of them, and pale in comparison to the others, these were probably the foremen of this terrible, sweating, stinking crew.

'You!' İkmen said, pointing to the closer of the two. 'Tell them to put their hands in the air!'

5

Everyone in the building had stopped working. Even those İkmen could now see were actually chained to their work benches had done that. But he and his colleagues needed to see exactly where all their hands were. After all, whether they were slaves or not, these workers would not welcome the police and what they represented, which was almost certain deportation back to their countries of origin.

'Tell them!' İkmen reiterated to the man who was now visibly trembling.

'I don't know what languages they speak!' he answered. 'They speak all sorts, they—'

'And you?' İkmen said as he turned his attention to the other pale man with his arms in the air.

'I don't know!' he said. Not obviously as frightened as his colleague, he added, 'How should we know? We just work here.'

'OK.' İkmen instructed his officers to go around the stinking shop floor and raise the arms of the workers themselves. As the uniformed men and women moved amongst the splintered wooden benches upon which the sewing machines stood, rats and mice scuttled towards the safety of the world outside.

'Who is in charge here?' İkmen asked as he watched a slow Mexican wave of raised hands begin in front of him. He looked at the two clearly Turkish foremen again and said, 'Well?'

'Sir!'

İkmen looked over towards one of his younger constables, Yıldız. 'Constable?'

'Sir, these people have been shitting where they sit,' the young man said with a disgusted look on his face.

İkmen sighed and then lit a cigarette in an attempt to calm his nerves. 'That's what happens when you chain people to their stations,' he said.

6

A female officer added that some of the women appeared to be bleeding.

'Allah!' He turned again to the Turkish foremen and said, 'Who's in charge? Who runs this concentration camp?'

The second man, the one with rather more courage than the other, said, 'I don't know. I needed a job. I heard there were jobs here. I got one.'

'Yes, but who gave you the job?' asked Süleyman, who along with İkmen was getting impatient with these men now.

There was silence.

'Well?'

Both of the foremen very pointedly looked away. İkmen turned to Süleyman and said, 'We'll just have to take the whole lot in.'

'Yes.'

Then addressing the two men once again, İkmen said, 'You know we will find out who you work for. If you don't tell us yourselves then these poor creatures you have exploited will give us descriptions that will eventually lead us to who is responsible for this outrage.'

Again there was a silence. This time it was broken by the sound of a pile of fake Prada handbags dropping from one of the benches and hitting the floor. After that a woman, somewhere, began to weep.

'Allah!'

İkmen was just about to give his officers the order to take everyone in the whole place into custody when the first foreman suddenly blurted, 'There's Tariq! He's in the office!'

He pointed to somewhere at the back of the factory floor. İkmen left Süleyman in charge while he and his sergeant, Ayşe Farsakoğlu, went to take a look.

\*　\*　\*

Neither of them saw the grenade at first. There was just this thin, foreign-looking boy sitting on a swivel chair in front of a desk heaped with paper, pens and pictures of handbags and watches. When İkmen and Ayşe Farsakoğlu opened the door and stepped into the office, he looked up, but otherwise he didn't move or look afraid initially.

'Tariq?'

He didn't answer. After a moment he looked down at something he was holding in his lap. It was Ayşe who first recognised what it was.

'Sir, he's holding a grenade,' she whispered nervously into her superior's ear.

İkmen took a big gulp of air in order to steady his nerves and then moved his head the better to see what the young man was holding. When he'd done that he turned towards Ayşe and said, 'Evacuate the building, Sergeant Farsakoğlu. Get those people off those machines. We have bolt cutters.'

Although the sight of workers chained, slave-like, to their machines had shocked İkmen, he had made sure that his team had come equipped for just that eventuality. This wasn't, after all, the first time that such a hellish factory had been discovered in the city.

'Sir.' Farsakoğlu left and İkmen watched for what seemed like an eternity as the boy rolled the grenade over and over in his hands. Out on the factory floor he heard Süleyman give the order to evacuate, followed by the sound of people moving from their seats and then the sharp snapping noise of bolt cutters biting through metal. Some were still crying and some cried in either fear or pain or both as the officers took hold of them and began to drag, pull or carry them out of the building.

The fact was, however, that there were probably in excess of a hundred people in that stinking space and it wasn't going to take just five minutes to move them out. İkmen had no way of knowing whether or not this boy now idly playing with a hand grenade was actually capable of using it. He had no way of knowing at that time whether or not the lad even spoke his language. What he did know, however, was that he had to find some sort of way to engage with him if his officers were to stand any chance of getting themselves and the slaves they had taken into custody out in one piece.

'Tariq.'

The boy looked up. İkmen smiled.

'Tariq, I don't know what part you have to play in this organisation. But I can see that you are a young man and so I can't imagine that you are actually running this place.'

The boy didn't respond, although İkmen did notice that his cheeks became flushed.

'We can help you,' İkmen continued. 'I know that we—'

'Shut up.' It wasn't shouted or said in any way aggressively. But by its tone and by virtue of what the boy was holding as he said it, it was clear that he brooked no argument. İkmen duly became silent. The boy was handling the grenade slowly and did not at that point seem to be unduly agitated. Meanwhile there was a lot of activity on the factory floor and people were clearly being moved out with alacrity. When negotiating with armed opponents, like this boy, it was as much about knowing when to be silent as it was about knowing when to speak and to act. There was also an element, İkmen knew, of recklessness on his part at this time too. Provided his officers and their poor broken-down charges got out, there was part of him that didn't care too much what happened then. Life had not been good in recent months; in fact life had been downright awful.

'I should have been dead months ago,' Tariq said. 'Then I would not be in this problem situation.'

At that moment, İkmen simply registered the foreign accent.

'We can help you,' İkmen reiterated. 'Those who have been exploiting you, and the others, will be punished.'

Tariq stood up and it was then that he began to tremble.

'Don't do this, son.'

The boy cried. The sounds from down on the factory floor were much reduced now. İkmen took a moment to sigh with relief about that. But then he looked at the boy's weeping face again and said, 'Don't!'

It was then that the final exchanges took place between them. Tariq pulled the pin out of the grenade, İkmen threw himself backwards and then, for İkmen, everything went black.

# Chapter 2

The doctor held up what looked like a piece of bone in front of İkmen's face. The inspector, still groggy from his latest shot of morphine, remarked upon it.

'It looks like bone because that is exactly what it is,' Dr Arto Sarkissian replied. 'To be exact, Çetin, it is the distal phalanx of an index finger. We think, your surgeon Dr Türkmenoğlu and myself, that it came from the boy who detonated the grenade.'

'Tariq?'

'If that was what his name was, yes,' Arto said.

'And that was what was lodged in my cheek?' İkmen asked as he automatically raised a hand up to the large dressing that now covered the right side of his face.

'People don't realise that when these characters decide to explode themselves, their bodily parts have to go somewhere,' Arto said. 'The force of the blast throws bits of face, leg, pelvis and whatever all over the place – sometimes into people unfortunate enough to be nearby.'

Police pathologist Arto Sarkissian had been friends with Çetin İkmen since they were both small children. Although very different in terms of income, the Sarkissian and the İkmen families had always been close. Arto and his brother Krikor had both followed their father into the medical profession, but neither of the İkmen boys had taken the road into academia as travelled by their father, though both Çetin and his brother Halıl were clever. Halıl had done well with his accountancy practice, but Çetin, although a high-ranking police officer, had only ever just got by. But then unlike either the Sarkissian boys or his own brother, Çetin had children – eight; it had been nine but one of his older sons had very recently died.

'Has Fatma been to visit?' Arto asked as casually as the cringing embarrassment he felt at asking this question allowed. İkmen lowered his gaze for a moment. The child who had died, Bekir, had done so as a result of a police operation against drug dealers in the south-east. Mehmet Süleyman had been one of the officers involved and, although Fatma knew that her son Bekir had been implicated in the drug running and had indeed killed an innocent man because of it, she could not forgive either Süleyman or her husband. It had been Çetin, after all, who had finally deduced Bekir's whereabouts and who had, according to Fatma, killed their son by revealing where he was to the authorities.

'Çiçek came yesterday with Bülent, Orhan, Kemal and Gül,' İkmen said as he attempted to turn his Armenian friend's attention away from his wife and on to his children – all of whom completely supported their father. 'Then in the evening,' he smiled, 'Hulya came with Berekiah and they brought my dear little grandson.'

'That's nice.' But Arto knew that even the arrival of İkmen's grandson hardly made up for the obvious absence of his wife. 'Sınan phoned.' İkmen's eldest son was a doctor who had just taken up a new job in London.

'Çetin . . .'

'Dr Türkmenoğlu says I'll probably be able to go home tomorrow,' İkmen said. It was obvious that he wanted, at all costs, to avoid any more talk about his wife. 'Back to work next week.'

Arto frowned. 'Do you think that's wise?' he asked. 'I mean, as well as the injury to your face, your legs are still badly bruised and then there is the shock—'

'I'll be OK.' İkmen looked up and smiled. 'So what news from the front? Do we know any more about our handbag factory in Tarlabaşı?'

'You'd have to ask your colleagues about that, Çetin,' Arto replied. 'But the young man who blew himself up appears to me to have been from either the Indian subcontinent or Afghanistan. When the DNA tests are complete we will know more. But by eye that is what I think. One thing I do know, however, is that he was suffering from tuberculosis.'

İkmen frowned.

'Yes,' the Armenian confirmed, 'seems strange these days, doesn't it? But then out in places like Afghanistan and even, to be truthful, in the wilder reaches of eastern Turkey not everyone is vaccinated as we have been, not even youngsters. The young man in the handbag factory was quite far on in his disease, he must have been very sick.'

'He said just before he blew himself up that he should have died some time before. I assumed at the time that he meant he should have martyred himself,' İkmen said. 'But maybe if he was sick he meant that his illness should, by that time, have taken him.'

'Possibly,' Arto said. 'Mehmet Süleyman will know more than I do about this case. Ask him.'

İkmen had already seen him, the man who had once, long ago, been his sergeant. But Süleyman, rather like his old friend Arto, hadn't been particularly forthcoming with regard to what was happening outside the confines of the Taksim Hospital. Everyone knew that what İkmen needed most now was rest. Everyone, that is, except Çetin İkmen himself.

'Yes, I will ask him,' İkmen said as he pulled his mobile phone out of the jacket that hung on the back of Arto's chair. 'In fact, my dear Arto, if you'd be so kind as to ask the nurses for a wheelchair, you can take me outside and I can do that right now.'

Arto Sarkissian sighed deeply and then went out to do as he was told.

Mehmet Süleyman watched the white boiler-suited forensic scientist gently tease away at one corner of what looked as if it might have been a poster. On the wall behind the ramshackle bench that had once served the illegal factory as an office desk, various pieces of paper, some of them documents, had been pinned. But it wasn't an easy site to investigate. The grenade that had blown the young boy apart in front of Çetin İkmen's eyes had also inflicted severe damage upon the surrounding area. Süleyman again thought about İkmen and how very lucky he was to be alive. By accident or design, İkmen had somehow managed to hurl himself to the far side of the great iron safe that now stood open in the middle of the charred floor. Built at the end of the nineteenth century, obviously to last, this massive box had taken most of the blast that in all probability would have eviscerated his friend. But luckily İkmen was alive and the safe itself, once opened, had yielded some very interesting finds.

Twenty blank United Kingdom passports were what they had found. They were not, according to the British authorities at the consulate in Beyoğlu, fakes. Issued out of the Passport Office at a place called Peterborough, these documents had somehow gone missing. And they had not been reported as missing. This seemed to imply that at least some of the Senegalese, Nigerian, Pakistani and Vietnamese refugees who had been found working in the Tarlabaşı factory were to be given the chance to go to Britain. If Süleyman's dealings with illegals and the gangs who trafficked them in the past were anything to go by, the passports and the transportation into Europe would not come cheap. Once in Britain the women would be handed over to gangs who would press them into prostitution, while the men would either have to work in dangerous or illegal industries, or pimp their own wives. Whatever they had come from, and he was the first to admit that he could probably not even imagine what poverty was like in a place like Senegal, a life of slavery in Turkey or Italy or Great Britain couldn't possibly be better? Could it?

'Sir.'

He looked up into the heavily moustachioed face of his sergeant, İzzet Melik. He was holding his notebook, the top of which he was tapping with a pen.

İzzet?'

'Seems, sir, that the actual owner of this site is, or was, a Serkis Yacoubian.'

'An Armenian.'

'Went to America sometime in the nineteen twenties,' İzzet said.

'And so this building . . .'

'On this site there was once a considerable house belonging to the Yacoubian family. But according to the local authority, it began to degrade badly in the fifties and then one day it just burnt down.'

'Mmm.' Something similar had happened to a house that had once belonged to Süleyman's own aristocratic forebears up in Nişantaşı. Just after his great-aunt, the Princess Gözde, had died back in 1959, her once great palace had burnt to the ground. Back then the city had been badly neglected and seemingly in inexorable decline.

'The site was used as a makeshift car park for some years after that,' İzzet continued. 'Then, sometime in the seventies, this place was put up.'

The factory was a large structure. It was also makeshift in the same way that the old gecekondu or slum dwellings on the outskirts of the city were. Basically the law used to state that provided a man could erect four corner posts and a roof within one night the land beneath that structure was his. That legislation, however, only applied to unregistered land. In this case the land, not the building, was still owned by the Yacoubian family. The factory, made up as it had been out of odd-shaped pieces of corrugated iron, splintered wooden timbers and fractured glass and plastic panels, had been thrown together like a gecekondu structure without actually being one.

'It was used as a car workshop until the nineties when it fell into disrepair yet again,' İzzet went on. 'The workshop was operated by a Mr Alpozen. Now nearly eighty and ill with cancer, he let the place out to someone called Ahmet Ülker who has apparently been there ever since.'

'Nothing in writing, I suppose?' Süleyman asked.

'Of course not. This Ülker, if indeed that is his name, doesn't rent his place from Alpozen legally. Alpozen doesn't even know where he lives. The land, legally speaking, still belongs to the Yacoubian family.'

Over the centuries many people – Turks, Greeks, Armenians, Levantines – had left the city of İstanbul. They hadn't always sold their properties before they set off for their new lives in America, Australia or Argentina. Sometimes they and their families had just gone, leaving their properties and considerable legal headaches behind them.

'I take it none of the people who worked here have named this Ülker?' Süleyman asked.

'No.' İzzet shook his head wearily and then equally wearily he lit up a cigarette. 'Poor bastards don't know anything much beyond the fact that we've shattered their dreams of a new life in Europe. That said, a couple of them have spoken, through their interpreters, about a boss. Some indistinct figure who occasionally comes by . . . A Turk, most seem to think. But no description.'

Süleyman, equally depressed by what seemed to be evolving into a familiar picture of a chimerical and untraceable people-trafficking operation, sighed and then also lit a cigarette. He was just about to give voice to his misgivings when the forensic scientist he had been watching turned towards him and said, 'Inspector Süleyman, do you have any idea what the letters E, P, P, I, N, G might mean?'

'No.' Süleyman walked over to see for himself exactly what the scientist was looking at. The paper upon which this word was printed was very much a fragment. The blast had ripped away the top layer of what had once been a poster, except for this word and the small red line that ran alongside it. 'I haven't a clue,' Süleyman said.

'Sir?' İzzet was looking impatient and was probably in need of some kind of direction.

'Right, İzzet,' Süleyman said. 'I take it this elderly man, this Mr Alpozen, hasn't been actually visited as yet.'

'No, sir, I've only spoken to him on the phone,' his deputy said.

'Take one of the uniformed officers and get over and see him.

17

Try to determine whether or not he's telling the truth and see if he can give us some sort of description of this Ülker character. Where, by the way, does this Mr Alpozen live?'

'In Yeniköy,' İzzet replied, naming one of the more fashionable villages that line the Bosphorus strait as it wends its way up towards the Black Sea.

'Very nice,' Süleyman responded. 'Obviously good money in car repairs.' His eyes glittered. 'Or something.'

His deputy smiled. 'I'll see what the man has to say for himself,' he said and then he left.

The forensic scientist very gently peeled the little fragment of paper he'd been working on away from the wall and put it into an evidence bag. E, P, P, I, N, G? Süleyman wondered what it meant and whether it was actually a word at all. He didn't even know what language it was in. He doubted it was relevant to anything much. However, if he'd learned anything since joining the police force, it was that things, even very small things, were rarely if ever of no significance at all.

Moments later his mobile phone rang. It was İkmen, still relentlessly working from his hospital bed. He wanted to know whether anything more had come to light about Tariq. It hadn't and so Süleyman told him about Mr Alpozen and the possible existence of Mr Ülker. Only when he'd finished the call did he remember the strange word on the fragment of paper and wonder whether he should have passed that by İkmen too.

It wasn't until later on that evening that the small fragment of paper from the back wall of the handbag factory found its way on to Commissioner Ardıç's desk. Someone at the Forensic Institute had recognised what the word was. Now, in light of that, İkmen and Süleyman's superior was talking to a Mr Nightingale from the British Consulate. A thin, dark man whose command of the Turkish language was second only to that of his command of Arabic, Mr Nightingale didn't actually have a job title at the consulate. But Commissioner Ardıç knew what he was even if he didn't really know *who* he was.

'Epping is a suburb of London,' Nightingale said without even bothering to look at the fragment. 'Your forensic man visited it at some time, did he?'

'She,' Commissioner Ardıç corrected. 'Apparently studied in London.'

'Epping's at the far eastern end of the Central Line, where the underground system hits the edge of the countryside.' He leaned over and looked at the fragment through its polythene bag. 'Looks like it's been torn from a tube map.'

'It was pinned up on the wall of the illegal factory we discovered in Tarlabaşı,' Ardıç said breathlessly as he attempted to lean forward over his immense stomach in order to tap the ash off the end of his cigar. Eventually, under the somewhat scornful gaze of the Englishman, he made it. 'The one with your passports in the safe.'

'Hardly my passports,' Nightingale responded acidly. But then he smiled and said, 'But I know what you mean. This was the place where the boy detonated himself after full jihadi battle cry, wasn't it?'

The question was rhetorical, he knew what the answer was only too well. But his tone made Ardıç smart. Though very far from being a fundamentalist, he was nevertheless a Muslim and he felt the contempt in the other man's voice sharply.

'One of my officers was wounded,' he said.

'Lucky not to be killed,' Nightingale said. 'But anyway, in light of this I will have to contact London again and it may well be that someone might want to come out and speak to your team.'

Ardıç shrugged. Cooperation between British and Turkish police forces was nothing new and of course the Europeans would be accommodated.

'On the face of it, a copy of the London Underground map on the wall of a factory transporting illegals into the EU would seem fairly innocuous,' the Englishman continued. 'One could argue that it would be very useful for them to memorise it in case they fetched up in London all on their own. Except that of course that is highly unlikely. As you and I both know, Commissioner, illegals only ever really go out alone once they've managed to escape those who have enslaved them to work in brothels, factories producing counterfeit goods or lap-dancing clubs.'

Ardıç nodded his agreement.

'The passports bother me,' Nightingale said. 'There is a discreet investigation underway across all of our UK offices as we speak. But what really concerns me,' he picked up the bagged fragment and looked at it again, 'is this.'

'Why?'

'Well, call me a ghastly pessimist if you must but when I put together the concept of a young man shouting "Allahu Akbar" with a map of the London Underground, I tend to feel my blood freeze.'

Ardıç took a long drag on his cigar and then nodded his head in agreement. On 7 July 2005 a group of fundamentalist suicide bombers had brought London Underground to a standstill. More importantly, they had killed not only themselves but a lot of innocent bystanders too. Like İstanbul, London bore the battle scars of numerous terrorist attacks.

20

At length, Ardıç said, 'I understand.' Then with a sigh of resignation he added, 'Get back to your people in London, Mr Nightingale. You will have the full assistance and cooperation of my department.'

Mr Nightingale smiled one of his thin, dark smiles and then left without another word.

# *Chapter 3*

The following Monday morning, Çetin İkmen went to work as usual. He was still sore in places and he wore a large plaster to cover the wound to his cheek. But apart from that, physically he was fine. And once he was outside his apartment, things improved psychologically too. Not that he could entirely forget how cold his wife was to him, but at least at work he could distract himself with other things.

On his way to the police station he gave his present domestic situation some thought. It had been six months since his son Bekir had died. It still hurt to think about; it always would. Within the İkmen family, Bekir had been the one who got away. Instilled from an early age, mainly by their father, with the idea that a person's goals can be achieved, albeit usually with some difficulty, the İkmen children were generally successful. Among them were doctors, flight attendants, A-grade students and a young parent, Hulya, who struggled to support her child and her disabled husband. At much cost to herself, Hulya did what she did well and her parents were immensely proud of her. Bekir had been quite different from the others. Bekir, his father now recalled, had been a lovely and loving child who had grown into a nightmare of a teenager. Some of his other boys had experimented with drugs and Bülent in particular had not had an easy adolescence. But Bekir had been on a different level. Not only had he taken drugs as a youngster, he'd also stolen from shops and even his own family in order to get cash for his habit. At fifteen and with the tacit agreement of his exasperated father, Bekir had left home. And although Fatma had cried for her absent son, everyone else in the İkmen apartment had breathed a sigh of relief.

But then, after seventeen years without any contact or news of him, Bekir İkmen returned. His mother cried, and his brothers and sisters listened awestruck – and with some scepticism – to his stories about begging, fighting with gypsies and battling drug dealers and his own heroin addiction. Only Çetin had totally distrusted Bekir. And Çetin had been right. Bekir had come home in order to hide from his father's colleagues, the police. Not only had he helped to spring a convicted murderer and drug dealer, Yusuf Kaya, from prison, Bekir had also been involved in large-scale dealing himself. Almost the last act Bekir İkmen performed on earth was to kill an entirely innocent man who opposed him. That was why the Jandarmes in the eastern town of Birecik, to where Bekir and his fellow criminals had been tracked by İkmen's colleague Süleyman, had shot him. For some reason that Çetin İkmen could not fathom, his son Bekir had gone wrong. To Çetin's recollection, he had never treated Bekir any differently from his other children – at least not until the drug taking and stealing began when he was a teenager. His wife Fatma disagreed.

'You always treated him badly,' she would say whenever the rein by which she held in her emotions snapped. 'You hated him and he knew it!'

Fatma blamed her husband entirely for what had happened and when she did not berate him, she was silent and broodingly resentful of his every breath. Their children, with the exception of the youngest Kemal who had been somewhat glamoured by his

24

bad-boy older brother, supported their father's point of view with regard to Bekir. But they could do nothing to move their mother who now, or so it seemed, hated their father with the same passion with which she had once loved him. Not even nearly getting blown to pieces in an illegal handbag factory in Tarlabaşı had, apparently, moved İkmen's wife to even a little sympathy for him. She did not visit him in hospital and when he came home, it had not been Fatma but her daughter Gül who had attended to Çetin's wounds and cooked special food for him. It was as if Fatma's love for her husband had died along with their son.

İkmen entered the station in dour mood and failed to acknowledge either of the two young constables who saluted him as he mounted the stairs up to his office. He knew that once he started working again he would become totally absorbed in his job and would be able to distract himself from his personal problems. But the walk up to his office was tiring and tedious and it made him painfully aware of how weak he still was from his injuries. He eventually arrived at his office door, aching and breathless. When he stepped inside, however, his sergeant, Ayşe Farsakoğlu, was not at her desk. Instead he found his superior, Commissioner Ardıç, in conference with a tall, blond, foreign man.

'Ah, excuse me, please,' he heard Ardıç say in English to the foreigner. Then struggling up from İkmen's own chair, Ardıç waddled across the office towards him and said, 'This is Inspector Riley from Scotland Yard in London. He wants to talk to you.'

'Talk to me?'

Ardıç turned towards the Englishman, smiled, and then said to İkmen in Turkish, 'About the Tarlabaşı handbag factory. There is a connection to London. This officer wants to talk to you about that.'

'Ah.' İkmen walked forward as the Englishman rose from his seat and extended his hand.

'Inspector İkmen, I'm Patrick Riley,' he said. There was an accent of some sort to his English which İkmen was later to discover came from Liverpool.

İkmen took Riley's outstretched hand and shook it. The Englishman smiled. He was, İkmen felt, probably about forty. Tall and thin, he wore a loose, rather cheap-looking suit and had the slightly rough voice of a smoker. The only really remarkable thing about him was his vast shock of white-blond hair which made his head look not unlike a particularly untidy hyacinth.

'Pleased to meet you, Inspector,' İkmen replied.

Ardıç grunted and sat down in Ayşe Farsakoğlu's seat. 'Your sergeant won't be disturbing us and nor will anyone else,' he said in Turkish as Ayşe's seat groaned in protest beneath his vast backside. İkmen walked round to his own chair and sat down too. It felt a little strange to be back, but to be back with Ardıç sitting in his office and this foreigner somehow on the scene too . . .

'Inspector İkmen,' Riley said, 'I've come all the way from London because we in the Met – that is the Metropolitan Police,' he smiled, 'we're currently involved in an investigation in north London into similar operations to your recent find here in İstanbul, involving counterfeit goods.'

'It is the mayor of London, is it not, Inspector Riley?' Ardıç said in English. 'He has a, what do you say, a fight against counterfeit things in London.'

'Our new mayor is very keen to deal with the gangs who produce fake goods in London,' Riley said to İkmen. 'It's run on slave labour—'

'As everywhere,' İkmen said. 'What we found in Tarlabaşı was not unusual, Inspector.'

26

'With the exception of the man who blew himself up,' Riley said. 'Not that that in itself is of interest to me.'

İkmen took his cigarettes out of his jacket pocket and offered them to Riley. The Englishman put out his hand to take one, but he looked surprised nonetheless. 'We can?'

'Soon it will not be possible to smoke in buildings,' Ardıç said as he reflexively touched the full cigar case in his trouser pocket. 'The government now, they don't like it. But for now . . .' He shrugged. 'İkmen always smoke. Please, Inspector Riley, do what will make you happy.'

With somewhat tentative fingers, Riley took hold of one of İkmen's Maltepe cigarettes and then allowed the Turk to light it for him. The strength of the cigarette caught him unawares and made him cough. Neither of the Turks seemed to think this was unusual and İkmen just waited until the coughing had ceased before he said, 'So what is of interest to you, Inspector?'

After swallowing hard, Riley said, 'A small fragment of a London Underground map was recovered from the scene of the explosion in the factory that you uncovered.'

İkmen hadn't been told this fact and it made him raise an eyebrow.

'Why it was pinned to the wall of the factory in the district of Tar . . . er, Tarl . . .'

'Tarlabaşı,' İkmen put in.

'Tarlabaşı, we don't know and neither do you,' Riley said. 'But in the light of the bombings on the London Underground in two thousand and five, it bothers me and my colleagues. What were those people, who were basically running illegal migrants and dodgy handbags in İstanbul, doing with a London Underground map?'

'Maybe they use the underground to distribute their products around London,' İkmen said.

27

Riley shrugged. 'It's unlikely. People don't transport large quantities of things on the tube, Inspector.' Riley leaned across İkmen's desk, his face very serious. 'Inspector İkmen, the man who blew himself up in Tarlabaşı did so with the words "Allahu Akbar" on his lips. Now I don't know if you are a religious man or not . . .'

Ardıç barely suppressed a snort of derision.

'I am not a religious man, Inspector,' İkmen said. 'And I can completely understand that you would immediately connect that statement and the act that followed it with Islamic fundamentalism. I do myself. But the fact is, sir, we don't know who the dead boy Tariq was or whether he was acting for an organisation or alone. According to our pathologist, he was a very sick boy. He had tuberculosis and was probably terminally ill. We are not in a position to say whether the boy was a fundamentalist or not. As far as we are concerned, he was part of an illegal counterfeit organisation that uses migrant workers who sometimes die in the hands of these people. We have some names, as I am sure the commissioner has told you . . .'

'Ahmet Ülker was the one that really struck us in the Met,' Riley said.

This was a name that İkmen knew. Süleyman had told him about Ülker. He was apparently the current landlord of the Tarlabaşı factory. But it seemed Mr Ülker had some interests abroad as well.

'An Ahmet Ülker owns and runs a couple of handbag factories we're watching in north London,' Riley said. 'He has dual Turkish/UK nationality on account of being married to a British woman. But he was born here in Turkey and we in the Met think it's too much of a coincidence that one Mr Ahmet Ülker should be running knock-off factories in London and an entirely different character of the same name doing it here.'

'I see.'

'Ahmet Ülker, according to the electoral register, lives in a one-bedroom flat in Dalston. This is not one of the better parts of London and the street he lives on is frankly a bit rough. His wife, however, is registered to a mansion on The Bishops Avenue in East Finchley. This is one of the best addresses in the city where houses can cost millions. Now Mrs Ülker, or Maxine Lee as she was before she married, does not come from money,' Riley said. 'Her folk were gypsies from down in Kent. When Ülker met Maxine she was working as a lap dancer in a dirty little club in Hackney. There's no way Maxine could have purchased that house in East Finchley. But we know that Ahmet is making a bundle out of his two factories in Hackney Wick. With nice little sidelines in legitimate production and retail as well as illegal people-trafficking and prostitution, he doesn't have to worry about how he might pay his bills.'

'But if you know so much about this man, why haven't you arrested him?' İkmen said.

'We have, for some time, had intelligence to suggest that Ülker's operation might be bigger and more far-reaching than we at first thought,' Riley said. 'What you have found here in İstanbul has confirmed that. In addition, we suspect he might have connections to larger organised crime gangs in the UK.'

'But are you certain this is the same Ahmet Ülker?'

'The business that Ülker's wife Maxine "runs" in London is called Yacoubian Industries. An Armenian name, I am told, and one that has a connection to Ülker here in İstanbul.'

'Yes.' Süleyman had told İkmen the familiar story of how the land the Tarlabaşı factory was on was in reality still the property of the long-gone Yacoubian family. 'Yes, that family still officially own the site of the Ülker operation here.'

'Exactly.' Riley cleared his throat. 'Our Ülker and yours have to be one and the same. We need to know how far his empire stretches. I think it might be very large indeed. In order to be able to buy a house on The Bishops Avenue and give Maxine her yearly dose of plastic surgery over in Los Angeles, he has to either be a big player or in bed in some way with big players. We have some very large and powerful gangs in London. An alliance with one of the eastern European outfits or a British/Albanian hybrid like the Gentlemen of Honour gang could be very serious. Then there is the question about what type of people Ülker might be bringing into Britain. Your young bomber and that tube map are worrying our security services even though we can't actually trace a solid link between Ülker and terrorism of any kind. Inspector İkmen, we need someone on the inside of Ülker's operation. We need an illegal immigrant of Turkish origin who can understand Ülker in his native language when he speaks to his henchmen. That person also needs to be able to understand and speak English very well even though he will have to pretend that he doesn't.'

'The Metropolitan Police would like you to do this for them, İkmen,' Commissioner Ardıç said. 'You have much experience. You have been to London. Your English is the best of anyone.'

'There is no pressure,' Riley interjected. 'This operation will not be easy, it could be dangerous and we have no idea about how long it might last. We know you are a family man and I understand you will need to consider them.'

Shocked, İkmen didn't say a word. His mind flew back over the decades to his only visit to the British capital back in the 1970s. It had been a grimy, dark place then, not unlike the İstanbul of the same period. Back then the London bobbies he had gone over to observe had usually finished their shifts drinking and smoking in pubs. Then, just like Turkey, Britain had been plagued by industrial unrest and political agitation. Now London, at least, was the shining heart of the global financial world and bobbies so he heard, were more likely to go to the gym than to the pub. But İkmen was no fool and he knew that this new, bright London had been bought at a very high price. He'd read about the miners' strike in the 1980s, about how Margaret Thatcher had dismantled the country's heavy industries. Now the British lived by their banks, their advertising agencies and businesses with odd names like hedge funds and futures – things he didn't understand.

After a few moments İkmen blurted, 'I have a son in London. He's a doctor. He recently got a job in Hounslow.'

Inspector Riley sighed. 'You won't, I'm afraid, be able to see or even contact your son,' he said. 'None of your family can know where you are or what you are doing. Not even your colleagues here can know. Ülker has a long reach. He will know what has happened here in İstanbul. What we don't want him to tumble is that a connection has been established between here and London. As far as we are aware he doesn't know we in the Met are watching him. That said, we have no real idea where Ülker's global influence begins or ends. That's why we're giving you time to think it through. It could be dangerous.'

'Yes, but—'

'Officially you will be working in the east,' Ardıç said in Turkish. 'You will be working in counter-terrorism alongside our colleagues and the armed forces. Your family will not be able to contact you except through me. Obviously if there is an emergency I will be able to contact the Metropolitan Police who will contact you. If you do this you will have to lie to your family about where you are going and what you are doing. You will have to lie to everyone you know.'

Just the thought of it saddened İkmen. To lie to everyone! And it wasn't even as if it was a comfortable lie. Going east into the provinces where the separatist Kurdish PKK, where Hezbollah and even, some said, al Qaeda operated was no soft option. Those he loved would worry. Although whether that would include his wife Fatma he didn't know.

'Something else you ought to know too is that you will have to enter the UK illegally,' Riley said. 'We cannot risk your coming into Britain legally and then attempting to disappear amongst the ranks of the truly dispossessed. Those who traffic people are always on the lookout for police plants. They know that we are constantly trying to break up their operations. This requires authenticity, total immersion. Commissioner Ardıç tells me that you speak German and so the idea is that you travel to Germany and make contact with people traffickers in Berlin. The German police know some of the areas where potential illegal immigrants meet these people. They will keep you under surveillance as far as they can but they, and we, cannot guarantee how the traffickers might bring you into Britain. It could be in a packed container full of hundreds of frightened and desperate people, it could be in a very leaky boat across the English Channel from France. That part of the job alone is dangerous and that's before you even start getting involved with Ülker and his people. Traffickers lose people all the time. I would be failing in my duty to you, Inspector İkmen, if I didn't tell you that you might not even make it to Britain. Even under surveillance, you could die before you got close to our shores. Think about it. Think about it very carefully before you give me your answer.'

# Chapter 4

Mehmet Süleyman hadn't managed to see very much of his friend Çetin İkmen on the latter's first day back at work. In the morning İkmen had spent a lot of time with Ardıç and some man no one seemed to know anything about, and then in the afternoon Süleyman had accompanied his sergeant İzzet Melik over to Yeniköy and the house of Mr Alpozen. The owner of what had once been a car repair workshop in Tarlabaşı, now the smoking ruins of a fake goods factory he had sublet to Ahmet Ülker, old Alpozen hadn't been very forthcoming about anything when İzzet had interviewed him the previous afternoon. So now Süleyman was going to try and impress upon him the seriousness of the situation. Normally the old man would have been brought into the station for questioning, but he was dying and leaving his bed was well nigh impossible.

'You have to know where Mr Ülker lives,' Süleyman said as he watched the old man take a swig from his bottle of oral morphine and then lean back against his pillows once again. Attached to some sort of drip that a nurse came in from time to time to tend, Alpozen was clearly on his last legs. The cancer that was killing him had started in his pancreas and then spread just about everywhere. The bedroom he had chosen to die in smelt of must, mould and death.

'Well, I don't,' the old man gasped. Then eyeing Süleyman

33

with some hostility he said, 'I told that hairy idiot you've brought along again to go away yesterday, now I'm telling you. Let a man die in peace.'

İzzet, the 'hairy idiot', cleared his throat.

'Mr Alpozen, a man died in the illegal factory Ahmet Ülker was running from your premises,' Süleyman said. 'Now I know that as the landlord of the building you are not directly responsible for that. You do however have an obligation to make sure that no illegal activity takes place on your premises.'

'The Armenians own the land!' Alpozen said. 'Ask them!'

'If by that you mean the Yacoubian family then, as you well know, Mr Alpozen, they are in America.' Süleyman began to feel his face getting hot with anger.

'They are legally—'

'On paper they are still the legal owners of the land,' Süleyman cut in, 'but you, sir, are the landlord of the building this Ahmet Ülker has been using. The Yacoubian family are irrelevant now.'

'Oh, I'm dying, what do I care! Leave me in peace! What can you do to me that my illness has not, eh? What are you going to do? Put me in prison?'

A middle-aged woman had shown Süleyman and Melik into Alpozen's house. Well-dressed and gravely polite, her name was Betül and she was the old man's daughter. In fact Betül was his only child and would one day inherit everything that belonged to him. This, as Süleyman then explained to Mr Alpozen, could include any offences relating to his property as well as any benefits. Betül Alpozen would, on the death of her father, take over responsibility for the Tarlabaşı property and all its attendant difficulties. When he heard this, the old man cried. Eventually he stopped weeping and when the morphine allowed him to speak, he demanded that the police officers provide protection for his daughter. He then gave them an address in the eastern city of Diyarbakır. Mr Ülker, apparently, was very rarely in İstanbul.

All of this information was passed on to Ardıç who then gave the address in Diyarbakır to the local police. Mehmet Süleyman hadn't yet managed to speak to İkmen. Strangely, his mobile was switched off and no one was answering his landline. This was very odd given that the İkmen apartment was always occupied by someone, even if it was only Fatma İkmen on her own. This lack of communication made Süleyman feel vaguely unsettled.

'You do as you please,' Fatma İkmen said as she looked at the telephone that had just rung for the third time in quick succession. To her way of thinking there was no reason not to answer it. As far as she was concerned, this conversation with her husband was over.

'Working in the east can be dangerous,' Çetin İkmen repeated yet again. 'I'm going to be liaising with army units directly in contact with terrorist organisations. I—'

'Our son died in the east. I know how dangerous it can be,' his wife cut in bitterly.

'Fatma, the PKK did not kill our son.'

'No, that was you, wasn't it?' Fatma said. And then as the telephone began to ring yet again, she got up and began to move towards it. 'I'm getting that.'

'No!' Çetin put himself between his wife and the phone and said, 'You have to know just how dangerous this is! You won't be able to contact me except through Ardıç and I have no idea how long I'm going to be away. I have no doubt you can cope on your own—'

'I've managed all these years with you being little more than a guest in this house,' Fatma said.

Her words hurt him. In a way the silence she had maintained with him in the months since Bekir had died had been easier than this. But he had had to tell her he was seriously considering going away for an indefinite length of time, even if what he told her was only the cover story – the only story she was permitted to hear.

'You can say no, I—'

'And why would I do that?' The phone finally stopped ringing and İkmen felt the tightness its insistence had produced in his head abate. 'You killed our son,' Fatma continued. 'I can't forgive you for that. Do what you will. You are nothing to me.'

'Fatma, our son was a gangster and a murderer.' The phone began ringing again and this time İkmen, enraged, picked it up and flung it against the wall. It fell to the floor in a tinkle of broken plastic and twisted metal.

'Oh, very good!' his wife said and stiffly adjusted her head-scarf. 'Very grown-up! But then what do I expect from a man who would sacrifice his own son for his career?'

İkmen put his hands behind his back lest he lash out at her and only then did he walk towards her. 'I will say this once more and once more only. Bekir was a gangster, a drug addict and a murderer. He killed an unarmed man, a defenceless Christian monk, and he almost killed Mehmet Süleyman. If the Jandarma from Birecik hadn't come along when they did, Mehmet would have died.'

'Bekir died!' She began to cry as she always did eventually when she thought about her lost child. 'You ordered his death.'

'I did not,' İkmen said. 'I did not do that, Fatma! As I have told you a hundred times, I asked Mehmet Süleyman to try and protect Bekir. But he couldn't. The boy was lost. He was bent upon murder and when the Jandarma came upon him and shot him they did the only thing they could do under the circumstances. He was about to kill a police officer, they had no choice!'

She knew that. Intellectually she had always known it. But the intellect has very little to do with feelings and the hate she had for her husband, even if based on no actual fact, persisted.

'Go to the east and do your duty,' she said after a pause. 'I don't care.'

She started to move out of the living room. Appalled and distraught, Çetin İkmen felt tears stinging the insides of his eyes. 'Fatma, we . . . we loved each other. I . . . I still love you . . .'

She looked at him with a coldness that was almost pity and then she said, 'Then you had better kill your love because it will never be reciprocated. You are a murderer and an unbeliever and it is a sin to live with either. This will always be your home, Çetin, your father bought this apartment for you. You still have children to feed and clothe and who love you. But I remain your wife in name only and if you choose to divorce me . . .' she very pointedly took off her wedding ring and put it down on the table beside the television, 'I will not oppose it. Our children are almost grown. I can take Kemal with me and go and live with one of my sisters.'

'Fatma!' His voice broke on the word but she didn't respond. She walked out of the room into the kitchen. Çetin İkmen sat down on the sofa, put his head in his hands and gave in to weeping.

It wasn't until the following morning that Mehmet Süleyman heard anything more about Ahmet Ülker's connection to the city of Diyarbakır.

'His mother lives there in an old house near the bazaar with a spinster sister,' İzzet Melik said as he looked down at the notes he had taken from the assistant to the chief of police in Diyarbakır.

'The old woman's a Kurd but her late husband, Ülker's father, was a Turk.'

'Does Ahmet Ülker own the house?'

'Apparently he does, although he hasn't been seen in Diyarbakır for years,' İzzet replied. 'The old woman pays the rent on the factory in Tarlabaşı on his behalf. The police in Diyarbakır say that she doesn't know why he's involved with that. Ahmet, apparently, travels.'

'Travels.'

'Yes, to Europe, to America, to China even. When she has to, the old woman sends things poste restante for him all over the world.'

'How quaint,' Süleyman said.

'Talks to him periodically on his mobile phone,' İzzet continued. 'Diyarbakır say that Ahmet Ülker has no record of involvement or even interest in terrorist activity. He finished high school, apparently. Hard worker. Started his working life in the Hasanpaşa Han in a jewellery shop, and moved to İstanbul in nineteen ninety-two.'

'Where we do not have an address for him.'

'Maybe he sleeps over the factory, or rather maybe that's what he did do,' İzzet said.

'Maybe.' Süleyman was still troubled by his inability to get in touch with Çetin İkmen the previous evening and was about to ask İzzet if he had seen him when suddenly İkmen was at his office door.

'Oh, Çetin, I—'

'I'm just off to see Ardıç,' İkmen said.

Süleyman left his desk and walked over to his older friend and colleague. İzzet Melik, sensing that they probably needed a

38

moment alone, looked down at the work in front of him in a very pointed manner.

'I tried to call you last night.' Süleyman took hold of İkmen's elbow and looked into his face with concern.

İkmen smiled. 'Oh, it was out of order last night,' he said. 'We didn't realise until this morning.'

'I tried to phone your mobile . . .'

'Charging. I was charging it last night.' He didn't like lying to anyone, especially not to his family and friends, but if he was going to take this assignment in London he would have to get used to doing just that.

'I see.'

Süleyman didn't believe him, İkmen could see that clearly.

'Well, I'd best be heading towards Ardıç's office,' İkmen said with a smile. 'Don't want to keep him waiting, do I?'

'No.' Just as İkmen began to move off, Süleyman said, 'Çetin, is anything wrong?'

'Wrong?' He shrugged. 'No. Should there be?'

'Well . . .' It would have been more to the point to ask whether anything was right. Since Bekir's death, nothing much apparently had been. 'Çetin, I've been concerned . . .'

'My life is as good as it can be,' İkmen said. 'I'm not unwell.'

'No, but I – I know you are tired,' Süleyman said. He didn't dare to even breathe the name of İkmen's dead son, especially not in front of İzzet Melik. İkmen, like most Turkish males, was uncomfortable about talk of personal things except with those closest to him.

'Well then you'll be happy to know that I'll be going away for a while soon,' İkmen said. 'A change of scene being as good as a holiday sometimes. I'm just going to tell Ardıç now. I've

39

been offered the chance to work out of town for a while. I've made the decision to take the opportunity.'

'Oh.' Süleyman was genuinely surprised.

'Where are you going, sir?' İzzet Melik asked.

'Away,' İkmen said. 'Out of the city.' And then on yet another smile, he left.

Süleyman looked at İzzet Melik and sighed.

'Out of town?' İzzet said gloomily. 'That to me smacks of a posting to the east. Why else wouldn't the inspector say the name of where he was going? Out there with all the heat and the violence and the sheer remoteness of it all.'

'Quite,' Süleyman said as he walked back to his desk, a frown now cutting deeply across his forehead. 'My thoughts exactly, İzzet.'

# Chapter 5

In the week that İkmen was given to wind up his affairs in İstanbul he made sure that he was generally too busy to talk very much. Ayşe Farsakoğlu had already been moved over to work with a team investigating a series of alleged child abductions. She knew that İkmen was going away for a while, and she was concerned about her future. She liked working with İkmen. She had never in fact enjoyed working with anyone else. But İkmen kept Ayşe and Süleyman and indeed all of his colleagues at arm's length now. He told himself that it simply made good professional sense, which it did, but it also allowed him not to feel – and he most certainly didn't want that. Feeling made him cry when he considered the fact that his wife apparently no longer loved him, feeling made him long for the touch of his children before he had even left İstanbul. And so, hard as they tried to engage him in conversation, Ayşe Farsakoğlu, Mehmet Süleyman and İzzet Melik could get nothing more than platitudes out of him. The only exception was İkmen's oldest friend, Arto Sarkissian. The day before İkmen was due to leave, the Armenian turned up at his office. It was lunchtime, it was quiet and İkmen was drinking tea and smoking a cigarette when his friend, without even knocking on the door, let himself in.

'Arto.' It was said with some warmth but without the usual expression of joy the Armenian's appearance generally elicited.

'So you go tomorrow,' Arto said and lowered himself into the chair in front of İkmen's desk.

'Yes.' İkmen looked down at his desk, pretending to read documents he had no concern with and which did not interest him.

'To the east, you say,' Arto continued. 'Is that the south or the north-east?'

He watched İkmen closely, knowing with certainty that his friend was not attending to what was on his desk in any way. He'd told him the previous day that he was going east, but he hadn't specified a location.

'Um, I don't know,' İkmen said. 'Not yet.' He looked up and smiled. 'They haven't told me.'

'They?'

'Ardıç.'

'Oh, so Ardıç—'

'Look, Arto, I can't tell you where exactly I'm going. I've told you this,' İkmen said. 'I can't tell you where I'm going, I can't tell you know long I'm going for. I can't even tell Fatma.'

'Have you sorted things out with Fatma?'

İkmen's face flushed immediately. 'Sorted things—'

'You know what I mean,' Arto said a little impatiently now. He and Çetin had never had secrets, they had always talked about everything. Except that when Bekir had been killed, Çetin had kept everyone out, including Arto. He knew that Fatma blamed Çetin for their son's death. Fatma had told her best friend, Estelle Cohen, who in turn had expressed her anxiety about the İkmen marriage to Arto's wife, Maryam. 'I just hope that wherever you are going you're not going just because you want to run away from the situation here.'

İkmen looked up at his friend with steady, lying eyes. 'No.' This was something he was going to have to get used to doing now.

'Because, Çetin,' Arto said, 'it is my belief that there are few things in life that cannot be sorted out in the end. You and I know this. There are ways and ways. Sometimes I identify a killer or a rapist for you using just one strand of hair I've picked up from underneath a dead body, sometimes you find a killer all on your own, using your experience, your skill or the magical insight you inherited from your mother. We solve things, Çetin. We always have.'

'Have we?'

'Çetin, I know you're not allowed to tell anyone where you are going. I mean, for all I know you could be leaving the country.'

Did he know? Or was he simply fishing for whatever he could find? He, like everyone else, with the notable exception of Fatma, was worried. They all knew now that he was going 'to the east' and they all feared he would die staring down the barrel of a terrorist's gun. What they didn't know, or rather what he thought they didn't know, was that he was more likely to die in an airless container on a ship crossing the English Channel. Just the thought of it made him shudder, something that Arto noticed immediately.

'Çetin?'

'Arto, I am leaving to go somewhere and I will return when I do. As to whether I'm running away from anything that is no more your business than the fact that your own marriage has been a front for years is mine.'

Childless and prey to numerous health problems, Maryam Sarkissian had been Arto's wife in no more than name for years. It was something the two men had spoken of only once, many years before when Arto had broken down during a conversation they had had in a bar. Nothing had been said since – until now. Çetin's words, spoken almost casually, hurt. Arto looked down at the floor and said, 'Çetin—'

'Arto, I am going for my own reasons and whenever I return, things will be as they have always been,' İkmen said. He could see his friend was hurt, there was no getting away from it, and deep inside he felt guilty for having inflicted such pain. But he also knew that it had been necessary. Arto, and only Arto, could so easily have wheedled everything about the London mission out of him, mainly because İkmen so longed to tell him.

After a short silence, the Armenian stood up to leave.

'Well, Çetin, whatever is happening, you know I wish you well,' he said. 'You know I . . .' He bit down on his bottom lip as if trying to hold back tears. It proved too much for İkmen who stood up, walked over to his friend and took him in his arms and kissed both his cheeks.

'You know that I will miss you,' Çetin said. 'You know I only say what I do because I fear I may tell you, and only you, what I mustn't. I'm sorry.'

The two of them stood in the middle of İkmen's office, in each other's arms, for a good five minutes before the Armenian finally left without another word.

When dawn broke over the great city of İstanbul the following morning, Çetin İkmen was already up and dressed. He didn't say goodbye to any family members still sleeping in the apartment. He didn't even look into what had once been his bedroom, where Fatma now slept alone. He didn't want even the slightest hairline fracture in his already shaky resolve. Then, in line with the instructions Ardıç had given him, he stepped out of his apartment, carrying nothing, not even his wallet, and walked away from Sultanahmet down the hill towards Sirkeci railway station. Halfway down he turned off on to Ebussuut Street where, just before reaching the main post office, he rang the bell of an

44

anonymous doorway beside a small electrical shop. After a short pause he was ushered up the stairs behind the doorway and into the flat above by a man of about thirty. Neither he nor the older woman with him said who they were or what they were doing and İkmen didn't ask.

'As you know,' the man said as he pointed İkmen in the direction of a group of chairs in the middle of the stark, blank living room, 'undercover work depends in part upon keeping your fake life story as close to that of your real life as possible.' He handed İkmen a Turkish passport. 'Your name is Çetin Ertegrul – your wife's maiden name.'

'Yes.' That had indeed been Fatma's name before she married him. Maybe, soon, it would be her name again. İkmen opened the passport and saw that it had no photograph.

'You're fifty-five years old, a widower, and you live in Laleli with your thirty-five-year-old daughter Çiçek and her husband Abdullah. My colleague here is going to change your appearance somewhat and then we're going to take your passport photo.'

'OK.' The woman came towards him carrying scissors, an electric razor and a bag of other things he couldn't yet see. She took the dressing off the wound on the side of his face. It was healing well. As she first shaved off his moustache and then coloured his hair what seemed to İkmen a most startling shade of black, the man kept on talking, telling İkmen who he was slowly but surely becoming.

Abdullah Karabas, Çetin Ertegrul's son-in-law, had – just like Çetin İkmen's real son-in-law, Berekiah – sustained an injury that meant that he could no longer work. Çiçek, Çetin's daughter, was newly pregnant. To make matters worse, Çetin Ertegrul himself had recently been made redundant from his job as a security guard at the Akmerkez mall in Etiler, possibly because his employers felt that he was too old to be seen amongst their younger and trendier customers. And so Çetin had made the decision to leave Turkey and seek more lucrative employment in the European Union. His hope was that by doing this his daughter would be able to stop worrying about money and enjoy her baby when it came.

'When you get to your destination, London, you will make contact with the person listed on this mobile phone as Ayşe,' the man said. 'This person will be your initial contact and your story will be known to that person.'

He handed a very slim and handsome mobile phone to İkmen and said, 'Keep this with you at all times.'

Once he was someone else, a person without a moustache and with very short, very black hair, the man took his photograph and then carried it and the passport away with him to another room. The clothes the woman gave him to wear were even cheaper versions of the already cheap and worn-out clothes that Çetin İkmen usually wore. The small suitcase he was provided with contained nothing that was any better. For his pockets there was a wallet containing eight hundred Turkish lire, a photograph of a woman who he was told was his daughter, a set of keys to 'his' flat in Laleli, the mobile phone and an ATM card in the name of Çetin Ertegrul.

'This ATM card will work anywhere in the world,' the man said. 'The PIN number is on your mobile phone. Draw in euros or sterling. You can take out up to five thousand euros at any one time.'

'Five thousand euros!'

'You're a police officer, you're supposed to be trustworthy,' the woman growled.

'Yes, but—'

'Wherever you go in the European Union, it will cost you,' the man said. 'Only the old ex-communist countries are cheap. You'll need money to pay whoever traffics you across the English Channel. It will be expensive. Now your mobile phone also contains two other numbers. One is listed under the name Wolfgang, that is your contact in Berlin. You call Wolfgang as soon as you arrive. The other is under the name Burak and that is your emergency number. You call that number if you are in trouble, if you're about to be unmasked, if your life is in danger. Understand?'

'Yes.' There wasn't much not to understand. There was, however, quite a bit to be worried about.

But the man smiled even if İkmen did not. 'Now . . .' He picked up a hand mirror and held it in front of İkmen's face. 'Say hello to Çetin Ertegrul.'

What stared back from the mirror was the very epitome of migrant Turkish desperation, thin and pallid, scarred, the short dyed hair a last-ditch attempt to appear younger. İkmen looked at his new incarnation with disgust. This person, this parody of a Turkish man, was going to go and plead to be trafficked out of Germany, beg for work in the UK. He started to feel angry until he remembered that Çetin Ertegrul wasn't real, was merely a part he was playing in order to expose a network of crime he had only glimpsed as yet.

# *Chapter 6*

Wolfgang was not what İkmen had expected. For a start he had not reckoned upon actually meeting his contact in Berlin. Maybe he had seen too many espionage movies. Berlin, what it had been and maybe what it still was, seemed to engender such notions. He'd imagined that when Wolfgang had told him on the phone to go to the Weissensee Jewish Cemetery in one of the old East German districts of the city, he would find some sort of message waiting for him there. A scrap of paper on a grave-stone, a bag with instructions underneath a tree. What he hadn't expected was a person – in this case a tiny, wizened and ancient Jewish man.

Wolfgang led İkmen between the large plain gravestones and into one of the most heavily wooded areas of the cemetery. 'You know that this is the largest Jewish cemetery in Europe.'

'It is?' German was very much İkmen's third language and he was not finding it easy to speak. He did not, he knew, prac-tise as often as he should. It made him feel nervous, edgy about both what he was saying and what he was hearing.

'So strange when you consider how many Jews the Germans transported and killed,' Wolfgang continued. 'But then central Europe has always had its problems, has it not?'

'Ah . . .'

'The Hundred Years War, all that business with Charlemagne

and the Holy Roman Empire, silly, silly Kaiser Wilhelm, the Nazis, then the Wall and all that aggravation.' Wolfgang cleared some ferns away from the side of the path and revealed a small, battered bench. 'Sit,' he said. 'Sit down, Herr Ertegrul.'

İkmen sat. He was red-eyed and shattered. It had taken him two days to get from İstanbul to Berlin by train and he had not travelled first class. Slumped for much of the time against the carriage wall, hemmed in by German Turks returning to their various home cities, he had been kept awake all night by blaring hip-hop music. This interspersed with ear-splitting attempts by various youths to rap in German had nearly driven him mad. When he'd arrived in Berlin he'd called Wolfgang straight away, stuttering in his schoolboy German, straining every nerve to understand what his contact was saying. After that he'd had to negotiate his way to Weissensee, a leafy, quiet area of the city that used to be part of old East Berlin.

'And through all of the silliness that has happened in this part of the world there have always been those who seek to move from place to place without let or hindrance,' Wolfgang continued. 'Of course this has not always been possible. For instance under Hitler, Jews could not go outside without wearing yellow stars on their clothing, they could not go to the next town, much less the next country.'

He was obviously building up to telling İkmen something about how he might secure his own illegal passage to the UK, but he was doing it slowly and for İkmen rather tortuously.

'I have, you know, lived almost my whole life in Weissensee,' Wolfgang said. 'There was of course a period of time, some years between nineteen forty and nineteen forty-five when I was . . . elsewhere, but that hiatus taught me much, Herr Ertegrul. I met people willing to sell almost anything to secure transport from one place to another. For a time I became such a person myself.'

Two small, round women, their heads covered by chiffon scarves, passed by and Wolfgang raised his hat. He was talking about the concentration camps. He had been in one. İkmen wondered how he had survived and wondered whether it had anything to do with this business of moving people from one place to another.

'But I came back to Weissensee,' the old man said with a smile. 'I would have preferred to live in the West but . . .' He shrugged his shoulders. 'What can you do? I was stuck with Russians, the GDR, the whole disaster. I would have been very depressed, not to mention poor, had I not remembered that earlier experience in the nineteen forties. I arranged for people to find alternatives to the GDR, Herr Ertegrul. Desperate people. I made their dreams come true and you know, in all the years that I did so, I never lost one person. Then when the Wall came down, of course I was very happy, but my business collapsed. Or rather it did for a while.'

İkmen had imagined that Wolfgang was some sort of police officer or agent. But it seemed not. He must have seen the confusion on İkmen's face because he smiled.

'Now, of course,' Wolfgang said, 'many of those who would be elsewhere come from Africa and they would really rather like to be here. Sometimes they need some assistance. Sometimes other people need assistance too. Nowadays one has such strange bedfellows, Herr Ertegrul. On occasion I even work for what they call the security services in what we all now call just Germany. I think that you should stay in Kreuzberg while you are here in Berlin. There are a lot of Turks in Kreuzberg.'

Kreuzberg, İkmen knew, was also known as 'Kleine Istanbul'.

'There is a bookshop on the main thoroughfare through Kreuzberg, the Bergmannstrasse,' Wolfgang said. 'It is called Eco. Books devoted to global warming, all the ecological nonsense. Above that is a small what you Turks call "pansiyon". It's run by a friend of mine. There is a room there that you can have tonight. Tomorrow the next part of your journey will begin.'

So much for first finding a trafficker and then paying him lots of money. Wolfgang himself was the people trafficker. 'But, er, Wolfgang, why then did we not meet in Kreuzberg? Why here in this cemetery?' İkmen asked.

The old man smiled. 'Oh, I always meet the people I move around here,' he said. 'Those who need me know it and so do the police. Fortunately these two groups do not always know each other.'

There was an arrangement obviously. On some level Wolfgang was allowed to do what he did best, what he had done for many years in the GDR under the noses of the hated Stasi. In return he did things like this, transporting people across borders for the police. The British policeman had told him nothing about this. But then maybe he had not known about it himself. Perhaps this was something between Wolfgang and the German police and them alone.

Slowly and painfully Wolfgang began to rise from the bench. 'Oh, and get some money out tonight,' he said to İkmen. 'Three thousand euros will be a start. I understand that you can draw anywhere in Europe. We will have some more in France. It has all been agreed.'

'Has it?' İkmen felt like a child. Alone, out of his depth, forced to go along with whatever was suggested simply because he didn't know any better.

'Trust me,' Wolfgang said with a smile and slowly walked away from the bench.

İkmen took his mobile phone out of his pocket and brought up the name Burak, his emergency contact. But he didn't call the number. After five minutes' cogitation he put the phone back in his pocket, stood up and began to walk out of the cemetery.

'Kleine Istanbul' was both familiar and unfamiliar. The streets were full of headscarfed women getting their shopping from grocers that sold everything one could ever want from 'back home'. But these places also sold German cigarettes, German biscuits and German lottery tickets too. The young people spoke German almost exclusively, even amongst themselves. Even men of İkmen's own age seemed to prefer to speak the language of their adopted country as opposed to their native tongue. A case in point was the owner of the pansiyon where Wolfgang had reserved a room. Shouting rather than speaking, he waved a hand in the direction of İkmen's small and rather smelly room and told him that he'd have to share the bathroom down the hall with a group of bricklayers from Albania. İkmen said that he had no problem with this at which the pansiyon owner shrugged and then walked back to his office.

That night İkmen dined alone at a restaurant in one of the streets off Bergmannstrasse. Probably because it was relatively quiet in the restaurant, he suddenly felt truly alone and very exposed. All around him people were speaking a language he could not easily comprehend. His lodgings, though adequate, were cramped and unsavoury, and he was moving on to another country he hadn't seen since the 1970s. How he would get to the UK he still didn't know. The mysterious Wolfgang was obviously involved but whether İkmen actually trusted the old man was a moot point. After he finished his meal, he returned to his room, lay on his bed, stared up at the brown-stained ceiling and smoked.

None of the irritations, fears and even anxieties about his immediate future that he had faced so far would have been half so bad had he not had Fatma on his mind too. She had known when he was due to leave, even if she knew no more than that, but still she had refused to utter one word to him. He'd spent the night before he left İstanbul in his son Bülent's old bed. He had been banished from his own bedroom since well before Bekir had been killed. After seventeen years on the streets, that boy had picked up where he had left off with his family – causing fights and divisions, encouraging his younger siblings to lie, cheat and take drugs. What a toxic waste of flesh Bekir had been! And yet İkmen had cried when he died. Bekir had been his son as well as Fatma's and he hurt as much if not more from the loss of him. Not that Fatma would ever understand that. It was clear now that she didn't want to. She blamed him for Bekir's death and that, now allied to the fact that she had only ever tolerated her husband's lack of faith in Islam, had apparently killed her love for him. And yet what a love it had been! Çetin and Fatma had produced nine children in their long, long marriage. She had been, he recalled, an enthusiastic and uninhibited lover right up until Bekir had come between them that final, fatal time. Now it was as if someone had turned a tap off. He couldn't get near her. With her headscarf pulled tightly around her face and her new, long Iranian-style overcoat, Fatma was not only someone unavailable, she was also, if only in appearance, foreign too. Alien and cold, she looked down at him as if he were something dirty, cheap and offensive. For the first time in nearly four decades, İkmen wondered what it would be like to make love to another woman. Strangely, just the thought of it made him shudder. How would that work? he wondered. How would he even begin to meet a woman? And, even if one were to come along, what would a smoke-dried, hard-up father of eight have to offer such a person? A meze in one of the restaurants on İstiklal Street, accompanied by a lot of rakı followed by a terrible, fumbling attempt at sex in the early hours of the morning.

Maybe he should go with a prostitute. There was plenty of money in Çetin Ertegrul's account. He could if he wanted to just order in some eastern European girl (there were easily as many Russians, Czechs, etc., in Berlin as there were in İstanbul) who would, no doubt, acquaint him with new and exciting sexual mores. But he knew that whatever this mythical person did, it would do neither him nor her any good. He couldn't just 'go' with anyone! He hadn't done that since he was a conscript back in the sixties. Even then he'd only done it once. Shortly afterwards he met Fatma, fell in love and had never had sex without love since. He knew that Mehmet Süleyman had had his share of illicit sexual liaisons, but he also knew that they had rarely, if ever, brought him joy. Recalling his colleague's name made him think about İstanbul again, made him wonder what Mehmet, Ayşe Farsakoğlu and İzzet Melik were doing now. He wished he had been able to bid them proper farewells, but even that had been denied to him. To Mehmet and the others his going was an absence, a strange vacancy. Even Arto had been baffled by it. He had been hurt too. He had of course understood but he had also, İkmen knew, felt upset. They had been friends all their lives, they had shared everything. Except this. But then in İkmen's 'new' world there was no Arto Sarkissian, any more than there was a Mehmet Süleyman, a Fatma İkmen, or even a Çetin İkmen. He was Çetin Ertegrul now: security guard, concerned father and general poor Turk. Çetin Ertegrul was not well-educated, he did not have friends in any of the professions and he only read the worst possible newspapers. Religious in the sense that

55

he regularly attended the local mosque and always kept Ramazan, Çetin Ertegrul was a conservative soul who hankered after his old life back in his ancestral village in Cappadocia. He was not someone Çetin İkmen really liked very much. But he knew he would have to learn to at least live comfortably with this character for the foreseeable future. Failure to do so could conceivably cost him his life.

Tired out by the events of the past three days as well as by his own very negative thoughts, İkmen eventually and mercifully went to sleep at around midnight. At 3 a.m. he was woken by someone shaking him and whispering in German. Alarmed, İkmen started to defend himself against this man until he said to him in Turkish, 'Get up, you fool! Get your things together! Tonight we go to Calais!'

A thousand miles to the east, in İstanbul, a sleepless Mehmet Süleyman stood in his garden and looked up at the moon. Where, he wondered, was Çetin İkmen now? More importantly, was he safe?

# Chapter 7

'The thing about buying counterfeit goods, Graham, is that when one does so, one is, if indirectly, funding international terrorism.'

Graham Amphill was one of the BBC's most feared and, in some circles, hated interviewers. As soon as the new and alarmingly young mayor of London had finished speaking, people all over the United Kingdom held their breath. What on earth would Graham say in response to *that*?

'Oh, lord,' Graham Amphill muttered as he looked wearily into camera four. 'Oh, come on, Mr Üner, not *that* old argument! You don't know that people selling knock-off watches and handbags on the streets of London are working for al Qaeda for God's sake!'

'No we don't know—'

'Well, if you don't know, Mr Üner, why are you spoiling it for poor Londoners who just want a fake Rolex or pair of slightly dodgy trainers to save a few quid? Isn't this really all about trying to stamp out what we in the west consider to be slave labour in the Third World?'

'I—'

'Isn't it all just about being judgemental and nannyish?'

'Graham, if you will let me speak . . .' Haluk Üner, mayor of London, leaned forward in the big black chair the BBC had provided for him and smiled. A good-looking man of only thirty-five, Üner was the first mayor of London to be the son of immigrant parents. Both his parents were originally from Adana in south-eastern Turkey. They had sent Haluk to the best schools that north London could offer. This had paid off when he won a place at Oxford to study law. Haluk Üner QC had been voted in on an Independent ticket as mayor of London only six months previously after a staggeringly fast progress into the upper echelons of the capital's local government organisation. 'I am not against people buying what they want,' he continued. 'But fake goods are, we know, produced in factories both here in Europe and in the Third World in appalling conditions. Those who work in these factories are slaves—'

'But is that our business if those factories are in Vietnam, Mr Üner? Isn't it a bit arrogant of us sitting on our well-fed behinds here in the west to tell people in places like Vietnam where and how they can work?'

'Possibly but—'

'And what about places where there is no alternative but to work in these factories? And by the way, you still haven't managed to explain where the funding of terrorism comes into this, have you?'

It wasn't the best interview Haluk Üner had ever given. But then Graham Amphill was not giving him an easy time – not that he ever really gave anyone an easy time. But Haluk Üner was a lawyer, he was a professional and he was mayor of London. He smiled.

'Graham,' he said, 'this connection doesn't come from me. I haven't just made it up in order to underwrite what some have described as my obsession with the counterfeiters. The acting commissioner of police tells me it is so. The Metropolitan Police, in concert with other forces across the country – notably Greater

Manchester – have established links between counterfeit production in the UK and abroad, and terrorist organisations they say may include al Qaeda.'

'May . . .'

'Al Qaeda is by its very nature a secretive organisation,' Haluk Üner said. 'What ordinary people like you and me know about it is minimal, Graham. But what our security services know is rather more extensive, thank God.'

'And so you just take their word for it?'

'Yes.' The mayor of London sat up straight in his chair and looked his interrogator square in the eye. 'I have to. Without other information to the contrary, I have no choice. If the police tell me that these counterfeit operations have links to terrorism then I have to believe them. I have to err on the side of caution, I have to protect Londoners, that is my job. What would you have me do, Graham? Take risks with people's lives? Good God, if I did that, people like you would come down on me like a ton of bricks!'

Inspector Patrick Riley of the Metropolitan Police raised his beer can in salute. Personally he hadn't voted for Haluk, not because he was Turkish but because he'd voted for the Liberal candidate. He always did. But in spite of his initial misgivings, he had to admit that Haluk Üner was doing a good job. Although he'd only been in office a few months, he'd already committed to new children's play areas and announced several affordable housing schemes, in spite of the fact that economists were forecasting a recession. Downturn or not, the capital had to have more homes, it was just a fact. And then there was his stand on knock-off goods. God, but he had the bit between his teeth about that! Maybe it was the connection to terrorism that got him so agitated. Some said that it was because he was a Muslim and so wanted to prove himself willing to tackle terror plots of all kinds. Riley didn't have any view on that, he didn't know Haluk Üner personally or otherwise. But what he had seen of the man he liked. Giving Graham Amphill a verbal run for his money was a joy to see in itself! But then he thought about counterfeit goods once again and his face dropped. What, he wondered, was Ahmet Ülker and the even more shadowy people who ran illegal goods in the capital doing while they watched Haluk Üner on the TV? Were they sneering, laughing, shouting threats at their fifty-inch flat screen digital God-knows-what entertainment hubs?

When Riley finally reached his sparse and lonely bedroom in the early hours of the morning, he wondered where that other Turk, his İstanbul colleague Çetin İkmen, was now. If everything was going to plan he was probably on his way out of Germany.

İkmen knew that his driver, who looked like a very much younger version of Wolfgang, would not make it to Calais on the French coast that night. He had no idea how many kilometres Calais was from Berlin but he knew enough geography to know that it would take more than just a few hours. Before they left Kreuzberg, the driver stopped at an ATM machine and told İkmen to withdraw three thousand euros. He'd known this was coming and so he handed the money over without complaint. Only then did the journey begin in earnest.

The truck was carrying bratwurst and other German sausages to the UK. They apparently liked them over there and the truck was refrigerated in order to preserve the meat on its journey across Europe. If, as İkmen suspected, this man whose name he never learned was Wolfgang's son, transporting pork products was rather a strange occupation for a Jew to be doing. But then he imagined that religion probably meant very little to someone like Wolfgang. How could anyone who had been through the camps, maybe even suffered at the hands of the Stasi afterwards, believe in anything even remotely divine?

While they travelled across Germany, İkmen rode up front in the cab with the man. Neither of them spoke although İkmen was heartened to see that his driver smoked almost as much as he did and so they both puffed the miles away in fairly convivial silence. Only on the approach to the Belgian border did this state of affairs change. The man pulled the truck into a deserted lane and told İkmen to get out. He also pulled a gun out of the pocket of his anorak. It had the instant effect of making İkmen's heart pound.

'What . . . er . . .' All his German banished by fear, he spoke in English now. Had he been cheated by Wolfgang and his son? Was this where he died, in some muddy German country lane? His head began to spin. But then he noticed that the man had something else as well as the gun in his hands. It was a sandwich. He thrust it at İkmen.

'You people don't eat pork,' he said. 'It's beetroot.'

'Beetroot?'

'Now you must get in here.' The man climbed up back into the cab and opened up a small hatch behind the driver's seat. It was a very small opening.

'You can take the sandwich with you, for the journey,' the man said.

'I get in . . .'

'It is dark and it is too small for you to do anything other than stand. But it will get you over the border into Belgium and then later across the English Channel to Dover. Get in.'

It wasn't easy, even for someone of İkmen's slight build. First

61

he had to bend double and then somehow thread his body through the hatch and into the pitch-black gap behind the cab. At one point he thought he couldn't actually do it, which was when he realised why his driver had a gun.

'It is get in there or I shoot you now and throw your body into a ditch,' the man said. 'We cannot have failure. Failure for us means that we are found out. Now get in. As soon as we have cleared the border you may get back into the cab again.'

In spite of the fact that bending that low hurt like hell, İkmen squeezed himself through the gap and then very slowly stood up in the narrow, airless space.

'Eat the sandwich,' the man said as he closed the hatch behind him. 'It will take your mind off things.'

And then there was utter darkness. İkmen, his hand still holding the sandwich, fought for what stale air there was in that tiny, terrifying space. Then the driver started the engine and, rendered totally blind, İkmen began his progress towards the Belgian border.

Although İkmen did eventually manage to wind down from his sojourn in the cramped compartment, it took some time. They were about thirty kilometres beyond the border when the man let him back into the cab. When he opened the hatch, İkmen felt his body literally ache to be through it. Trembling and panting from the lack of oxygen in there, he scrambled out of the hatch and sat down, blinking in the grey Belgian light, his fingers stained by the beetroot sandwich.

'You'll have to go in again when we cross the border into France and then you'll have to go in and stay in for the crossing to Dover when we reach Calais,' the man said. 'But you won't be alone.'

İkmen looked at him in horror. Alone, he had barely been able to breathe in there. With other people, that might well become impossible.

'But—'

'No one has ever died in there yet,' the man said irritably. 'You suddenly don't want to go to Britain? You know what I will have to do.' He patted the pocket of his anorak and then he smiled. İkmen felt his face drain of blood. In order to calm himself, he lit a cigarette and kept quiet.

Just outside Brussels, they stopped at a transport café where İkmen bought himself a very strong cup of coffee and a cheese sandwich. When he returned to the truck he saw that the driver had picked up some more passengers. A thin black man and a girl, also black and very obviously pregnant. As he approached, the girl pulled the scarf that covered her head over her face. From his small experience of Africans, İkmen deduced that they were probably Somalis. But he never found that out for certain, not even when the three of them were caged up together for eight hours while the truck driver boarded the ship at Calais, crossed the Channel and cleared the port of Dover. Engulfed by darkness and fighting for every breath, İkmen heard the man speak gently to the girl in what he just about recognised as Arabic. But the girl never once replied to whatever he said to her. She just wept and, when the driver finally dropped them off somewhere near Canterbury, she was still crying. İkmen, who thought that his drop-off point was to be the same as the Africans', made to try and jump down from the cab, but the driver put his hand out to stop him.

'You're going to London,' he said.

'Why do you drop those other people here?' İkmen asked.

'Because they have jobs here,' the driver said.

As the truck pulled away, İkmen saw another vehicle pull up beside the African couple and stop. Three men, all big and leather-jacketed and blond, pushed the pair roughly into their truck and then took off at high speed. Who knew what kind of work those men had lined up for them? İkmen guessed the man would do something either dangerous or illegal or both, and the girl? She had been a pretty little thing and the men in the van had leered at her. Once her baby was delivered, he didn't like to think too hard about what might happen to her. The man driving beside him, Wolfgang's son as he inwardly thought of him, didn't show a flicker of emotion, much less concern. But Wolfgang himself, İkmen felt, did really believe that he was doing some good by this. He had in the past helped people to escape from East Germany to the West. He had also intimated that he had assisted some in their flight from Hitler's concentration camps. His view of refugees and their need to move on at any cost very obviously coloured his view. Whether or not he knew about the crime and prostitution rings that his son delivered these people to, İkmen didn't know. Whether Wolfgang really did work in some instances for the German police he didn't know either. Whatever the truth of the matter, he was now in the United Kingdom and as soon as he was alone, there was a phone call he had to make.

He settled back into his seat and watched the other cars, vans and lorries on the motorway. Unlike in Turkey, where most motorists sounded their horns most of the time, here the vehicles were relatively quiet. But as he watched the traffic he noted that it was no less aggressive for all that. The British drove quietly but with a very evident and smouldering passion to be superior, fastest and best. It was then that he began to actively recall his previous visit to the UK back in the 1970s. How polite and kind he had thought the British to be at first. But then he'd gone to

64

a few pubs and seen another side to that quiet character he did not find so impressive. The cars they drove now were much sleeker and shinier than the old Morris Minors and Ford Anglias they had driven back in the seventies; they were quite clearly much richer now than they had been then. But as the truck was passed by a madly speeding Subaru complete with passengers making rude hand gestures out of the windows, he could see that money had probably not improved them.

# Chapter 8

'I don't want nothing what makes me look common, you get me?' the young girl said from inside the folds of the scarf that enfolded her head and the lower part of her face. 'Them little diamonds are well nasty.'

The woman decorating the girl's nails, the so-called 'nail technician', sighed. Why did so many of the London Turkish girls sound like Jamaicans? They didn't *really* sound like that at all. In fact as soon as either their parents or other older extended family members came on the scene they reverted either to Turkish or very well-spoken English. Of course they did! Those parents had worked very hard to send these girls to schools where they were taught to speak like the late Princess Diana. Her own parents, two hundred and fifty miles to the north in Manchester, had been just the same. 'You speak like that nice Gail from off *Coronation Street*,' her mother had told her. 'She's northern but she speaks really nice.'

'I quite like them little butterflies there,' the girl said and pointed to a small plastic tray full of tiny, nail-sized metal butterflies. 'They're nice I think, ain't it.'

'Yes.' She smiled. She didn't like this job. It was rather too girly. It was at this moment that her very girly pink mobile phone began to ring. Luckily most people had more than one mobile these days and so she knew that none of her colleagues, other nail technicians, would think anything of her taking a previously unseen phone out of her bag. She excused herself to her client and answered it.

'Hello, Ayşe here.'

'Hello, Ayşe, it's Çetin Ertegrul here,' the smoke-dried voice on the other end replied.

'Oh, Uncle Çetin!' she said excitedly in Turkish. 'How lovely to hear from you! Where are you at the moment?'

The client shuffled through the boxes of nail adornments once again and sniffed slightly impatiently.

'I'm outside a place called the Toulouse Patisserie. Very nice cakes, by the look of them. Anyway, it's off Soho Square. I haven't been to London for thirty years, I don't recognise that much.'

Ayşe laughed. 'Oh, poor uncle! Listen, do you have any money?'

'Yes. I took some sterling out at an ATM across the road.'

'Then put yourself in a black cab and ask the driver to take you to the Marmaris Nail Bar on Stoke Newington Church Street,' she said. 'It'll probably cost you about twenty pounds.'

'Twenty pounds!'

'Uncle, you're in the UK now, everything costs!' Ayşe said. 'Just get here and then we'll sort things out.' She finished the call and looked at her client. 'Sorry about that, my uncle . . .'

'From Turkey?'

'Yes.'

The girl sniffed again and then said, 'I think now I'll go for butterflies on the fingers and then one of them Chanel logos on each of the thumbs. That is cool.'

Ayşe smiled as she assembled her materials. Well, at least her colleague from İstanbul had finally made it. Soon, with luck, her 'Uncle' Çetin would become integrated into the community and maybe get a really dodgy job. Then, hopefully, she could ship out of this hellish 'beauty' parlour and get back to doing what she did best. Ayşe Kudu was one of Greater Manchester police force's few female officers trained to carry and use firearms. Fiddling about with tinfoil butterflies was most definitely not what she was accustomed to.

'So why did we come here?' İkmen asked as he sat himself down on the cold wooden bench beside her. While the light still held, his 'niece' had taken him to a place called Abney Park, which was actually a graveyard. They each had a small doner kebab. Quite what it was with these people in Europe and meetings in graveyards, İkmen didn't know. But the kebab was nice.

Ayşe said, 'Because on a weekday no one else comes here. There's the odd drunk and the occasional jogger but the illegals are generally too superstitious to hang out in a foreign graveyard and there's no need for any of those who exploit them to come here. You and I can talk.'

'And so you are . . .'

'I am a nail technician. I'm thirty-three, I'm single and I come originally from Manchester where my parents run a kebab shop. My name is Ayşe Ertegrul and you are my uncle, my dad's brother from İstanbul. You've come in illegally to find work because you've got money problems back home.'

'My son-in-law cannot work and my daughter Çiçek is pregnant,' İkmen said. 'I'll take anything I can get.' Now that he'd finished his kebab he lit a cigarette. Ayşe pulled a face.

'You know that smoking has been banned in all enclosed spaces over here, don't you?' she said.

İkmen nodded. 'And yet you see many people smoking on

69

the street, outside offices and pubs,' he said. 'Everyone smoked when I came here in the nineteen seventies. Many people still seem to do so.'

'It'll take years yet to get rid of the habit completely,' Ayşe said with rather more glee than İkmen liked. 'But anyway, look, I've managed to get you a room in a place called the Rize Guest House which is basically a big house on Leswin Road. My own bedsit is on the same street and so I'll be near at hand if you need me. The Rize is owned and run by a man called Abdullah Yigit. He's not too bothered about who takes rooms in his place, which is why I've put you in there. Also we know that at least two of the men currently living in the Rize are working for Ahmet Ülker. Both illegals. One is called Reşat Doğan and the other Süleyman Elgiz. Doğan works at what is the public face of Yacoubian Industries which is a leather clothes shop here on Church Street. Basically he sells intricate and over-the-top leather jackets to Turkish teenagers and very tailored and smart versions to British middle-class mummies. Elgiz, however, works at one or other of Ülker's factories in Hackney Wick. Ülker owns two big old industrial units down there. It's where the leather clothing he sells in his shop and elsewhere is made. It is also, we believe, the source of the vast numbers of fake handbags, purses and sunglasses that Ülker's gang, and others, flood this city with. In recent weeks we've also received some intelligence to suggest that Ülker may well be importing fake drugs from Africa and storing them in these units. Basically, these places are slave fac-tories. Süleyman Elgiz works there and enjoys the luxury of living out in Stoke Newington. We know that most of the illegal workers down at Hackney Wick also live on the site.'

'You want me to get a job in one of those factories.'

'Get to know Süleyman Elgiz. He, too, is originally from

İstanbul. Ask him about work. Also,' Ayşe continued, 'there is someone else in the Rize we need you to get to know.'

She took a small photograph out of her handbag and gave it to İkmen. It showed a thin, dark man probably in his late twenties. His long, pointed chin was covered with a sparse, wispy beard.

'This man is Ali Reza Hajizadeh,' she said. 'He is a British national, the son of Iranian refugees who came to this county in the nineteen eighties. He was introduced to radical Islamic thought while a student at Birmingham University. One of his peers at Birmingham blew himself up while making a homemade bomb in his room. The people he mixed with there were serious. He rejected his parents and devoted his life to the pursuit of radicalising other young Muslims. He, too, lives in the Rize Guest House. Officially he is in receipt of sickness benefit from the state. Unofficially and interestingly, he also works for Ülker. When not attending various Shi'a mosques across the city, he drives Ülker's wife Maxine around. Hajizadeh has been seen in the company of known jihadists, he contributes to radical newsletters and websites. He hates the west and all its works with a passion but he also,' she smiled, 'it is said, sleeps with Maxine Ülker from time to time.'

'Very pious,' İkmen said gloomily.

Ayşe smiled. 'Cultivate Hajizadeh. He speaks Turkish. Part of his mission is to radicalise the Turks of Stoke Newington,' she said. 'You're bitter about how your life has turned out so far. Maybe a renewed interest in religion might help.'

'Maybe.' İkmen put his cigarette out on the ground beside him and then lit up another.

'Yigit, the landlord of the Rize, is also important,' Ayşe continued. 'He knows Ahmet Ülker and it was through him that

Süleyman Elgiz got his job at Hackney Wick. Yigit is sly and acquisitive and it is well known that he charges new immigrants for "introductions" to prospective employers.'

'Charming.' İkmen sighed. 'But then these poor people get exploited by everyone, don't they?'

'They shouldn't come,' Ayşe said, İkmen felt somewhat harshly. 'By the way, how was your journey?'

İkmen breathed in deeply. 'Frightening, arduous. I came in with two Africans. A man and a pregnant girl. Some very heavy-looking men picked them up just outside Canterbury. To be honest, I feared for them.'

Ayşe neither responded nor commented. 'You must be tired,' she said.

Still frowning, he said, 'You have no idea.' He had been convinced he would die in that tiny compartment in the German truck. Dead, with only unintelligible Africans and thousands of bratwurst sausages for company!

She stood up. 'Keep your mobile phone with you at all times,' she said. 'In the next twenty-four hours your handler will call you.'

'But I thought—'

'No, I'm not your handler,' Ayşe said. 'I'm like you. I've been embedded here for nearly six months.'

Six months! İkmen got wearily to his feet. How long did the Metropolitan Police want him to spend on this job?

'I've a handler of my own,' Ayşe said. 'Now come on, let's get you to the Rize. Oh, you'll need this.' She shuffled around in her handbag for a moment and then took out what looked like a blue credit card. 'It's called an Oyster card. It's a pre-pay travel card like Akbil in İstanbul. We've put one hundred pounds on it for you. Use it on tubes, buses, the Docklands Light Railway.'

İkmen took the card from her and put it in his pocket.

'Does the rule about not smoking indoors apply to guest houses?' İkmen asked as they crunched down the leafy pathway through the gravestones back towards Church Street.

Ayşe, in spite of herself, smiled. 'It's a cheap Turkish pansiyon, uncle,' she said. 'What do you think?'

The room the landlord Abdullah Yigit gave to İkmen was a little bit better than the one he'd had in Berlin – at least it didn't smell. But the bedclothes were grey, the cupboards dusty and broken and the small sink was rough to the touch and heavily stained. But there was a small television, tuned to MTV. İkmen immediately changed channel to the main state broadcaster, BBC1. This he remembered from his first visit back in the 1970s. And although the presentation of the evening news programme he was watching now was much slicker than it had been back then, BBC1 news still possessed a certain gravitas that he liked.

İkmen sat down on his bed, took an ashtray from the bedside cabinet and smoked as he watched TV. He kept the volume down not because he was worried about disturbing others (the kid in the room next door had been listening to full blast rap music when he'd first arrived – no one cared) but because he didn't want anyone to know that he spoke any English. Any hope of success as a potential spy inside Ülker's organisation depended upon that.

Initially the news broadcast focused on the various conflicts in the Middle East as well as some rather gloomy economic forecasts for the coming six months. Then there was a feature on the new mayor of London, Haluk Üner. He was at a rubbish dump in a borough of east London called Barking and the mayor, together with a lot of rough-looking men in high-visibility jackets, was igniting an industrial incinerator.

'I want the gangs who produce this counterfeit trash and use the money they make from it to kill others to know that their time in London is coming to an end,' the mayor said as he flicked a switch to light the vast machine. He smiled at the men around him. 'Half a million pounds worth of fakes up in smoke!'

The men around him cheered. The piece then cut to Üner being interviewed outside the incinerator by a serious young female reporter.

'So, Mr Üner,' she said as she held the microphone up to his mouth, 'are you happy with what's happened here today?'

'The destruction of an estimated half a million pounds' worth of fake clothes, bags, watches and electrical goods?' He smiled. 'I'm delighted, Kirsty. And this is just the start! Londoners are hitting back. Through the good offices of the Metropolitan Police and through the "Condemn a Counterfeit" scheme I initiated myself whereby people can anonymously call my office and tell us about shops and businesses selling or making this rubbish, Londoners are fighting this menace.'

'Mr Üner,' the reporter continued, 'what do you say to people who see this war you're waging against the counterfeiters and their alleged terrorist masters as just window-dressing. I mean, it is well-known that you are Muslim and—'

'Yes, I am a Muslim and proud of it,' Haluk Üner said. 'My parents came here from Turkey back in the nineteen fifties. I am both British and Turkish and I am proud to call myself a Londoner too. But Kirsty, when you talk about Islam you have to understand that Islam as a religion has nothing whatsoever to do with terrorism.'

'Yes, but the terror organisation that has most threatened London in recent years is a radical Islamic one. These counterfeiters are, it is thought, bankrolling organisations like al Qaeda.'

'And other terrorist groups too. Some Islamic, some not.' He smiled again. 'It is my mission to protect all Londoners from terror threats wherever they come from. If we can cut off just one source of income that emanates from this country then we are winning. My message is simple: fakes hurt people, money from them translates into bombs and guns. Those who make the fakes are little more than slaves. This has to stop and I am going to make sure that it does.'

İkmen hadn't known that the new mayor of London had a Turkish background. He came across as very gutsy and seemed very young to be holding such a high office. He was also very handsome and reminded İkmen of Mehmet Süleyman when he was younger. But Üner seemed to have much more energy than Süleyman had ever had. And unlike his İstanbul colleague, who was lugubrious by nature and disillusioned by life, the mayor was a man with a mission. Like an American-style superhero he was going to 'clean up' his city and make it safe for old people, women and children, and he was going to do so with his Islamic credentials out for all the world to see. İkmen admired him even if he couldn't help feeling that the mayor was being really very naïve. The fakers and their terrorist backers, if such parties really did exist, wouldn't put up with Üner having their shops raided, breaking into their factories, destroying their goods and seizing their money. He had declared war on them on TV and probably via all sorts of other media too. İkmen could not help but feel a little fearful for Mr Haluk Üner.

# Chapter 9

'Mr Riley sends his best,' the man, whose name was Terry, said to İkmen. Terry was about his own age, a coppers' copper who smoked, swore and wore clothes that looked sorely in need of a good dry-clean. He was a type that was familiar to İkmen from his first visit to the UK in the seventies. The only other member of the British police he had met so far had been Ayşe and she was very unfamiliar indeed. Terry was İkmen's handler while he was undercover.

'My regards to him also,' İkmen replied with a smile.

'Yeah.'

Terry had told İkmen to meet him at a place that had turned out to be a very long way away from Stoke Newington and its environs. Brixton was the last and most southerly stop on the Victoria underground line, with a large Afro-Caribbean population. Back in the seventies Brixton had had a reputation, İkmen recalled, as a place where cannabis was easy to get, where parties were known to last for days and where some of the black men grew long and intricate hair locks.

'Called dreadlocks,' Terry explained when İkmen told him what he remembered about Brixton from his first visit. 'Worn by the Rastafarians.' Then seeing the puzzled look on İkmen's face he said, 'It's a Jamaican religion. The hair's all part of it.'

When he'd arrived at Brixton tube station, İkmen had followed the instructions Terry had given him to Brockwell Park. This had been a considerable walk for İkmen who generally tried to avoid any sort of exercise. He had turned up out of breath, which had evinced a smile from Terry who had been sitting on a bench smoking when the Turk arrived. What had also made Terry smile was the automatic way in which the gasping İkmen had lit up himself. In Terry's opinion, fags were rapidly giving way to intense jogging and occasional cocaine use amongst the young. He didn't approve.

'Now then, Çetin,' he said, 'I know Ayşe has told you what you have to do and, in your guise as her uncle, you can pass on information to her at any time. She'll help and advise you as much as she can. But I'm here to watch your back and to make sure that you stay focused and also as safe as you can under the circumstances. I can have you out of your role within minutes, believe me. The people who come to get you won't probably know who you are or what you're doing but they will get you out. Understand?'

'Yes.' They were speaking in English. That was one reason why they were so far away from Ahmet Ülker's patch.

'As you know, it's vital that no one finds out you can speak English,' Terry said. 'We want the people around Ülker to talk freely in front of you.'

'Terry, you don't speak Turkish . . .'

'No, I don't. So if you find yourself in a situation where you need to speak to me urgently but you're around people who mustn't know that you speak English, call Ayşe,' Terry said. 'Tell her you've a message for Uncle Ali, she'll understand.'

'For Uncle Ali.'

'Yes.'

Terry put his number into İkmen's phone and also provided

78

him with a street map of the city. Then there was a talk about what Terry felt İkmen needed to know about the Met in the twenty-first century. It was by no means comprehensive, but it did give İkmen some sort of idea about who he was now working for. As they talked, joggers and dog-walkers passed them by without apparently taking any particular notice. Later, they parted. İkmen now knew both of the officers he would be dealing with. The rest was up to him.

He decided not to go back to the Rize until the early evening. There had been a lot of activity in the pansiyon between six and seven o'clock that morning and İkmen suspected that most of the other men had gone out then. And so armed with his *A to Z* he decided to spend the day visiting some of the places he had seen in the 1970s. This could not of course include Scotland Yard, but he could go and see what they called the West End, where the theatres were. In addition, going in and out of stations, shops and cafés would give him the practice he needed in pretending to be a monoglot. As well as having a very good English teacher when he was at high school, İkmen's late father Timür had been a linguist. Timür could speak German, French and Russian as well as English, but the latter had been his favourite language. His sons Çetin and Halıl had been exposed to English from birth. In fact it had been Çetin's almost native ability in the English language that had kick-started his rise through the ranks of the İstanbul police force. Back in the late sixties when he had first joined up he had been one of the very few officers who was fluent in English. Back then, due to the many, many Turks who went to Germany to work, most people could 'do' German; the old aristocracy still 'did' French. But English had not been so widely spoken. Back then only people who called themselves 'travellers' ventured from Western Europe into Turkey. Now millions regularly descended upon resorts like Bodrum, Kuşadası and Marmaris where even the most lowly waiter could get by in English. Pretending not to know a word was going to be difficult.

Using his *A to Z* and his Oyster card, İkmen managed to get from Brixton, via the Victoria and Piccadilly lines, to Piccadilly Circus. Back in the seventies Piccadilly Circus had been the scene of considerable drug activity. Together with the two other Turkish colleagues with whom he had travelled to the UK, he had watched the British police raid the men's public toilets at the tube station. He remembered the terrible smell of the place, the shouting and screaming as the police banged on cubicle doors and, in some cases, broke them down with their truncheons. Then there had been the addicts themselves, pale and thin, blood sometimes running down their arms or thighs or both, the used syringes the police found all over the floor, down the toilets, sticking out of people's bodies. It had been a shock back then. Of course there were addicts in İstanbul too but not nearly so many and very few youngsters. But now when İkmen rode the escalator up from the platform and into Piccadilly Circus station, he could either not remember where the toilets were or they had gone. The place was still tatty and a little dirty, but it was no longer swathed in cigarette smoke and the people, his fellow travellers, were in general smarter than they had been.

Walking up the stairs and out into the street, he was hit by a wall of familiar sound. Traffic just got worse and worse wherever one was in the world. But he was happy to see that the statue of Eros was no longer in the middle of the Circus but had been incorporated into the pavement to the south and so was now much easier for visitors to access. Just like all the other foreigners, he walked over to the statue and had a look at it.

Some very excited Japanese teenagers were taking seemingly endless photographs of each other standing underneath the winged figure. Eros, the life force, the source of the erotic . . . Had it been some sort of joke on the part of the city's 1970s rent boys when they had set up what the Met had told him they called the 'Meat Rack' around the statue all those years ago? In the daytime, Eros had been a tourist attraction just as it was in the twenty-first century but at night it had turned into something a lot more seedy. He remembered going out on patrol one night and seeing the young boys lounging around the statue, looking up and pouting at every man that passed. There had, as he recalled, been a telephone box nearby too. He'd seen a couple – a girl and a boy – kissing inside it. That had seemed so daring to him at the time! What the British had called then 'permissive'. How innocent it had been in reality. He couldn't see the box now. It had gone, victim of the all-conquering mobile phone.

With £100 on his Oyster card, İkmen was free to roam. He did after all have to familiarise himself with London. He was interested, it wasn't difficult. What was hard, however, was pretending not to speak the language. At midday he was hungry and so finding himself up by Leicester Square station he walked into a little café, what in İstanbul would have been called a büfe, and sat down. The waitress, a young blonde girl who spoke English with a heavy eastern European accent, came over and said, 'Yes please, sir, would you like to order?'

İkmen had seen a rather inviting looking dish of spaghetti and meatballs in the café's window. He wanted to ask for just that. But he couldn't.

'Er . . .'

He looked foreign. She said, 'Can you not speak English?'

Again he wanted to say, 'Yes, of course I can and a lot better than you!' But he made himself sit, look blank and then after a couple of seconds he shrugged.

The waitress said something to him in a language he felt was probably Polish. He shrugged again. Then she said, 'Coffee? Tea? You want—'

'Coffee!' He smiled.

She wrote it down on the little order pad she had in her hand. 'And to eat?' She made a motion with her hand towards her mouth and then made chewing noises.

İkmen got up from his seat and beckoned for the girl to follow him. He went outside the café and pointed to the meatballs and spaghetti through the window.

'Ah.' The girl smiled. 'You'd like meatballs.'

'Evet,' he said – Turkish for yes. She didn't have a clue what it meant but she did now know that he wanted meatballs which, when they finally arrived, he ate with relish. When he had finished, the girl took his plate away, talking all the while to another waitress, apparently an English girl.

'I don't have any idea where he comes from,' the Polish girl said to her companion. 'Maybe he is something like Iranian or something? He said a word that was very strange.'

'Looks a bit like an Arab to me,' her companion said. The urge to jump up and say, 'I'm a Turk!' was very strong, but somehow İkmen managed to resist it. He concentrated on keeping his features as blank and unmoving as possible, but it wasn't easy and he knew he was struggling even with this small and unimportant foray.

He spent the rest of that day in and around Leicester Square and Tottenham Court Road. At the famous Foyles bookshop he practised his monoglot act again and consequently took nearly fifteen minutes to buy a Turkish-English dictionary.

He got back to the Rize at just after 6 p.m. that evening. He was tired and his back hurt from all the unaccustomed exercise. But he did not go straight up to his room; instead he sat with the men who were sharing bread, cheese, olives and black tea in the foyer. Apart from one, who was tall, slim, young and bearded, they all looked like middle-aged, overworked Turks. They looked just like he did.

Mehmet Süleyman knocked on the door of Commissioner Ardıç's office and then walked in.

'Sir?'

'Yes.' The commissioner lifted his great meaty head from contemplating a document on his desk and motioned for Süleyman to sit down.

'I've just had another call from the assistant chief of police in Diyarbakır about Ahmet Ülker,' Süleyman said as he sat down in front of Ardıç's desk. 'Apparently there is a belief amongst some of Ülker's contemporaries that he has business interests abroad.'

'Oh?' Of course Ardıç knew full well that Ülker had business interests in Britain at least but he couldn't tell Süleyman that.

'It's generally believed that he has some sort of involvement with a factory in Cambodia. Although rumour has it that he is a somewhat junior partner or minority stakeholder in that,' Süleyman said. 'A stronger lead is to an operation in London. Ülker, it is said, is married to an English woman and runs a legitimate business there in her name. But some men from Diyarbakır, it is alleged, have been employed by him in London illegally. They've gone over without jobs or visas, entered illegally and then worked for Ülker. Now if his business is legitimate, that would be quite difficult. The UK, I believe, has quite stringent

83

employment legislation. So what I think may be happening is that Ülker could be running an illegal operation alongside his legitimate business. I mean, if he's knocking out fakes here in İstanbul and in Cambodia then I don't see why he can't be doing that in London too.' And, of course, there had been that fragment of the London Underground map found just behind where Tariq had detonated his grenade. Süleyman looked at Ardıç expectantly.

The commissioner, who knew all about the London connection, was nevertheless intrigued by the idea of Ülker providing foreign work for the men and boys of Diyarbakır. The Cambodia connection was new too.

'Do you know,' he asked, 'whether any of these Diyarbakır men Ülker has given work to in London have returned?'

'No, I don't, sir, but I can try to find out,' Süleyman said.

'Do that,' the commissioner said.

'Sir, do you want me to contact Scotland Yard about a possible connection between Ülker and London?' Süleyman said.

'My English is adequate, I'll deal with Scotland Yard,' the older man said. 'You concentrate on interviewing those illegals we found at the Tarlabaşı factory and on Diyarbakır.'

'Sir, there was part of a map, the London Underground map—'

'I have informed Scotland Yard about that already,' Ardıç said.

'Quite a few of the illegals we have interviewed so far have told us that their ultimate aim was to get to an English-speaking country. The UK was of course one of those. Now if Ülker is operating there and living there then—'

'Inspector Süleyman, you can rest assured that there is a very good line of communication between myself and my opposite number in London,' Ardıç said. 'If you must know, I contacted him as soon as that map fragment was found. You need not worry about that in any way. Just continue with your own investigation and keep me informed.'

'Yes, sir.' Had İkmen been around, he would probably have been the one making contact with London, Süleyman knew. İkmen's English was so good. But İkmen was 'out of town' somewhere and so Ardıç was taking it all, apparently, upon himself. There was also talk that a European had been to see Ardıç just after the explosion at the Tarlabaşı factory. Süleyman wondered how much of what he had just told Ardıç was already known to him. As he made to leave, Ardıç said, 'Oh, and Süleyman, we still don't have any idea about who the boy who killed himself was.'

'Tariq.'

'The boy with tuberculosis, yes,' Ardıç said. 'The workers in the factory are being checked for the disease and so far all have been negative, fortunately. Inspector İkmen was of the opinion the boy was either an Afghan or a Pakistani. Every effort must be made to try and locate where this boy was staying. None of those he worked with either know or are prepared to tell. Apart from anything else, tuberculosis is a notifiable disease and we do not want an outbreak of that amongst the poor and dispossessed – or anyone else, come to that.'

'Yes, sir.' Süleyman turned at the door. 'Sir, with regard to Inspector İkmen—'

'He is out of town and currently beyond our jurisdiction, Süleyman,' Ardıç said. 'The man has other things to do for a while.' He waved a dismissive hand at his inferior and added, 'Now go about your business.'

Süleyman left. He had much to do, what with the illegal factory workers, liaising with Diyarbakır and trying to track down traces of Tariq. But he also resolved to find some time to go and speak to Dr Sarkissian too. After all, he had always been Çetin İkmen's best friend and Süleyman was far from happy about what Ardiç had told him. İkmen, he felt, was not where anyone would expect him to be. He was also possibly at some risk. Lately things between Çetin and his wife had, he knew, been very bad. And if Fatma İkmen really was freezing him out because of Bekir's death, it was possible that his colleague had volunteered for something very unwise and reckless.

# Chapter 10

It was the owner of the Rize Guest House, Abdullah Yigit, who asked İkmen to sit down with him and the others to share food. A wide, short man in his sixties, Yigit wore a pair of tattered striped pyjamas just like a lot of traditional café and pansiyon proprietors did in the far east of Turkey. Yigit, according to İkmen's 'niece' Ayşe, was a full UK citizen but he spoke English really badly. It was his wife, apparently, who did all the business and was the brains behind the operation. Mrs Yigit it was who would personally remove those who did not pay their rent. Abdullah Yigit, it seemed, was the (almost) acceptable face of the pansiyon.

'I understand you are from İstanbul, brother,' Mr Yigit said as he passed a plate over to İkmen and then gestured for him to sit on the floor beside the low table with the other men.

'Yes,' İkmen said. 'My niece—'

'The young lady from the nail shop.' Mr Yigit smiled. 'Yes, she spoke about you to my wife. How long do you hope to be in England, brother?'

İkmen wasn't accustomed to people calling him 'brother' but he knew that migrants from Anatolia often used the word freely amongst themselves.

'I don't know yet,' İkmen replied. 'It depends how things work out.'

'What things?' The man who asked was thin like himself. He wore rather more tidy and fashionable clothes than the others.

'Well . . .' İkmen didn't want to come straight out with some sort of request for work. But then again he knew that they knew the only reason he was in the UK was for just that reason. 'I used to be a security guard, back home,' he said. 'They got rid of me.'

'They?'

'I worked at a shopping mall,' İkmen said. 'Now I'm here. A man must do what he can to support his family.'

'That's true,' an older, very hairy man said miserably. 'We all have to do that.'

'Can you speak English?' asked the young bearded man who stood leaning on the reception desk to one side of the eating group.

İkmen finished the olive he had been eating before he said, 'No.'

'Oh, well, then you won't stand a chance,' the young man said. 'You might as well pack up and go home now.'

'Ali!' Mr Yigit said angrily. 'How can you say such a thing?'

'I can only say what is truly in my heart,' the young man said. 'He doesn't speak any English, what can he do?'

'Well, I don't know, but . . .' Mr Yigit shrugged and then smiled at İkmen and said, 'A security guard, you say? Mmm. I am sure that Allah will provide an answer for you, my brother.'

İkmen thanked him politely and they all began eating again. The young man turned away and İkmen heard him mutter something in English, which sounded like 'Stupid fool!' He wore Islamic dress, and İkmen recognised him from the photograph Ayşe had shown him. He was the Iranian, Ali Reza Hajizadeh. Who the other men were he didn't know and didn't discover because the rest of the meal passed in silence.

When he climbed into his lonely and slightly greasy bed that night, İkmen could not help but feel despondent. In spite of her coldness towards him of late, he missed his wife. He missed his children too and at one point he felt very tempted to call his son Sınan who was only a few miles away at his new home in Hounslow. But he knew he wasn't allowed to make contact with anyone from his real life. Only Çetin Ertegrul existed in London. The other men who lived in the pansiyon were not communicative and in his current mood his mission seemed like a huge mountain that was impossible to climb. His thoughts turned to the Iranian Ali Reza Hajizadeh. İkmen had spent a great deal of his working life around young men who were troubled and so he knew the signs very well. Ali Reza was definitely of that ilk although quite how that would manifest itself in the future he did not know. But he found the contemplation of it interesting.

'Mr Ertegrul! Mr Ertegrul!'

İkmen, sleep-sodden and exhausted, couldn't make out at first why someone was banging on his door calling out a name that wasn't his.

'Mr Ertegrul it is Mr Yigit, your landlord!' the voice said. 'You must come downstairs! It's very important! You must come!'

Realising that he was in fact Mr Ertegrul, İkmen said, 'All right, Mr Yigit, I'm coming.'

'Good. Come quick.' This was followed by the sound of heavy footfalls on the landing outside and afterwards on the stairs. İkmen quickly grabbed his clothes from off the back of a chair and after running a comb quickly through his hair he followed Mr Yigit downstairs. There in the lobby he found his 'niece' Ayşe.

His heart pounding, İkmen said, 'What—'

'Oh, Uncle Çetin,' she said, 'I thought that maybe you'd like to come for breakfast with me. I can introduce you to the İstanbul Büfe, it is my favourite place to eat.'

İkmen, still a little shell-shocked from Mr Yigit's frantic wake-up call, said, 'Allah protect me, I thought it was an emergency!'

'Well, it is,' Ayşe said, 'mainly because my first appointment is at nine thirty which gives us only forty-five minutes for break-fast.' She turned to the landlord and said, 'Thank you, Mr Yigit.'

The landlord smiled. It was at this point that İkmen realised that Mr Yigit was not alone. Standing beside him and about the same height as the landlord was a nondescript man of about thirty-five. He had a rather doughy face which didn't really suit the very modern spiked haircut that he sported. He was very smartly dressed in a dark three-piece suit.

'Come on, Uncle!' Ayşe said as she took hold of İkmen's arm and pulled him towards the front door. 'You must be hungry. I'm starving!'

Out on the street, İkmen noticed a Ferrari parked outside the Rize. Ayşe pulled him into an alleyway on the opposite side of the road and said, 'That Ferrari over there belongs to Ahmet Ülker. It was Ülker who was standing beside Mr Yigit.'

'Oh.' The nondescript man.

'Look!'

Ali Reza Hajizadeh came out of the pansiyon and stood beside the Ferrari holding a small remote control in his hand.

'The Iranian,' Ayşe said.

'Yes, I met him last night,' İkmen said. 'He wasn't very friendly.'

Ayşe pulled İkmen back a little further and then said, 'When I saw Ülker go into the Rize I knew I had to find a way for you to see him. He doesn't come here that often. It was an oppor-tunity not to be missed.'

'Hence the breakfast.'

'Hence the breakfast. Talking of which,' Ayşe said, 'we will have to go to the İstanbul for breakfast now. If we don't, someone will tell someone else who will tell Yigit – you know how it goes. This is a small community here in Stoke Newington. Everyone knows everyone else.'

'I understand.'

'I have something to tell you too,' Ayşe said without explaining what.

After taking a last look at the figure of Ali Reza Hajizadeh they set off in the direction of Stoke Newington High Street. Ayşe took İkmen's arm. 'Have you met either Süleyman Elgiz or Reşat Doğan yet?' she asked.

'I met a group of men last night,' İkmen said. 'Together with Mr Yigit they shared their food with me. But I didn't discover any of their names.'

'Only Ali Reza.'

'You showed me a photograph of him. And he sticks out somewhat,' İkmen said. 'He's young, his Turkish accent isn't that good and he slips into English which the others don't. He's trouble.'

'Yes, we know,' Ayşe said.

'I think it may take some time to get in with these men to the extent that I can ask them about work,' İkmen said. 'They seem very closed off.'

'Well, they're illegal.'

'Yes, which means it will take them some time to trust even innocuous old Çetin Ertegrul,' İkmen said. 'Ayşe, I don't think that they are necessarily going to help me.'

Now on Stoke Newington High Street, Ayşe turned into a rather greasy and nondescript-looking doorway and said, 'This is the İstanbul. They do the best *menemen* outside Turkey.' She scanned the restaurant to see if there were any tables free where they could talk undisturbed and finding that there weren't, she told İkmen what she needed to tell him on the doorstep. 'We won't need to bother about either Elgiz or Doğan soon. Ahmet Ülker will be needing some new security guards for his factories in a few days' time. We need to move forward with this investigation now. Make sure that Mr Yigit knows what you do.'

'It came up in conversation last night actually,' İkmen said. 'I told them all what I do. Not that I think it impressed Ali Reza. But they know.'

'Good.' Ayşe smiled. 'Make sure you're around Stoke Newington and the pansiyon a lot in the next few days. Yigit sees himself as a fixer and he and Ülker know each other. If Yigit likes you, it will help. But he will rip you off royally, so be prepared.'

Ali Reza Hajizadeh slipped into the driver's seat and looked across at the woman in the passenger seat. The competing perfumes from her many and various cosmetics nearly made him cough. But he took one of her hands and put it on his crotch.

'Your husband wants his cigarettes. They're in the glove compartment,' he said.

Maxine Ülker opened the glove compartment with one hand while she pulled on his penis with the other. Doing men in cars was something she was very familiar with although with Ali Reza there was an added element. With him, there was love too, at least on her side. That said, he was young and as soon as she went down on him it was all over in a second.

'You're a dirty bitch, Maxine,' he said as he leaned back in the luxurious leather seat, panting.

Maxine fixed her lipstick and said, 'It's what you love about me, isn't it?'

She handed him her husband's cigarettes and lighter. He looked at her with the usual mixture of lust and loathing. With her long, sleek blonde hair and her big tits she was like an animated sex doll. But that, although it made him feel dirty and guilty, was what he liked about her. She'd been a whore when her husband met her and so she knew her way around what men liked in the sack. Ali Reza had no doubt that Maxine still did it with Ahmet all the time, but she did it with him too and that was the point. She'd fallen for him, which was exactly what he had wanted her to do. With Maxine besotted, Ali Reza knew that she would do whatever he asked of her, including spying on her own husband. And Ahmet Ülker needed watching. Although nominally a Muslim, he wasn't a 'soldier' like he himself was. Ahmet was necessary for the moment, but in the long run he was expendable. Like Maxine. And because she was little more than a used tissue to him, that was OK. Had he loved her, a foreigner, an infidel and a whore, that would have been a sin. But he didn't and so that was OK.

# Chapter 11

The Sılay brothers were not stupid. Uneducated and a bit rough and ready at times but they knew what was what and how to survive. They'd both known Ahmet Ülker back in Diyarbakır and so since coming to England they'd had help from him. But before he'd taken them on to guard his Hackney factories, the brothers had done their fair share of ducking and diving in order to make a crust. Zeki, the older of the two, had laboured for a building firm whose boss had not been too fussy about the law. He'd not been very fussy about paying his workers either and so Zeki had moved on to first waiting at table in a café and then cleaning in a massage parlour. Yaşar Sılay, Zeki's brother, had taken a rather different course. Just as he had done back in Diyarbakır, he'd made his living dealing drugs, cannabis mainly. Yaşar wasn't trustworthy and Ahmet Ülker had known it when he took him and his brother on as night security guards for his factories in Hackney. But Zeki had assured Ahmet that he would keep his brother in line and make sure that he didn't deal drugs any more.

'Because although you have the title security guard at my factories, what you really are is an early warning system,' Ahmet had told Zeki when he took him and his brother on. 'You watch out for the police, you watch for suspicious people hanging around, you make sure that none of my workers leaves my buildings under any circumstances. I need you and Yaşar to be

95

completely trustworthy and completely straight. No drugs, do you understand? No drugs.'

Zeki had readily agreed. He hated cleaning up after what he considered to be the vile things that went on in the massage parlour. Persuading Yaşar to swap his casual drug dealing for something more regular and demanding had not been easy, but he had done it. Yaşar had stopped dealing. What he hadn't stopped doing was smoking drugs himself. He didn't do it at work. True to his brother's promise to Ahmet Ülker, he did not jeopardise the operation of the factories by being off his face on the job. With goods coming in and going out sometimes all night long, not to mention quite a few problems with the people Ahmet got to work for him, he couldn't afford to be drugged up. But on the journey to work, which the two brothers made from their flat on Clissold Road to the factories at Hackney Wick, he would have one small joint. This he always lit as he walked from the flat to the battered old Vauxhall Cavalier the two of them used to get to work. Zeki had told him again and again that that wasn't a good idea, that neighbours might smell the weed and shop them to the police. But Yaşar said it would be all right. He was convinced that the neighbours neither knew nor cared what they did. It was therefore quite a shock to Yaşar when he came out of his flat and felt a heavy and unfamiliar hand upon his shoulder. Over by the car he could see his brother Zeki, his face a grey picture of terror, being frisked by two uniformed police officers. The officer who had his hand on Yaşar's shoulder said to him, 'Now what is that I can smell, sir? Not an ordinary Marlboro Light, is it?'

'Tuberculosis isn't an easy disease to catch,' Arto Sarkissian said to Mehmet Süleyman. 'We don't see it that often these days although it is making something of a comeback now.'

'Why is that?'

The Armenian shrugged. 'Population movement is part of it. In countries like Afghanistan where health care is perfunctory to say the least, people are not vaccinated and therefore vulnerable. People flee from places like Afghanistan to make homes in other, safer countries and so the disease spreads further than it would under normal circumstances. I don't blame those who flee for doing so but it does give us problems.'

They were standing outside what looked like a derelict house in the district of Cihangir, opposite the Taksim Hospital. The house, which local talk said was occupied by men generically described as 'Indians', was being searched by uniformed officers.

'I may be wrong but I think it unlikely that the boy Tariq came into the country alone,' Arto said. 'He was sixteen at the most and from the look of his teeth, he'd probably lived in some remote place for most of his life. I doubt very much whether he could have negotiated his way to İstanbul all on his own. And if he was with others then there is a higher than usual chance that those people have tuberculosis too. We have to find them, and soon.'

They both looked up at the tall stone house, its once elegant internal spiral staircase visible through holes in its external walls. Already officers had found some evidence that people slept there: small amounts of food, ashes from wood fires, the occasional tattered bedroll. But so far no people had been found. The security guard at the hospital had told Süleyman that smoke came out of the old house on most evenings and the patients in the wards opposite sometimes saw lights, probably from torches, at the glassless windows.

Süleyman turned back to Arto Şarkissian. 'Doctor, have you heard from Çetin?'

'Oh, my friend is completely off the radar as far as I am concerned, Inspector,' Şarkissian replied. 'His destination, so I understand, is police business. Don't you know where he is?'

'No,' Süleyman said. Without thinking he bit his lip.

'It makes you anxious?' the Armenian asked and then without waiting for a reply he said, 'I've always been close to his son Bülent. I've met him a few times since Çetin left. The family are managing.'

Neither the doctor nor the policeman mentioned the difficulties they both knew Çetin and Fatma had been having. To talk of the personal life of a friend is not something polite Turkish men do. After a few moments Süleyman burst out with, 'I just wish I knew he was safe!'

'Sir! Sir!' called one of the constables.

Süleyman looked towards the house again. There was a lot of activity around the small door underneath the main entrance. He walked over to the constable, Yıldız. 'What is it?'

'There's a man in the basement, sir,' another constable said. 'Look.' He pointed through the low door into the chamber where Süleyman saw a pair of bright eyes looking at him out of a very dark face.

'Hello,' said Süleyman. The man looked old and scared and very, very thin. 'Do you—'

'Don't hit me! Please do not to hit me!' the man said and threw his skinny arms up and across his face in panic. 'I will tell you about the boy who blew himself up! I will tell you about Tariq!' Oddly, he spoke in English.

Had he been able to go to the West End or the City it would have been easy for İkmen to amuse himself. In Stoke Newington it would have been possible for him to have a good time had he

98

been able to use his English. There were bookshops, small art galleries, cafés full of interesting-looking people. Some of course were Turks and he could have spoken to them, but remembering what Ayşe had said about the smallness of the Turkish population in Stoke Newington, he didn't really want to forge relationships. Çetin Ertegrul was an illegal Turkish migrant who wanted to work and send money home. The last thing he needed was for some new male friend to invite him back to his house and introduce him to his recently widowed sister. And so for two days after Ayşe had taken him to breakfast he drifted aimlessly around damp streets. He looked in shop windows that advertised Turkish foodstuffs, poked around in hardware shops that looked exactly like such places did back in İstanbul, and occasionally sat in Clissold Park, smoking and drinking Coca-Cola from cans. And although he knew that Ayşe and Terry were available to him, until he was somehow inside Ülker's organisation there was really nothing to talk about. Apparently the Met were engineering a situation whereby Ülker would soon need one or more security guards. All he could do was wait.

When he returned to the Rize that evening he found Mr Yigit in halting conversation with a thin Englishman whose face was badly scarred on one side. He was probably around İkmen's own age but much better dressed, although the hand with which he held a smoking cigarette was yellow and rather dirty-looking.

'Oh, Mr Ertegrul,' Yigit said as İkmen passed by his desk in the lobby. 'Did you find any work? Did you have a good day?'

'No, I didn't find any work,' İkmen said. 'The day was OK.'

'Ah.' Mr Yigit turned towards the Englishman and said, 'He looks for work.'

'You all look for work, old son,' the Englishman replied. 'That's what you lot do. How much of it do you think we have over here?'

The accent wasn't broad but it was definitely London. What was also definite was the clear distaste this man had for İkmen's 'lot'.

'But Mr Harrison,' Mr Yigit said, 'you must not to make the complaining. Turkish man, Mr Ülker, he give it a job to you.'

'Don't give me a load of pony about how I should be grateful to Ahmet Ülker!' the Englishman said angrily. 'He should be fucking grateful to me!'

'Ah, but I mean nothing to it, Mr Harrison,' the pansiyon owner said. 'Only fact, he give job to you when really is difficult for you—'

'What the fuck are you staring at, Abdul?' The Englishman's face was suddenly puce with anger. Startled, İkmen took a step backwards. 'Uh . . .'

Yigit walked over to him and put an arm round his shoulders. 'Oh, Mr Harrison,' he said, 'sorry, sorry. Mr Ertegrul, he speaks no English.' Then he turned to İkmen and said, 'Don't stare at him, please, Mr Ertegrul. He is an ill-mannered bastard, like so many of them.'

'I'm sorry, I didn't mean—'

'Oh, pay it no mind. Pay it no mind.' Yigit smiled. 'He's an annoying man but one that a person has to be polite to.'

'Speak bloody English, will you, Yigit!' the Englishman growled. 'God help us!'

'Sorry! Sorry!'

'Harrison looked İkmen up and down with some distaste, 'So what does he do, this new mate of yours? What is he? A waiter? Who among you lot isn't? Or is he some bloody idiot who thinks he can lay bricks?'

100

'Security guard,' Yigit said to the Englishman. 'Back in
İstanbul Mr Ertegrul is security guard. Mr Harrison, I think
maybe that—'

'What, with no bloody English?' Mr Harrison puffed on what
was left of his cigarette and then put it out. 'Five foot and a fag
paper and without a word of English! What bleeding use would
he be? Christ Almighty, Yigit, even them stupid druggie brothers
could do their "good mornings" and their "please" and "thank
yous". This one looks like he's fucking brain dead!'

'Oh but—'

'What's going on?' İkmen asked. 'What's he saying?'

Yigit pulled up his baggy pyjama bottoms and smiled again.
'Mr Ertegrul, this man's employer now has some vacancies for
security guards.'

İkmen opened his eyes wide and said, 'Does he?'

'Yes, he has good Turkish employer,' Yigit said. 'Mr Ertegrul,
if I can get you in, maybe to meet this man's employer . . .'

'I would be interested,' İkmen said.

'Of course, and if I help you, there would naturally be a consider-
ation . . .'

Money. Of course.

'Yigit, if you're telling him you can get him a job, you can
stop that right now!' Harrison said. 'He can't speak English!
Don't tell him you'll get him something when you can't! Don't
ask him for money to do it either. I know you, you old twister!'

'Mr Harrison, I don't never ask people for money!' Yigit said.
'And why he don't make the security guard anyway? He don't
need English.'

'Yes, he does!' the Englishman said. 'How's he going to—'

'Many peoples work in factories for Mr Ülker don't have no
English,' Mr Yigit said. 'Thousand, thousand languages there.'

'Yeah, but the security guards are a bit different,' Harrison said. 'What if the old bill come along in the night and try to speak to him? They're gonna suss what he is straight away and then we're back to square one again.'

'This man, Mr Ertegrul, is a decent man,' Mr Yigit said. 'He don't smoke drugs. Not like Sılay brothers.'

'I'm not saying he isn't decent! What I am saying is that he's got no English!'

'What's he saying?' İkmen asked. 'What's going on, Mr Yigit?' He looked genuinely bemused.

'Nothing. Nothing,' Yigit soothed. He clearly wanted to make a few pounds out of him if he could. 'There now, Mr Ertegrul, don't you worry. This Englishman is nothing, just a stupid pig. You know he works for Turkish people five years, still he speaks not a word of our language. I know his boss, he is a personal friend of mine. Don't worry, I will get you an introduction.'

# Chapter 12

The old man's name was Abdurrahman Iqbal and he was a Pakistani citizen. His passport stated that he had been born in 1920 which meant that he was eighty-seven years old.

'I was born in India, Calcutta,' he told Süleyman. 'Before partition, you see. There was no Pakistan before nineteen forty-seven.'

'I know, Mr Iqbal,' Süleyman said. 'Now, you told Dr Sarkissian here and myself that you knew the boy Tariq, the boy who blew himself up in Tarlabaşı.'

Unusually, Arto Sarkissian had come into the interview room with Süleyman and İzzet Melik. He'd come because the Pakistani was very old, very thin and could possibly need medical attention. He would also at some point need to explain to him about Tariq's illness and what that might mean for him.

The old man shrugged. 'I knew that the police would come sometime,' he said sadly. 'I told the other Afghans as soon as Tariq did what he did. I said, "You must go now or the police will catch you!"'

'You live in that house with illegal Afghan—'

'I used to,' Iqbal said. 'But you have me here now and the Afghans when they know you have been there, they will disappear.'

'Do you know their names, these Afghans?' İzzet Melik asked.

Iqbal shook his head. 'No. I knew only Tariq,' he said. 'The

103

others are all grown men. They didn't want an old man with them. But Tariq? He was so young and alone and sick too – always coughing. The others ignored him but to me he was a poor confused boy. I tried to help him. I failed.'

'Mr Iqbal,' Süleyman said, 'we need to know everything you know about Tariq. It is very important. You also need to consider when you answer that you are an illegal immigrant into this country. What you tell us may make those in immigration look more favourably upon you.'

The old man smiled. 'You mean, sir, your immigration people might help me to stay?' He shook his head. 'With great respect, I do not want to stay here. I am in transit only. My hope was to move on soon.'

'Into the European Union?'

'To Great Britain,' he said. 'That was where Tariq was going too, you know.'

'All right, before we speak of your plans, let's get back to Tariq,' Süleyman said. 'What do you know about him?'

Iqbal told them that Tariq, a Sunni Muslim, was an Afghan from a village to the north of Kabul. All of his family with the exception of one older brother had been killed in the various battles that had taken place between the Afghan army and the Taliban. Left with a hatred for both the American-backed Afghan army and the Taliban, Tariq had left Kabul and was making his way to London to be with his brother. Already very sick, his condition had deteriorated by the time he got to İstanbul. He had also run out of money. Abdurrahman Iqbal had found the boy begging on İstiklal Street. At first he had thought that he was a fellow Pakistani, but when he found out that he was an Afghan he took him into the house opposite the Taksim Hospital. It was, after all, a haunt for others of his kind even if they wanted little to do with him. In the limited way that he could, he nursed Tariq and got him on his feet again. The boy had been grateful. When he'd heard about the possibility of getting some work at an illegal factory in Tarlabaşı, he had jumped at the chance. He needed money to go on further and he also wanted to get some cash for Iqbal.

'I was a little short of money myself by then,' the old man said. 'And so the boy went to work. He spoke some Turkish on account of his mother having been a Turkoman.'

And for a while he got on with his job very well. His father had been a tailor and had taught him to sew when he was little. Stitching leather handbags wasn't so much different. But as the weeks passed, Iqbal began to see a change in his young friend. Not only did his cough get worse again but he began to come out with things that the old Pakistani wasn't sure were true.

'At first he was very happy because he said his new bosses were going to arrange transport to England for him. I told him to be careful,' Iqbal said, 'because you know, gentlemen, what some of these people traffickers can be like. People who make false goods are criminals and so if they also traffic people, those people sometimes end up as their slaves in their new country. Prostitution and things like that.'

But as time went on it became apparent that something even more sinister was happening to Tariq at his place of work. Someone at the factory, Tariq never said who, began to talk to him about fundamentalism. He told Iqbal that the way it was presented sounded just like the Taliban and at first he was appalled. But as time went on he began to feel more and more guilty about leaving his country in the hands of 'infidels'.

'I told him they were poisoning his mind,' the old man said. 'But Tariq said that they had promised not only to take him to

London but to give a considerable amount of money to his brother there.'

'What did they want from Tariq in return?' Süleyman asked.

The old man lowered his eyes. 'Tariq knew that he was very sick. His only desire was to see his brother before he died.' He looked up sharply and said, 'They wanted him to explode a bomb somewhere in London.'

'A suicide attack?'

'Yes.'

Süleyman leaned across the table and looked deeply into the old man's eyes. 'Where?'

He shrugged. 'I don't know. London. I have never been there.'

Süleyman turned to İzzet Melik and spoke in Turkish. 'İzzet, the two foremen we arrested at the Tarlabaşı factory—'

'Awaiting trial, sir.'

'Contact the prison and tell the authorities we need to speak to them,' Süleyman said.

'Now?'

'Right now,' his superior said. As İzzet Melik rose to his feet, he added, 'And tell Commissioner Ardıç that we may well have some more information the police in London will find interesting.'

'Yes, sir.' İzzet left.

'Carry on, Mr Iqbal.'

'I told Tariq to leave that place and somehow I would get us both to London,' he said. 'But he was in two minds. On the one hand he knew I was right. He was a good Muslim who knew that violence and Islam are two ideas that just cannot be connected. A good Muslim is a peaceful and kind person, caring of everyone and prejudiced in no way against anyone. But growing up in that terrible country . . .' He shook his head.

'The people in that factory told him that if he blew himself up, his soul would go straight to Paradise. They gave him guns and grenades to make him feel powerful. Young men like such things. He brought them home! Allah, but I nearly took them from him and threw them into the Bosphorus. I wish now that I had. Two weeks before he killed himself he talked of opening his veins to get himself out of pursuing their plan. I told him not to. Maybe I was wrong in that.' He looked over at Dr Sarkissian. 'I know you know what was wrong with Tariq, sir.'

'Tariq was in the final stages of tuberculosis,' the doctor said. 'That's why we need to find everyone he came into contact with. I will need to X-ray your chest and do blood and skin tests. Tuberculosis is a notifiable disease. We have to protect the public.'

The old man smiled. 'I have no problem with your tests, doctor,' he said. 'If I could find the Afghans for you I would but . . .' He shrugged. 'You know, in my life I have known various people who make fake goods for their living. But I have never ever come across any who do that and are also involved in jihad. It's a very strange combination, don't you think?'

The knock on the door burst into İkmen's dream as someone hammering on the entrance to his apartment back in İstanbul. In his dream it was his son Bekir, back from the dead, shot and bleeding. In reality it was Mr Yigit.

'Mr Ertegrul,' he said. 'You must get up!'

'Get up?'

İkmen looked at the small travel clock he kept beside his bed and saw that it was 2 a.m.

'What's the matter?'

'Mr Ertegrul,' Yigit said excitedly, 'I have secured you a job interview! That stupid Mr Harrison was wrong and I was right.

Of course Mr Ülker would want to see you for a job at his factory! He needs security guards! You are a security guard. Get your clothes on and come now.'

İkmen sat up and blinked at the harsh light that Yigit had let in from the corridor. 'Now?'

'Of course now!' Yigit replied. 'You must work at night. It is night now! Come along, Mr Ülker is waiting!'

Ten minutes later İkmen found himself inside an old Ford Escort with Yigit leaning heavily across the steering wheel and squinting so that he could see the road ahead. It was neither raining nor snowing and so İkmen could only conclude that Yigit's eyesight was not all that it could be. It didn't take them long to get to some scrubby wasteland that was just beyond a railway station called Hackney Wick. The area, which was criss-crossed by dirt tracks and pot-holed roads, was semi-derelict. There were buildings everywhere but most of them were little more than skeletons and those that were not were generally leaning at crazy and unsafe angles. This was not the shining landscape of Canary Wharf or the City. No, this was like the old London of the seventies that he had known when he was young. Dark and dirty, reeking of poverty and despair. And not just figuratively either. İkmen wrinkled up his nose and said, 'What on earth is that smell?'

'Oh, many apologies,' Yigit said. 'That, Mr Ertegrul, is a farm. A pig farm, I am afraid. But it is a way from here, over the other side. I promise you faithfully you will never so much as have to look at the filthy animals. No.'

'Right. OK.' It was faintly touching the way that Mr Yigit was so concerned for İkmen and any possible contact between himself and forbidden pigs. Looking out for his soul. İkmen smiled. But then his landlord changed tack and was much more upbeat.

108

'This area is where we will have the Olympics in a few years' time,' Yigit said as he pulled up beside a very long, very scruffy-looking wooden building. 'An Olympic village! I think it will be most spectacular.'

Between his own tiredness and the down-at-heel hopelessness of wherever they were, İkmen couldn't imagine how anyone could clear the place up, much less build an Olympic village on the site. Outside the wooden building İkmen could see two men. One of them was clearly the Englishman he had seen with Yigit earlier, Harrison. The other was shorter and darker, seemingly rather better dressed, and İkmen recognised him immediately. It was Ahmet Ülker. Before either of them got out of the car, Yigit leaned across to İkmen and said, 'Now look, brother, that is Mr Ülker there. If he does give you the job you will owe me two hundred and fifty pounds. That's one hundred and fifty Turkish lire. Job-finder's fee. But Mr Ülker is a good employer. You will make good money. And don't worry, I won't take my fee until you have been paid.' He smiled.

They got out of the car and walked over to the two men. İkmen could see light coming through the various cracks in the wooden boards the building was made of. There was noise, too, the sound of many industrial sewing machines. The sound that had greeted him just before he had broken into the illegal factory in Tarlabaşı.

'Mr Ertegrul?' That spiky haircut Ahmet Ülker had didn't look any better now than it had done in the lobby of the Rize.

'Yes.'

Ülker didn't smile which was probably just as well. Doughy faces like Ülker's did not, İkmen had always felt, suit levity very well.

Ülker pointed at the building behind him. 'This is one of my businesses,' he said in English. 'The other one is behind it.'

'Eh?'

İkmen heard the sound of a deep sigh, which came from Mr Harrison. 'Ahmet, I told you he doesn't speak any English!' he said angrily. 'God Almighty, this is such a waste of fucking time!'

'Oh, but Mr Ülker, my friend Mr Ertegrul is very willing to work and . . .' Mr Yigit looked at İkmen and said in Turkish, 'You will learn English, won't you, Mr Ertegrul?'

'As soon as I am able,' İkmen said. 'Yes.'

Ahmet Ülker frowned. 'This job doesn't just involve guarding this place,' he said in Turkish now. 'You have to take deliveries and you have to make sure that the workers inside do their shifts and don't call attention to themselves. In other words, you have to keep them all inside.'

'I can do that.'

'With no English?'

'He can! He can!' Mr Yigit said on İkmen's behalf. 'Mr Ülker, almost none of the people who work for you speak English!'

'In the factory that doesn't matter,' Ülker said, 'but out here—'

'But Mr Ülker, the other man that you have, he can speak English, can't he?'

'Mustafa? Yes,' Ülker said. 'I have taken him on to guard the other building. But—'

'Mr Ülker, you said that you would give my friend here a try,' Yigit said. 'Maybe when deliveries come, Mr Ertegrul can ask Mustafa to help him with that.'

Ülker frowned.

'It's a fucking ridiculous idea!' Harrison persisted. 'It'll be like employing a retard!'

For a moment no one said anything. But then Yigit, who had been thinking rather rapidly about how he might save his precious

110

£250, said in English, 'Mr Ülker, there can I think be benefit to Mr Ertegrul no speaking English.'

'Oh?'

'What fucking shit are you talking now, Yigit?' Harrison said.

'All suppliers speak only English,' Yigit said. 'Everyone speak English! You do not know Mr Ertegrul, I do not know him either. He is uncle to Ayşe at the beauty shop, but who is she? He say he is guard in İstanbul. But . . .' Yigit shrugged. 'Try him, Mr Ülker. All I say. Then get rid of him if he no good. He see things but he understand nothing. He tell nobody nothing. You say whatever you want in front of him.'

Again, no one spoke. Ülker put his fingers up to his lips while he regarded İkmen closely. For his part, İkmen lowered his eyes. Maybe he feared that Ülker would see in them the light of comprehension and intelligence. The man from Diyarbakır wanted a thick, mindless peasant with no education. That was what İkmen hoped he was giving him.

'All right,' he said after a while. Then he said it again in Turkish and added, to İkmen, 'I will give you a try.'

'Christ!' Derek Harrison pulled Ülker towards him and hissed, 'What the fuck will our partners—'

'Derek, go and get Mustafa,' Ülker interrupted angrily. 'He can show this man the ropes.'

'Ahmet!' Harrison tugged on Ülker's arm once more.

'Just do it!' Ülker shrieked. Reluctantly, Harrison left. Then Ülker looked at İkmen again and said, 'Let me down, try to cheat me or fail in your job in any way and I'll break your legs. Understand?'

İkmen, his eyes still lowered, said, 'Yes, sir.'

'I'll pay you two pounds an hour for a twelve-hour shift,' Ülker said.

'Two pounds an hour is twenty-four pounds for just one night's work, that is very good money,' Yigit told İkmen. 'You will very soon have paid me back my two hundred and fifty. It will go in a heartbeat, Mr Ertegrul.'

Ülker looked sourly at Yigit and said, 'That and whatever you owe to whoever trafficked you into this country will mean you'll be able to send maybe five pounds home every week. Not that that is any of my concern.'

İkmen didn't answer. Ülker said, 'Your niece told Mr Yigit you came in from Germany.'

'Yes, sir. An old Jewish man, he—'

'Yes, I know of an old Jewish man in Germany,' Ülker said. 'Ah well.'

He was well-informed. But then he would have to be, given what he did for a living, given what had just happened to his previous two guards. Obviously Wolfgang back in Berlin passed some sort of test.

Harrison returned with a tall, thick-set young man who looked like a particularly vicious grease wrestler.

'This is Mustafa,' Yigit told İkmen. 'He will look after you.'

Ayşe Kudu woke up to find a very gratifying message on her phone from Çetin İkmen. Ahmet Ülker was apparently trying him out for a job as a security guard at one of his factories. He had been recommended by Mr Yigit. This, together with the news that Ülker could apparently be involved with some other people, namely business partners, was progress. She would have to ask İkmen just how much Yigit had charged him for his 'services' as a fixer, she thought with a smile. A second message told her she should call her 'Father', in other words Scotland Yard. News from that quarter was sobering. Apparently the police in İstanbul had discovered that someone had been grooming Tariq, the boy who had blown himself up at Ahmet Ülker's Tarlabaşı factory, to be a suicide bomber in London. But apparently Tariq had had doubts; in reality he didn't want to kill anyone.

'Whether or not the attempt to radicalise the boy involved Ülker himself, we know that people connected to him are radicalising kids,' Riley said. 'Tariq failed. But if they really want to bomb London, a little setback like this won't stop them.'

'No.'

'Tell your Uncle Çetin to keep his ear to the ground when you see him, won't you?' Riley said.

Ayşe said that she would. Shortly afterwards she received another text from İkmen which said, 'Ülker has a man called Derek Harrison. Please check.'

# Chapter 13

Derek Harrison knew all about Maxine Ülker and that barking mad Persian of hers. As Ahmet's assistant he sometimes had to go up to his house on The Bishops Avenue to pick stuff up his boss couldn't be bothered to get for himself. The lazy bastard was half Derek's age, but then that was how it was, how it had been for a very long time.

About a year back he'd caught them. In one of the many spare bedrooms. Maxine had been on top, eyes closed, licking her lips as she moved up and down on the Iranian's cock. Later, Derek had stuck around, he was good at that, he'd watched her suck him off, and the Persian had talked dirty to her as she did it. So much for Ali Reza's supposed piety. Obviously sinning for him did not include shafting his boss's wife or having her give him a blow job. Not that Derek gave a shit.

Ahmet Ülker was just one in a long line of nasty and unscrupulous employers he'd had since the late seventies. Unskilled and with a whole host of health problems that were not his fault, Derek Harrison had been forced to seek such employers, forced to become the kind of thing that tortures, grasses and maims. No firm with any standards wanted people like him. Derek had only one foot, he was diabetic and his ticker was more than a little dicky. The government said that people with all sorts of disabilities could get and were entitled to jobs, just like everyone else. But in practice that didn't happen, certainly not in the line of work Derek had wanted to do. They didn't let you drive a train with a dodgy heart and only one foot. And because he didn't want to become some sort of poof behind an office desk or a grunt on a building site, Derek had become an enforcer for people like Ahmet. He was bitter, and pulling out people's fingernails or burning them with cigarettes didn't cause him stress. His heart didn't even race when he did things like that. What did make his heart race was when he considered what he had wanted to be and why he hadn't been able to do it. That was what stopped him shopping Maxine and Ali Reza to his employer. Ahmet was putting things in hand to right the wrong that had been done to Derek all those years ago. Ahmet was doing it for his own reasons, to increase his standing with people he was in the process of getting into partnership with, but Derek was glad. Derek also knew that what his boss didn't need as he brought his wonderful, terrible plan to fruition was the distraction of an unfaithful wife and the bother of having to kill and then dispose of some bloody mad Iranian. The Iranian wouldn't be around for much longer anyway, not if everything went to plan.

'It isn't a lot to show for a life, even a short one like Tariq's,' Abdurrahman Iqbal said as he showed Süleyman the few poor things the boy had possessed. They were back at the house opposite the Taksim Hospital, now cordoned off by police tape and guarded by two constables. Abdurrahman had had his blood and skin tests for tuberculosis, all that remained was the X-ray, which Dr Sarkissian had arranged to take place later at the hospital.

Süleyman looked down at the pathetic bedroll, the few tattered jumpers and the thick leather satchel. This latter item he picked up and opened. 'So, Mr Iqbal,' he said, 'why were you on your way to London? Do you have family there?'

The old man sighed. 'I don't have family anywhere,' he said.

'Then . . .'

'Inspector, I was born in a country that is on hostile terms with the country that I live in now. I am an Indian. I was born in Calcutta, my first language is not Urdu as in Pakistan, but Hindi as in India. I speak Hindi first, English second and Urdu third.'

Süleyman was frowning as he looked through the satchel. 'So you feel rootless.'

'Yes. I cannot go back to India because Pakistan and India do not enjoy good relations. I would not be welcome there. But many years ago, before partition, I worked as a driver to an English army captain. He was called Captain Jackson and he said to me that if I was ever in England I should regard his home as my home. I do not feel comfortable in my country of Pakistan any more and so it is my very sincere wish to visit Captain Jackson in England and stay with him.'

Süleyman found a pen, some paper tissues, an Afghan passport and a notebook in the bag. 'So why didn't you just visit this captain as a tourist?' he asked the old man.

'Because I am not a tourist!' Abdurrahman said. 'I want to stay in England.'

At first Süleyman opened the notebook the wrong way round. Then he remembered that Afghans wrote using the Arabic script and so read from right to left. He turned the book round. At the top of every page were some printed characters he thought just might be dates. 'Mr Iqbal,' he said, 'can you tell me anything about this book, please?'

He handed it over to the old man who took a pair of spectacles out of his pocket, put them on and then looked at the item.

'His diary,' he said. 'Tariq's.'

'You saw him write in it?'

'Yes, although I can't understand it, if that is what you were hoping. The Afghans speak Dari. I do not. Or rather I can read the letters while not understanding the words, if you know what I mean.'

'So you cannot tell which month is which or—'

'Oh, I know that this word here is equivalent to this month, April, this year,' the old man said as he pointed to a selection of marks at the top of one of the pages. Only since the coming of Atatürk's Republic back in the 1920s had Turks been using the Latin alphabet. Before that people like Süleyman would have been familiar with Arabic characters. But so thoroughly had the new alphabet taken hold in the country that only the very old and Ottoman scholars could still decipher Arabic script in the twenty-first century.

'Mmm. We will have to get it translated,' Süleyman said and he held his hand out to take the book back.

But Abdurrahman didn't give it back immediately. 'I am just wondering,' he said, 'whether he wrote down any details about the journey to London his employers had promised him.'

He flicked through the pages rather heavy-handedly. Süleyman frowned. 'Yes, but if—'

'Ah, here is something,' the old man said. 'May the third.'

'That is in five days' time.'

The old man squinted at the page. 'The problem with Dari, and with Arabic and Urdu for that matter, is that one must know the context. This says either Merk or Mark and then the other word could be Lene or Lana or Lena. I don't know. But there is something here in your Latin script.'

Süleyman leaned over his shoulder. 'EC3?'

'Yes.' The old man looked grave now. 'My friend Captain Jackson, the address I have for him from nineteen forty-seven is WC2. It means west city two. There are also east city codes. I think that EC3 is a district of London.'

When Çetin İkmen returned to the Rize after half a night over at Hackney Wick, Mr Yigit was the first person to ask him how it went.

'Mr Ülker has not yet offered me the job,' İkmen said as the pansiyon owner barrelled towards him, his hands outstretched in anticipation.

In fact neither Ülker nor Harrison had stuck around long after İkmen had been given over into the care of the thuggish Mustafa. Rough and boorish, this creature had told him all about 'the ropes', which seemed to consist solely of walking around the factory all night long and beating any people inside who tried to get out. Deliveries of unspecified things would happen from time to time and İkmen would be required to carry goods into the factories. But he wouldn't be able to talk to any of those making the deliveries and if he saw any police he was to call Mustafa immediately. He'd been given a mobile phone just for this purpose. It was similar to the one the police had given him.

İkmen went to his room, sat on his bed and called his handler, Terry.

'Well, with any luck Ülker will give the nod for you to carry on,' the policeman said. 'Have you told Ayşe yet?'

İkmen said that he had sent her a text to that effect. He then went on to tell Terry about his co-worker Mustafa.

'You don't have a surname?'

'No,' İkmen said. 'But he looks to me as if he might be a

119

professional thug. I don't think he's a UK national though. From what I heard, his English is adequate only.'

'OK.'

'If I get the job I will apparently be working seven nights a week,' İkmen said. 'I think Ülker maybe finds it difficult to fill these security positions.'

'They're out in the open,' Terry said. 'He can't put a Somali or someone from Cambodia on it, they'd stick out too much. Brits would be ideal, but he can't get them, and so Turks, preferably who can speak English, are the next best thing. But if, like Çetin Ertegrul, they can't – well, he just has to make do, doesn't he?'

'There is one Englishman working for Ülker,' İkmen said. 'Derek Harrison. I asked Ayşe, by text, to check him out.'

Terry cleared his throat. 'Oh, I can tell you about Derek. Got a record stretching back to the late seventies. Robbery, robbery with violence, aggravated burglary.'

'I first saw Mr Harrison with the owner of this pansiyon, Mr Yigit,' İkmen said. 'It seemed from what Yigit said that Ahmet Ülker had done Harrison a favour in giving him a job.'

'Because he's an ex-con,' Terry said. 'People don't readily employ them here, just as they don't in Turkey, I imagine. Also Harrison is disabled. He's only got one foot. Lost it in an accident on the tube. There's all sorts of other health problems he's supposed to have too.'

'Supposed to have? You don't believe him?'

'I wouldn't say that,' Terry said. 'But he's supposed to have a dodgy heart and yet I can't see too much evidence of that myself. Let's put it this way, it doesn't stop him robbing or beating people up.'

'He's a very angry man too,' İkmen said. 'But Ülker trusts him. Something he said suggests he knows Ülker's business partners.'

'No names, I suppose.'

'No,' said İkmen. 'Just something about "our partners". Ülker got quite angry.'

'OK. Listen, I'm going to be in Hackney from now on and I'll try and sneak a look at this Mustafa tonight,' Terry said.

'Provided I still have a job.'

'Provided, as you say, you—'

'Mr Ertegrul! Mr Ertegrul!'

İkmen dropped his voice and said, 'That's Yigit. I have to go.'

He ended the call and walked to the door, wondering how long Yigit might have been listening to his side of a conversation performed in a language he wasn't supposed to be able to speak. But if Yigit had been listening, he covered it well. In his customary excitable fashion he threw his arms in the air as İkmen opened the door and said, 'Excellent news, Mr Ertegrul! Mr Ülker has given you the security guard's job on a permanent basis! I will take my two hundred and fifty pounds in instalments. One hundred the first month, one hundred the second and on the third only fifty pounds!'

The first of the two ex-foremen of the Tarlabaşı factory that Süleyman and İzzet Melik spoke to was adamant that he knew nothing about either who owned the place or any radicalisation happening on the premises. Cemal Dinç was just a man who had done a job that was illegal because he was poor. That was the story he was sticking to and he was fully prepared to serve any prison time coming to him. Süleyman noted that he came from Ahmet Ülker's home city of Diyarbakır. The other foreman, one Can Arat, originally from Adana, was rather more amenable. Prison had clearly had a profound effect upon him and as he entered the room the governor had allocated the police for this

121

interview he was visibly shaking. Not that Süleyman or Melik alluded to this when they began questioning him. What they did make plain was his position as someone who would not be leaving prison any time soon.

'We know that the Tarlabaşı factory was run by a man called Ahmet Ülker,' Süleyman said. 'We know quite a bit about him now. We know he comes originally from Diyarbakır, that he has illegal businesses in İstanbul and Europe and that he has business interests in the Far East. We also know that he is ruthless, cruel and that he doesn't give a damn whether those who work for him live or die or indeed rot away in prison.'

'What the inspector is saying,' İzzet Melik said, 'is that you, Can, don't need to shop Mr Ülker because we already know about him.'

Can Arat looked terrified and said absolutely nothing.

'What we don't know, however,' Süleyman continued, 'is who radicalised the young man who blew himself up. We know that he was introduced to this violent and wholly erroneous version of Islam at the factory, but we don't know who did this or why. The workers, or slaves as I call them, know nothing about this. There were some Pakistani men among them but they claim that radicalisation was not something they had experienced. Tariq, however, we know was radicalised at your factory. How do you think that might have happened?'

Can Arat looked around the room wildly and then, seeing that İzzet Melik was smoking, he asked for a cigarette.

'Oh no, I don't think we can give you a cigarette,' Süleyman said with a smile. 'You only get a cigarette, and possibly a chance to reduce your sentence, if you help us.'

'Help you?' His voice was husky and dry. 'How?'

'Tell us who radicalised Tariq,' Süleyman said. 'We know the boy was an Afghan. He hated in equal measure the foreigners who had come to supposedly liberate his country and the Taliban. He had lived under Taliban rule and he didn't like it. It would have taken a lot to radicalise him.'

The man shrugged. 'I don't know.'

'Was it Ahmet Ülker himself?' İzzet Melik asked. He put his cigarette out and then immediately lit up another. 'Not that I see a businessman like him as some sort of religious fanatic but . . .'

There was a silence. The two policemen looked at the man sitting opposite them who was sweating heavily.

'We know, Can,' Süleyman said, 'that Ülker is out of the country at the moment. As far as we are aware the Tarlabaşı factory was his only Turkish business interest. He isn't here. This is a private conversation which he is not privy to.'

'Maybe not but he has people,' Can Arat said. 'Everywhere!'

'People? What people?'

'People he's involved with, people who work for him!'

Süleyman shrugged. 'If you tell us their names . . .'

'Tell you their names? Tell you . . .' Can Arat leaned across the table and said, 'He doesn't just have men who duck and dive, or even simply gangsters on his payroll. Some are, some are . . .' He stopped, put his head down and then breathed in deeply.

'Some are what?' İzzet Melik asked. 'Foreign gang bosses? Hitmen? Terrorists?'

Can Arat looked up.

'Who radicalised Tariq, Can?'

Can shrugged. 'I don't know.'

'Don't know or won't say?' İzzet Melik said.

'Can, it's up to you,' Süleyman continued. 'You can serve whatever sentence is eventually handed down to you and wait, maybe quite some time, for Mr Ülker to thank you for doing that.'

'Some of those slave workers were near to death,' Melik put in. 'That, I can guarantee, will be taken into account when it comes to your eventual punishment.'

'Or you can help us,' Süleyman said, 'and have *that* taken into account when your case comes to court.' He leant across the table. 'I can see you're not having a very easy time of it here, Can. I am told by those who know about such things that prison doesn't get any easier with the passage of time.'

Bad food,' İzzet Melik said, 'smokes hard to come by if you've got no money, the noise . . .'

'Hot in the summer,' Süleyman said, 'cold in the winter. Few blankets, you see.'

İzzet Melik looked over at his boss and smiled. 'And then, sir, there are the men serving life who want to make every new boy their girlfriend.'

'Indeed.'

Can Arat was nearly crying now but he said, 'Look, you can say as much of that stuff as you like, I can't tell you anything! I can't tell you anything about *them*!'

'About who?'

'If you are withholding information about an individual terrorist or terrorist organisation and we find out, which we will,' Süleyman said, 'then the sentence you will get for that will make what you are facing now look like a holiday. At home or abroad, it makes no difference, if you know about a terrorist plot and you do not tell us and people die—'

'Oh, Allah!' Can Arat pulled his filthy fingers through his filthy hair and said, 'There was an Iranian. An old man. With a beard. Like your grandfather, you know?'

'What was his name?'

124

'He knew Mr Ülker. They embraced as friends. Sometimes he came with some young men, like a bodyguard. They carried guns.'

'Do you know who this man was, Can?' Süleyman asked. 'Can you recall his name?'

Can shook his head. 'No. But Mr Ülker let him come to the factory often and he seemed to take to Tariq.'

'Do you know why?'

'They used to talk about religion. The old man always carried a copy of the Koran. He was from some organisation I'd never heard of, the Brothers of the Light. Iranian, I suppose.'

'How did you know he was Iranian?' İzzet Melik asked as he wrote down what Can had just told him.

'Because he spoke with an accent I didn't recognise and so I asked Mr Ülker where he was from and he said Iran. He said he was in Turkey to spread his religious message and that he'd come to the factory to gather souls for Islam.'

'And did he succeed in your factory, Can?' İzzet Melik asked.

'He did speak to some people,' Can said. 'But a lot of our people were Christians and Hindus. He spoke to some of the Pakistanis but they weren't interested. Tariq listened. I think he did it out of politeness at first. But then the old man just kept on coming back. Mr Ülker let Tariq off his work so he could talk to him.'

'So Ülker allowed this Iranian holy man to come into his factory and talk to people about religion.'

'Well, Tariq.'

'Did you ever hear what the old man said to Tariq, Can?'

'No. Stuff about Shi'a Islam, I suppose. They're all Shi'as over in Iran, aren't they?'

'Generally, yes,' Süleyman said. 'Which makes me wonder why this old holy man, a Shi'a, was welcome in a factory belonging to a Sunni Muslim, Mr Ülker. Further, is it not strange that another Sunni, Tariq, should find his words so interesting?'

Can shrugged again. 'I don't know,' he said. 'I'm an Alawi, what do I know?'

Süleyman leaned over the table again and said, 'Can, we think that Tariq, via this old man and with the help of Mr Ülker, was planning a suicide attack on London, England.'

Can Arat's face went white. 'I don't know anything about that!' he said. 'I don't know anything about any terrorism!'

'And yet it was the threat of being prosecuted for terrorist offences that got you to talk to us about this Iranian, his brothers of light and his interest in Tariq,' Süleyman said. 'You knew this Iranian was suspect, you knew that he was radicalising or attempting to radicalise . . .'

'I didn't know that he and Tariq were about to bomb London!' Can said. 'I was as shocked as anyone that Tariq had a grenade!'

'Now listen to me, Can,' Süleyman said. 'You must tell us everything you know about this old man and about Mr Ülker. We know he is abroad. When did he leave the factory?'

'Er, about, er, two weeks ago, I think,' Can said. 'About that.'

'And do you know if the old Iranian went with him?' İzzet Melik asked.

'No. No, he kept coming after Mr Ülker had gone away on business,' Can said. 'He had been in, to see Tariq, the night you lot raided us. He came with his bodyguard. Very serious all of them, bowing to Tariq and patting him on the back.'

Preparing him maybe for his 'holy' mission in England, Süleyman thought. Tariq's diary was currently with a translator who specialised in the Dari language. Maybe soon they would know where in London EC3 the attack was supposed to be taking place – in just five days' time.

When Süleyman and İzzet Melik finally left the prison, the inspector said to his sergeant, 'OK, İzzet, it seems we are now looking for an elderly somewhat avuncular Iranian.'

# Chapter 14

İkmen hadn't been sleeping when Ayşe called him at 2 p.m. to meet her for a late lunch. Lying on top of his bed, fully clothed, he'd been thinking of home, his family, and feeling acutely how much he missed them all. In a way, being in a place like Stoke Newington, where every second business was Turkish-owned, didn't help. Because of the food everyone ate, the language everyone spoke, the fact that the woman he was working with was called Ayşe, he felt at times that he could almost be back in İstanbul. But he wasn't, everything was just that little bit wrong, like the television that was of course in English and the cars which drove on the left as opposed to the right-hand side of the road.

He met Ayşe in a restaurant on Church Street called the Turkish Chimney, which was clearly aimed at the native British market. It was staffed by Turks but the clientele were to a man and woman middle-class Brits. Ayşe treated her uncle to a late lunch meze which included his favourite, Albanian liver.

'Your colleagues in İstanbul have been very busy,' Ayşe said. 'It seems that the boy Tariq had been groomed to blow himself up in a suicide attack on the third of May. If that is the case, your role in this operation may be shorter than we envisaged. You will have to be extremely vigilant from now on.'

'I see.' İkmen was trying not to look surprised or animated

so as not to draw attention. 'Do we know where this was to take place?'

'Intelligence suggests EC3,' Ayşe said. 'That's the City of London, the part down by the Tower, Leadenhall Street, that area.'

'Was the Tower the target?' İkmen asked.

'We don't know. But my bosses and yours are concerned that this could still be going ahead. Your colleagues in İstanbul reckon that Ülker allowed radicalisation to take place at his factory over there. An Iranian cleric came in apparently.'

'An Iranian cleric?' İkmen frowned. 'They're usually Shi'a, aren't they? Ülker is a Sunni. Also, Ayşe, he doesn't strike me as a person with any sort of religious leanings.' He put a piece of liver into his mouth and for a second savoured the flavour. 'Very good,' he said. 'Just like home.' And then his face momentarily dropped.

'For whatever reason, it would seem that Ülker has entered into some sort of pact with this Iranian cleric and his organisation, which is called the Brothers of the Light apparently.'

İkmen shrugged.

'No, we've not heard of them either. But they were recruiting in Ülker's İstanbul factory apparently with his blessing.'

'But Ülker is a businessman,' İkmen said. 'I can't imagine why he would want to ally himself with fundamentalist fanatics. What good would that do him? I mean, I know your mayor here in London believes that money from the production of counterfeit goods finds its way to terrorist groups, but I don't see the connection in Ülker's case.'

'Basically the terrorists get their cut from gangster organisations in exchange for providing extra muscle to the criminals,' Ayşe said. 'They often provide security at the illegal factories in places like Cambodia and Vietnam.'

'But not here.'

'Not as far as we know and clearly not in Ülker's case,' Ayşe replied. 'But then his factories are rather more visible than places in the jungles of South-east Asia. The Brothers of the Light can't be a big organisation or we'd know about them. But if they are or were planning a suicide attack on London then they are clearly ambitious.'

İkmen frowned. 'But Ülker has muscle of his own,' he said. 'Why ally yourself with a bunch of fanatics you don't need? Surely that is just inviting trouble?'

Ayşe's mobile phone began to ring and she turned aside in order to answer it. İkmen took a swig from his tea glass and then scooped a load of fava bean paste into his mouth with the rather odd flat bread they had in the UK; he imagined it was supposed to be lavaş. It was called pitta and was rather floury and dry, in his opinion. But it sufficed. As he chewed, İkmen considered Ahmet Ülker. The man wasn't obviously religious – he was married to a lap dancer and he dressed like a western gangster. But then there were unsubstantiated rumours of Ülker's business interests in the Far East – that was one of the reasons why the Met were treading so carefully, in order to locate all of his empire – and so maybe the 'Brothers' helped him out over there. That was possible even though it didn't seem to really sit right. Why recruit Tariq from İstanbul? Why would the Iranians want to be in bed specifically with Ülker?

'Your people in İstanbul think that the intended target was or is Mark Lane,' Ayşe said as she closed her mobile and put it back into her handbag.

'Mark Lane?'

'Mark Lane, EC3,' she elaborated. 'It runs from Fenchurch

Street down to Byward Street which is almost opposite the Tower of London.'

'Is there anything of particular interest on this street?' İkmen asked. 'I mean, apart from its proximity to the Tower of London?'

Ayşe shrugged. 'It's one of those City streets dedicated to commerce,' she said. 'There are lots of companies down there: insurance companies, brokers, accountants.' She frowned. 'Maybe one of those firms is the target for some reason. My colleagues will be looking at those companies and seeing where their business interests lie.'

'But with Tariq dead . . .'

'We have to assume that the attack is still going ahead,' Ayşe said. 'We have to protect people, that is our first priority.' She leaned across the table and lowered her voice a little. 'And you, Uncle Çetin, you must pay very close attention to what goes on over at Hackney Wick. Ülker isn't going to take any potential terrorists to either his flat in Dalston or his posh home on The Bishops Avenue. We know that most of his slave workers sleep on the premises at the Hackney factories. The bomber or bombers could be doing that too.'

'I hope this new bloke of yours really is as pig thick as you think he is,' Derek Harrison said to Ahmet Ülker. The two of them were having a late lunch at the celebrity chef Jamie Oliver's Fifteen restaurant in Old Street. Ahmet fancied himself as a bit of a gourmand. Harrison thought he was a pretentious ponce.

'He is an Anatolian peasant,' Ülker said. 'I know the type. The blank eyes, the deference, the only thought in his head for the immediate need. He has to send money home to his family in Turkey. He'll focus only on that.'

132

'I don't like the way he just conveniently appeared when them pot-heads of yours got themselves arrested.'

'The man is nothing,' Ülker said. 'You don't understand Turkish people, Derek. He'll be fine.'

'Provided he doesn't see too much.'

'We've a consignment coming in from Abuja tonight. If he deals with that . . .' He shrugged and then said, 'What do you think of the ceps?'

'The mushrooms?' Harrison snorted. 'All right.' He pushed his half-finished meal away from him. 'Wish you could smoke in here. Fucking hell, you'd think for all this money . . .'

'Can't smoke anywhere,' Ülker said. 'It's the law. Mr Blair and now Mr Brown—'

'Fuck Mr Blair and Mr Brown!' Harrison said. 'Mr Blair was the one who started the war your mates take such exception to. How is your old Iranian friend anyway?'

Ahmet Ülker winced.

'Likes our young nutter, does he?'

Ülker finished his meal and then laid his cutlery down on his plate. 'It was a pity we lost our young man back in İstanbul. But at least he had the sense to kill himself. As for Ali Reza, I think the Ayatollah finds his enthusiasm inspiring,' he said.

'Doesn't think he's a fucking nutter then?' But Ülker did not reply. 'Not that I'm complaining about that meself.'

'No, Derek, you shouldn't.'

'I am grateful, to you and to him,' Harrison continued. 'Not that I believe in his reasons of course. But then neither do you, do you? Nor our partners neither.'

Ahmet Ülker blanched. 'We don't talk about them, Derek. Not here.'

Derek Harrison shrugged. 'Whatever.' He looked out of the

window into the street below and said, 'You having a sweet, are you?'

Ülker smiled, the tension suddenly released from his face. 'I thought I might have a little something.'

'I'm going off to see John, finalise things,' Harrison said. He rose quickly from the table, took his suit jacket off the back of his chair and put it on.

'OK,' Ülker said. 'But leave the car, please, Derek. I haven't had a drink and so I'm fine to drive. Take a taxi.'

Harrison smirked. 'What, on to the estate?' he said. 'You want me to get mugged before I even leave the cab?'

'I'm sure you can handle yourself, Derek,' Ülker said with a weary sigh. 'But if you're that bothered then take a cab to Barking station and then walk. The exercise will do your heart some good.'

'What, with five grand in my pocket? I don't think so,' Harrison said. 'I'll get John to meet me at Barking station, give it to him there.'

Ülker lowered his voice. 'Well, just make sure that no one sees you and that you are well away from the CCTV cameras. I haven't forgotten about how my operation came to an end in İstanbul. The police got there on a tip-off. We can be dis-covered at any time.'

Harrison snorted contemptuously. 'What do you think I am? A bloody amateur? I'm not like those local yokels back in your country.'

'No, but . . .' Ülker caught the eye of one of the waitresses across the room and beckoned her over. 'Just give him the money and get the code,' he said. 'Oh, and tell your friend nothing about our friends – any of them. Also, if he does have any intention of double-crossing us, I know where all his children live. Our partners would decimate them, as you know.'

Derek Harrison picked up the holdall that had been under the table by his feet and with a sour look at his boss's hard face walked away.

Mustafa came to check on İkmen every hour. On one occasion they'd had to chase away a gang of kids that Mustafa said had come down to the waste ground to sniff lighter fluid. It wasn't easy shooing away people who were shouting at him in English. He'd wanted to yell at them in kind, but he couldn't and so he had to leave Mustafa to swear at them very ineptly in their native tongue. Most of the time, however, Mustafa just asked him questions. How İkmen had come into the country was a subject frequently discussed. It made the policeman wonder how much of this was curiosity on Mustafa's part and how much Ahmet Ülker's. But then if Ülker was indeed planning something big then he had to be sure that everyone in his organisation was who he said he was. İkmen again rolled out his 'German Jew' and this time told Mustafa a little about his nightmarish journey across the English Channel.

'I too came in with Africans,' Mustafa said when İkmen told him about the terrified African couple he had shared the journey with. 'They were very dirty.' He wrinkled up his nose in disgust. 'Tonight we have a delivery from Africa.'

'Do we?'

'I think it is medicine,' Mustafa said. 'Mr Ülker is very keen to provide cheap medicine to people.'

'Oh. Good.'

If it was what İkmen thought it was, it would all be counterfeit and of no clinical value whatsoever. Fake Viagra to leave

135

you impotent, painkillers to leave your pain undiminished whilst toxifying your kidneys – the list was endless. Much of this stuff came out of Africa and it was a logical move for Ülker as he extended his counterfeit portfolio across the planet.

Mustafa left, leaving İkmen alone with the hum of many sewing machines from inside the factory and his thoughts. If anything was going to happen it would most probably be on 3 May, which was only four days away. Four days to find out as much as he could about this possible attack on London and hopefully help the Metropolitan Police to do something about it. Then, with luck, he could go home. Not being himself was giving him problems he hadn't even considered before he went under-cover. The loss of status bothered him. It wasn't something he had even considered before. Had someone asked him how he would feel about play-acting a poor and destitute man, the last thing that would have come to mind was that he would feel unhappy about it. But he did. Çetin İkmen wasn't used to being talked down to. People, including his boss Ardıç, did that at their peril. But Çetin Ertegrul was another matter. He was a poorly educated illegal immigrant and everyone talked down to him. Everyone also took money from him for all sorts of reasons whenever they felt like it. They took him for an ignorant fool. He was helpless and alone. He thought about Fatma and how much he missed her in spite of the fact that they were no longer on good terms. He missed his children, his friends and his colleagues. He thought of Süleyman working his end of the Ülker case back in İstanbul with no idea that he was in London doing this awful security job with a man who looked like a retarded grease wrestler.

'Çetin!' He looked up and saw said grease wrestler running towards him. 'The delivery! It's now!'

A large truck was parked up beside the factory that Mustafa guarded. As İkmen approached, his colleague pulled a large sliding door in the back of the building open and then whistled to the driver to take the thing inside. İkmen followed and found himself inside a carbon copy of Ülker's factory in Tarlabaşı. Row upon row of people bent over sewing machines, heaps of leather down on the floor beside their thin, usually brown, feet. The noise was bad but the smell was worse. Just as in İstanbul, these people pissed and defecated where they sat, the women bled. Most of them seemed to be African. They hardly looked up as the truck drove into the big space at the back of the building and came to a halt. The driver jumped down from the cab and went over to Mustafa.

'Stuff for arthritis,' he said as he handed İkmen's colleague a piece of paper, presumably a delivery note. The man was black and spoke English with a very strong London accent.

'Arthritis?'

'Painkiller for it,' the man said.

'Oh?' Suddenly there was another man, a small, pale individual with a trim grey beard and a large white turban on his head. He had emerged from a small office at the back of the building.

'Don't work,' the driver said. 'Load of crap. Why? You got arthritis have you grandad?'

Mustafa took in a sharp breath. 'Wesley,' he said, 'you cannot speak to Ayatollah Nourazar in that way! He is very holy man!'

Wesley shrugged. 'Not to me, he ain't. You lot want this delivery or what?'

İkmen and Mustafa began unloading boxes of something that declared itself 'Percodan'. İkmen wondered whether Percodan was a real drug or just a name the counterfeiters had made up. The boxes, of which there were hundreds, looked very new, clean and professional. As the two men worked, the man Mustafa had referred to as Ayatollah Nourazar looked on. He smiled beatifically at the two men and then went back into the small office.

'Who's that?' İkmen asked Mustafa during one of the frequent breaks he had to take in order to catch his breath.

Mustafa smiled at İkmen's lack of fitness. 'That is a very holy man. Ayatollah Hadi Nourazar, from Iran.'

'From Iran?'

'Why do you look surprised?'

'Well . . .'

'He is a holy man,' Mustafa said. 'You have a problem with Shi'a people? I am Shi'a. My family name is Kermani. They come originally from Iran. Shi'a is a most noble path.'

İkmen shrugged. He was about to say that religion meant nothing to him, but then he changed his approach. After all, Çetin Ertegrul was not the secular person that he was. 'I am Sunni,' he said, 'but I have no problem with Shi'a. What does your holy man do here?'

'Oh, he has business with Mr Ülker,' Mustafa said. He unloaded the last two boxes on his own and then pulled the shutter down on the back of the truck. 'Wesley!' he called over to the driver. 'Truck is ready now!'

The driver ran over to the truck, climbed into the cab and drove out of the building. 'Be lucky!' he said with a smile out of the cab window.

İkmen and Mustafa returned to their duties outside. İkmen wanted to know more about Ayatollah Nourazar but he was glad to be out of that building. The stench and sheer hopelessness of it was almost beyond endurance. And now Ülker and his company were peddling more misery. Fake drugs that would bring no relief to those already unfortunate enough to be crippled by arthritis. İkmen's own father had suffered from the disease and so he knew how bad it could be. Thinking about the fake Percodan tablets made him angry. Terrorism or no terrorism, he would get something done about that when this was all at an end.

# Chapter 15

It was almost lunchtime before Terry got in to see Inspector Riley. But then engineering a chance meeting with the Turkish copper after his shift had finished at Hackney Wick hadn't been easy. Then he'd had some work to do based upon both what he had himself observed and what İkmen had told him.

'Seems that Iranian holy man they've been looking for in İstanbul could very well be here, guv'nor,' he said as he sat down on the chair in front of Riley's desk. 'According to our Turkish friend who saw him last night, he's called Ayatollah Hadi Nourazar. About sixty years old. Born in Isfahan.'

Patrick Riley looked up and narrowed his eyes. 'What's his story then?' he said. 'Any idea?'

'The Israelis have him down as an agitator,' Terry said. 'Fiery speeches at rallies on the West Bank. Deported from Egypt nineteen ninety-seven. Again political agitation. Religion-wise he's one of those "born again" types. He wasn't involved in the revolution of seventy-nine, he came to religion later.'

'Probably frightened not to,' Riley said.

'Anyway, he's got a following of sorts. Call themselves the Brothers of the Light. Rabidly anti-Semitic. Interestingly, the Iranian government aren't too keen on him or his "brothers". Off message with them maybe.'

Riley shrugged.

141

'He's very down apparently on Muslims who give up their faith or who seem to side with the likes of us,' Terry went on. 'Also, he was heavily involved in the purges that took place once the Shah left and Khomeini took over. No involvement with terrorism as far as we know.'

'And yet suddenly he is here,' Riley said.

'Illegally.'

'Oh.' Riley raised an eyebrow.

'No record of entry. Back in İstanbul he had a posse of heavies. Çetin hasn't spotted them here so far. He may or may not be alone. According to the other security guard at Hackney Wick, this Ayatollah Nourazar has "business" with Ülker. The other guard, by the way, is Mustafa Kermani. Turkish parents but Iranian forebears. Çetin thought he was illegal but he's actually a UK citizen now. Entered illegally, but then married a Rachel Halliwell in nineteen ninety-six. He was twenty at the time, she was fifty-six.' Terry shrugged. 'They're now divorced. Mustafa has got form for affray. One of those periodic things that take place outside the Israeli Embassy.'

'Gawd.' Riley rolled his eyes.

'He's a nothing, Kermani, and even this Nourazar isn't exactly a big fish,' Terry said. 'It's all low-key as far as I can see, guv'nor. Mind you, they took a delivery last night of a load of counterfeit Percodan – painkillers for arthritis. I was watching. The truck they were in was being driven by an old friend.'

Riley frowned.

'Wesley Simpson,' Terry said. 'Everyone's favourite getaway driver. Obviously given up on cars and has gone into the HGV business.'

'Mmm. Could be useful to know as we get nearer to when we think these people are going to make their move,' Riley said.

'My recollection of Wesley is of a basically peaceable bloke who just wants to turn a quick quid.'

'He's a lazy bastard, guv'nor.'

'But not a violent man,' Riley said. 'We'll keep an eye on Wesley. What we must also do now, I think, is mount surveillance on our other Iranian connection.'

'Ali Reza Hajizadeh?'

'Yes. He, like this ayatollah chap, was born in Isfahan,' Riley said. 'I want to know if they meet. What, if any, connections they may have. Tell Çetin to keep his ear to the ground. This may or may not be the same holy man the police in İstanbul came up with but for the moment I think it's safe to assume that it probably is. I'll contact them to that effect.'

'Yes, sir.'

'We know that Ülker has some business involvement in the Far East,' Riley went on. 'There's talk of business partners who may or may not be this cleric – maybe another gang. But if we haven't managed to pin him down by the third, Terry, we are going to have to stake Mark Lane out and then if it looks in the least bit dodgy take Ülker down. I don't care what the bloody mayor says. I hate all this fake stuff, especially the medication, as much as he does. But if Ülker is directly associating with terrorists then we can't put the public at risk.'

'No, sir.'

Riley sighed. 'Well, as long as we're all working off the same page . . .' Then he looked up at Terry and said, 'I know we could blow it with regard to getting at Ülker's other business contacts. But we can't have another seven/seven or the events that followed it.'

Terry looked down. He knew what Riley was referring to, the

death at police hands of the innocent Brazilian man Jean Charles de Menezes.

'Given time, Çetin İkmen could have given us a lot of information about Ülker's operation. I feel we'll probably under-use him, which is a shame but what can you do?'

Terry shrugged. 'Inspector İkmen strikes me as a resourceful sort,' he said. 'I'm sure that one way or another he'll play his part.'

Things came to Abdurrahman Iqbal, so he said, in fits and starts.

'My memory isn't what it was,' he told Süleyman. 'But I do now recall that Tariq was obliged to study a map of the London Underground before he took part in his "mission". He wasn't allowed to take it out of the Tarlabaşı factory. But he did have to study it.'

Süleyman was walking with the old man along Meşrutiyet Street towards the British Consulate. Given Abdurrahman's high level of cooperation, they had looked into his claim to know a person called Captain Jackson. The consulate had news about this which was why Süleyman was escorting the old man there now.

'Given the boy's poor state of health,' Abdurrahman went on, 'as well as his absolute foreignness in a place like London, I thought they would not leave him on his own there. But apparently he had to learn to move around alone.'

'Do you know where he was going to obtain the explosives he was due to use?'

'No,' the old man said. 'Although I do not imagine they were going to risk crossing borders with them. These people have sympathisers in England. I think that Tariq would have been given what he needed there.'

As they drew level with a small grocer's shop, Süleyman saw

144

Çetin İkmen's son Bülent coming out, clutching a new packet of cigarettes.

'Excuse me, Abdurrahman,' Süleyman said to the old man. Then he called out to the young man. 'Bülent!'

'Mehmet!' The young man came bounding over and then reached up to put his thin arms round his father's friend. 'So good to see you!'

'And you too,' Süleyman said. 'I'm just escorting this man to the British Consulate and so I can't really talk now. But, quickly, have you heard from your dad?'

'I haven't,' Bülent replied. 'Mum hasn't mentioned it, but then my mother wouldn't.' He sighed impatiently. The feud between his parents was getting Bülent down. 'I don't think that anyone else has heard. But then Dad said that he wouldn't be contactable. I worry.' He sighed again and then asked, 'Mehmet, you don't know where Dad is, do you?'

'No, I don't,' Süleyman said. 'On my honour.'

'I fear he's somewhere out east,' Bülent said. 'There's always trouble out there.'

'Your father is not a man easily outwitted, Bülent.'

'He can be shot as easily as anyone else, though, can't he?' Bülent said. He lit a cigarette and went on his way. Süleyman and the old Pakistani continued in the opposite direction towards the British Consulate.

Working at night wasn't easy for Çetin İkmen. He had worked many night shifts in the past but never as a matter of regular routine. And he had to keep his wits about him. Terry had called to say that it was now more important than ever to report anything and everything that went on both at his residence and his place of work. Mustafa, his fellow security guard, had a police record, albeit minor, and Ayatollah Nourazar was a known fundamentalist agitator.

İkmen didn't have a great deal of experience with terrorist offences. His speciality was murder. Furthermore, he was uncomfortable with the context in this case. He wasn't a religious man by any means, but nominally he was a Muslim and it offended him to see the faith of his fathers, and of his wife, distorted to create prejudice and pursue acts of violence. He felt sympathy for Christian and Jewish Britons caught up in all this but he feared them too. What if a major incident did take place in Mark Lane? What if the people of Britain all became insanely anti-Islamic as a result? Clearly that was what the terrorists wanted and the thought appalled him.

It was pointless trying to sleep now that the sun was shining directly into his window. Also, Mr Yigit was vacuuming the stairs to a tuneless rendition of 'Kiss, Kiss' by Tarkan, and that alone was death to sleep. And yet the landlord knew that some of his tenants worked only at night. There was a Kurdish man who worked as a bouncer at a nightclub in the West End, and then there was also Süleyman Elgiz who Ayşe had said worked in Ahmet Ülker's factories. He was out all night but thus far İkmen hadn't seen him at Hackney Wick. Since most of the workers there were Africans who slept on site, Elgiz had to be a foreman or at least something a little bit more elevated than just a stitcher. İkmen wondered idly where the Iranian ayatollah laid his head at night. The vacuuming, and the singing, stopped, and İkmen heard the voice of another man.

'Yigit, you know you've got to find a room for Mr Harrison, don't you?' It was Ali Reza Hajizadeh, speaking in English. 'He needs to be here until Friday morning. He's working with me.'

146

'Why? Mr Harrison has house,' Yigit said. 'In south London I think.'

Ali Reza clicked his tongue in aggravation. 'Just do it, Yigit,' he said. 'Orders of Mr Ülker.'

'Yes, but I don't have—'

'Chuck one of the Kurds out,' the Iranian interrupted. 'You're a Turk, you don't like them anyway, do you?'

'Ali Reza, I like all people!' Yigit protested. 'I have no problem with no one!'

'Well, good for you, Yigit,' Ali Reza said. 'What a fine man you are! Just remember that this is Mr Ülker we're talking about here. You know what will happen if you refuse him.'

İkmen heard Mr Yigit sigh very deeply.

'Mr Harrison will be wanting his room at six o'clock tonight,' the Iranian said. 'Just make sure that one of your Kurds is on the street by then. Oh, and change the sheets before Mr Harrison gets in there, won't you? And don't give him the terrible nylon things you give to me!'

İkmen heard footsteps descending to the floor below and then the vacuuming started up again. This time Mr Yigit did not sing while he worked. He was no doubt puzzling over who he could move and under what pretext. Clearly, Ahmet Ülker's word was law.

İkmen wondered why Harrison needed to move into the Rize and why the date of his departure was Friday, 3 May. Whatever Terry and Ayşe said, he couldn't quite believe that Ahmet Ülker and his associates would plant bombs in London on exactly the same day they had planned to do so when Tariq had been involved. Ülker's İstanbul factory had been raided in the interim and that surely would have made him nervous. Turks at the factory had talked – eventually. Whether or not Ülker knew about that, he would realise that if anyone had talked to the police in İstanbul, they would most certainly pass the information on to London. So the idea of mounting the attack as originally planned with Tariq seemed ridiculous. And why was Mark Lane the target? It wasn't as if the Israeli Embassy or anything significant like that was down there. İkmen resolved to go to Mark Lane the following day and have a look around. He would have to be careful in case any of Ülker's people saw him. Maybe he would run that by Terry first. He would have to speak to him anyway to pass on what he had just heard. He also wanted to express his doubts about the date, although the news about Harrison suggested everything was still on course for Friday.

'It's my day off tomorrow,' Ayşe said as she sipped her cappuccino. 'I could take you to the Tower of London. Nothing wrong with me showing my uncle the sights.'

İkmen smiled. 'If I can stay awake,' he said. He hadn't managed to get any sleep since he'd listened in to Yigit and Ali Reza's conversation in the hall.

'You've got to try and get a look inside those factories tonight, Çetin,' Ayşe said. 'We need to know if that cleric and maybe some of the bodyguards reported to us from İstanbul are staying there. Keep your ears open.'

'Unless he speaks Farsi and then I will be lost,' İkmen said.

He'd asked to meet Ayşe in the İstanbul Büfe at the end of her working day and an hour and a half before the start of his. He'd spoken to Terry during one of his long, lonely walks around the Abney Park graveyard but his handler had just reiterated what had been said before. A covert surveillance operation on both Ülker and his associates and Mark Lane itself was scheduled for Friday. Those involved had to be apprehended with explosives or weapons of some sort before an incident took place. According to UK law, just finding such items on someone's property did not mean that person was guilty. And the Met really wanted to take Ülker right down. If he was aiding terrorists he would have to give them up to the police completely in order to come out of the process with any sentence less than life. If he gave up information about his business dealings with other gangs or in other parts of the world as well, so much the better. Just thinking about it made İkmen frown.

'I still don't know why Ülker wants to get into bed with terrorists,' he said. 'He could just carry on making and distributing fake goods and keep his head down. He isn't religious. Why does he need to ally himself with people like this Iranian cleric?'

'Fakes are being cracked down on here,' Ayşe said. 'The mayor's "Condemn a Counterfeit" scheme means that people can just ring up City Hall anonymously and tell the mayor's office who is producing or selling fake goods. And if an actual gang member wants to provide the police with information, he will get a reward for doing so.'

'Your Mr Üner is a very determined man,' İkmen said.

She smiled. 'He's a bit of a hero – with the Met. And let me tell you, there isn't a British woman of Turkish descent who doesn't have designs on him. That includes me!'

'Mr Üner isn't married?'

'No.' She lowered her voice. 'To be honest with you, Çetin, I tend to think that the rumour one sometimes picks up that Haluk Üner is gay may well be true. It would make perfect sense in terms of his abhorrence for fundamentalists.'

İkmen frowned. 'And yet it still can't be comfortable for him. I have seen him interviewed and he is obviously a believer and proud of it.'

'So am I,' Ayşe said. 'We all are. I am not, believe me, happy about spying on and reporting fellow Muslims. But the belief that I cling to and that Haluk Üner lives by also is that these extremists are wrong. I don't believe that stoning homosexuals or denying women an education takes you closer to God. We're Muslims, we are enlightened, we're above such things!'

İkmen shrugged. 'I don't know about any of that . . .'

'Yes, but you are a Muslim.'

'That is what it says on my identity card, yes,' İkmen said with a shrug.

Ayşe changed the subject. Now was not the time to be discussing what each of them did or did not believe. 'The counterfeiters are under threat here,' she said. 'What we fear is that those gangsters who fund terrorists or are in some way connected with them are now calling in favours because of the crackdown. If bombs start going off in London and people think it is because of Mr Üner's initiative, they will withdraw their support for him and the gangs will grow even more powerful. When Mr Üner started this campaign, he was really putting his neck on the line – and ours, of course.'

# Chapter 16

Ayatollah Hadi Nourazar was deeply offended that Ahmet Ülker had denied him and his men proper accommodation. In İstanbul he had given them the use of a very nice apartment. Here in London they all had to sleep in one of his nasty factories. The noise was appalling and the smell of the people who worked for Ülker not much better. But then physical comfort was not really what Nourazar craved. What he really wanted was respect, something the Turk Ülker did not seem over-keen to give him. But then Ahmet Ülker, like most Turks, was a Sunni Muslim and so he wasn't at all impressed by a Shi'a cleric – not that Hadi Nourazar was a real cleric. He used the title ayatollah because that was what he had been – once. Not now. The Islamic Republic of Iran didn't want people whose beliefs and practices echoed those of the Afghan Taliban, and Ayatollah Nourazar gave the impression of being a Shi'ite Talib in all but name. He was of the opinion, for example, that women should be denied shoes; they walked far too noisily when shod, something that could disturb men at their devotions. And although the Islamic Republic did not exactly publicise the fact that Nourazar was no longer a significant person or even wanted in Iran, he had been denied entry back into his own country for over five years. And so he and his disciples, who he called collectively the Brothers of the Light, agitated in Palestine, Egypt, Afghanistan and Syria.

He and some followers had ended up in İstanbul while travelling from Syria to Egypt. A two-day stopover in the city on the Bosphorus had turned into a week, during which Nourazar had met Ahmet Ülker. The new mayor of London had just started his campaign against the counterfeiters and Ülker had been worried. It was a concern he shared with Hadi Nourazar. The ayatollah had told his new friend that Mr Haluk Üner was nothing to worry about; some well-placed explosive devices would fix the problem.

But Ahmet Ülker had been sceptical and worried. He wanted the mayor of London off his back with regard to his businesses but he didn't really want to harm or endanger anyone else. The ayatollah was of the opinion that assisting a suicide bomber to kill infidels would attract blessings from heaven as well as resolve Mr Ülker's business difficulties. None of his own people could be spared for such work but he could recruit people who would take on that role. And so Mr Ülker had let him recruit the Afghan boy Tariq. Unfortunately that had not worked out and a new suicide bomber had had to be recruited in England. This had not been hard but as far as Hadi Nourazar was concerned it was not entirely satisfactory. A young Iranian known to Ahmet Ülker had been approached with a theoretical scenario and had apparently been most enthusiastic about the idea. He came from one of those old Isfahan families who had benefited from the rule of the Shah. Radicalised at university in England apparently, this young man could not be faulted for his zeal. But Nourazar distrusted Ali Reza Hajizadeh's blood. He and his family had been amongst the elite. People like them had drunk alcohol and worn jewels and not even really been loyal to the Shah, much less the subsequent republic – just like Hadi Nourazar and his family. Now Ali Reza wanted to take jihad to the people of

London and Ahmet Ülker was happy for him to do so. But then Ülker himself was not a believer. He drank, he had a big ostentatious house, a loose western wife. The ayatollah for different reasons didn't trust him either. But Ülker was just a means to an end, and Hadi Nourazar felt that the end justified the use of such people. After all, if he, Hadi Nourazar, brought enough death to enough infidels, then the world, not just the Iranian government, would have to respect him. And then of course there was the money. That, more than anything, made Hadi smile. That, as nothing else about him, was real.

Derek Harrison had always had problems with sleep or, rather, he'd had problems since 28 February 1975. The Moorgate disaster was what everyone had called it. But 'disaster' hardly did it justice. Hell, more like. He'd been going to see his sister Phyllis down at the Barbican. She'd married a posh doctor and had a flat in that dull but expensive complex. Derek had still lived with his mum and dad in Highbury at the time. He'd just been taken on to do the underground driver's course – his dream job – and so he was on top of the world. He'd quite naturally taken a tube down to Moorgate. He thought he'd walk to the Barbican from there, it was easy enough then. But when the train arrived at Moorgate, it didn't stop. It ploughed into an overrun tunnel, hit a single hydraulic buffer and then smashed into the brick wall behind. The second and third carriages concertinaed into the first carriage and the driver's cab. Forty-three people died immediately. But not Derek Harrison in carriage number three. Bleeding and terrified, he was in total darkness; all around him people were moaning and screaming but he himself seemed to be injured in only one foot. He couldn't move his left leg below the knee at all. He had no idea about the internal injuries he had sustained.

It took the fire brigade four hours to free him. It was 120 degrees Fahrenheit down there by that time and he was boiling hot and ice-cold by turns. A doctor put him out for it because they had to cut off his foot at the scene. Then at Barts Hospital they took out his gall bladder and his spleen. By the time he left Barts, he had one foot and a stack of medication the doctors told him he would have to take for the rest of his life. London Underground was very sorry, both for the accident and for the fact that they could no longer consider him for a driver's job. Would he consider maybe working in one of their ticket offices?

Derek Harrison, as he so often did, woke up screaming. Mr Yigit, who had never heard the like before, was ordered by his wife to go and see what on earth the matter was.

When he got to the door of Mr Harrison's room, all Mr Yigit could hear was bitter weeping.


'What are you doing?'

İkmen whipped round from watching the old man and his group of followers in the corner and found himself face to face with Mustafa.

'I was cold,' he said.

'You're paid to watch this place,' Mustafa said. He took hold of İkmen's arm and pulled him outside the factory.

'As I said, I was cold,' İkmen repeated.

'Well, too bad,' the bull-necked younger man said. 'I know you're getting on in age but Mr Ülker doesn't pay you to snoop around.'

'I wasn't snooping, I was—'

'Cold, yeah.' Mustafa lit up a cigarette and then breathed out slowly, observing İkmen closely as he did so. 'You were looking at the old man talking to the young men in the corner.'

'He has a turban,' İkmen said. 'I thought that maybe he was a Hodja.'

'I told you, he's from Iran,' Mustafa said.

'The young men were very interested in what he was saying,' İkmen said.

Mustafa frowned. 'And what was that?'

'I don't know.' İkmen shrugged. 'I couldn't understand.'

'Mmm.' Mustafa looked at his watch and realised that he should get back to guarding his own factory. 'I must go. Don't go inside again. There's no delivery tonight and so there's no need for you to. If you feel cold, rub your hands together or light a cigarette.' Then he left.

İkmen breathed out slowly in order to calm his nerves. It had been unfortunate that he had been caught inside the building. Thank goodness the ayatollah had been speaking English to his little band of disciples, which as far as Mustafa was concerned meant that İkmen hadn't understood a word. Some of the disciples seemed to be boys of Pakistani origin who could speak neither Turkish nor Farsi. The Iranian had spoken English very well and, İkmen thought, with a cultured accent.

In the main, what the ayatollah had said to the boys was inconsequential rhetoric but one thing he had said seemed significant: he would be leaving to 'spread my word of truth yet further' on Saturday morning. He didn't say why he was leaving or where he was going but it seemed odd to İkmen that he should choose Saturday to move on. If an attack was planned for Friday then surely that was when the ayatollah would leave – if he was taking part. If he wasn't taking part, it would make more sense for him to be clear of London before the attack took place. People around Ülker were making arrangements that did not seem to add up.

İkmen sent a text to Terry with this latest piece of information and then went back to doing his job. Not that there was much to do, with no deliveries and apparently no one lurking around the area taking drugs or drinking. There were, however, ominous sounds from inside the factory – people being shouted at and beaten.

Although he knew full well that his wife had gone downstairs and that she was upset, Ahmet Ülker did not leave his bed to follow her. She was drinking gin, smoking and crying in the kitchen not for him or anything he had done but because of her boyfriend Ali Reza. The Iranian was now telling those around him that, from Friday, he was going away for a while. Maxine, besotted with him, was devastated.

Ahmet had known about their affair for months. One didn't get to run a massive organisation like his without knowing every-thing about everyone all of the time. He knew, for instance, that his right-hand man, Derek Harrison, was fully aware of the affair between Maxine and Ali Reza Hajizadeh. He could understand why Derek hadn't passed this on to him – he didn't want distrac-tions until the job was done. All the same, he needed to be taught a lesson in loyalty – but that could wait. Maxine was going to get the surprise of her life when Ali Reza not only left her but made the national headlines also – that is, if he let her see them. Ahmet pulled a disgusted face. How awful these fanatics were! But dealing with a small organisation like the Brothers of the Light wasn't like getting into bed with something like al Qaeda. There was no one behind the Brothers. The Iranians had kicked Hadi Nourazar out and what he did was in no way controlled by them. Ahmet could, in theory, dispose of the cleric and his men in any way he chose once they'd fulfilled their purpose. In fact that might be something to ask his new partners about.

Maxine came back into the bedroom with a glass of water and was surprised to see her husband sitting up in bed.

'Oh . . .'

'Don't worry, you didn't wake me,' Ahmet said with a smile. 'Are you OK, my darling?'

Maxine looked down at the floor. 'Just a bad nightmare,' she said and slipped back into bed.

Ahmet put an arm round his wife's shoulders and leant across to kiss her. 'Let me take that nasty thing away for you,' he said. And then gently and slowly he made love to her. While he did it, all he could think about was how he was going to enjoy killing her when all of this was over. No one had ever got away with cheating on Ahmet Ülker and no one, especially not some cheap lap dancer, ever would.

Just before he went to sleep he said, 'How about we take the covers off the swimming pool tomorrow? It's nice weather now.'

'Pool needs cleaning,' a half-asleep Maxine replied.

'Oh, well then I'd better get the pool man in, hadn't I?' her husband replied.

# Chapter 17

Çetin İkmen had often wondered how it would feel to be a citizen of another country. He was Turkish and proud to be so, but what if his parents had moved somewhere else when he was little? What if they had gone to Germany or England? If that had happened, where would his loyalties lie now? Unwittingly, Ayşe answered the question. They were standing outside the Tower of London and İkmen was looking somewhat askance at the Beefeaters.

'Why do they wear clothes that surely are from the time of Henry the Eighth?' he asked. 'And if they are supposed to be guarding the Tower, why do they only carry pikes?'

'You'd like to see them carry guns?' Ayşe asked.

'No. But if they're guarding the place, I mean given current realities . . .'

'The Tower is very well-protected, believe me,' Ayşe said. 'As for the Beefeaters and their clothes, well, yes, they are Tudor, and why not? It's tradition. In İstanbul you have the Mehter, the Ottoman military band. I don't see them wearing modern clothes. Here we have something that reflects our past.'

'Our past?'

'Like it or not, Uncle Çetin, I am both British and Turkish,' Ayşe said with a smile. 'As a police officer in this country I have sworn allegiance to the Queen. I am proud of my Turkish heritage but that doesn't stop me from being a true Brit, or rather a particular type of Brit.'

İkmen frowned.

'I'm a Mancunian,' Ayşe said. 'You talk about wanting to go home to Turkey and your family, I can't wait to get back to Manchester and my folk. Apart from the odd inter-gang incident, the Met didn't have too much to do with the Turkish community until Ahmet Ülker started flexing his muscles. At first they thought they'd just shut him down. But when it became apparent that he had other business interests in other places, the decision was taken to keep him under surveillance until such time as he could be taken down properly.' She pointed to the great yellow and grey castle and said, 'Do you want to go in?'

'I would like to,' İkmen said, 'but I don't think there's enough time. I need to see this Mark Lane and the area around it.'

Ayşe held her arm out to him. 'OK. Why don't we just walk beside the river. I can show you the main features – Traitor's Gate, the White Tower – and you can see where the mayor of London lives too.'

'Ah, Mr Üner. He lives by the river?'

They began walking down in front of the Tower gift shop towards the River Thames.

'Practically,' Ayşe said. 'His office, City Hall, is over there, on the southern shore of the Thames.' She pointed to a most peculiar modern building fashioned, İkmen thought, rather like a misshapen cone. 'Haluk Üner is a workaholic. He always arrives for work early, leaves late, works on Saturdays. He is very fit but sometimes when he is under a lot of stress, you can see him outside City Hall having a cigarette. He's quite open about it. But I don't think he handles stress well.' She smiled. 'Poor man. Poor boyfriend or girlfriend of that man.'

Great walls of stone reared up to their left as Ayşe and İkmen began walking on the cobbles beside the Thames. Along the way İkmen noticed ancient cannon facing out from the Tower across the river, towards City Hall. It was as if the might and majesty of a semi-divine monarchy were ranged against the power and modernity of the secular authorities opposite.

'So how long have you been embedded in Stoke Newington?'

'For almost eight months,' Ayşe said. 'They couldn't use a local copper because, as you know, in Turkish communities we all know each other. So I was brought down from Manchester. At first the plan was to have me infiltrate Ülker's organisation by getting a job in one of his factories. But it soon became apparent that he only employs male foremen, and those that do the actual work are all illegals. Of course I could have come in as you did, as an illegal myself. But the high command here in London deemed that too risky for a woman and so the plan was that eventually I work for Ülker in one of his shops. I was putting out feelers to that effect. But then it all went off in İstanbul and you came along. It's much better with you anyway because you can pretend you don't speak English. That has already proved useful.'

'Your superiors were quite right about not allowing you to enter this country illegally. I came in with an African couple and although I didn't see anything untoward happen to them – well, no more than what was happening to me – I fear for them, especially the woman. Our driver delivered them to some men on the motorway near Canterbury. The men who took the couple in looked at that woman in ways that made me shudder.'

Ayşe shook her head sadly. 'So you said, and I know it bothers you. Illegal women get raped,' she said. 'If they put up a fight, they could be killed. And I would put up a fight. There are many things I will do for my country but . . .'

'Fortunately your country doesn't expect that of you,' İkmen said. And then he stopped in front of a large gated aperture in one of the Tower's walls and read a sign that was standing in front of it. 'Traitor's Gate.'

Ayşe smiled. 'This is where those accused of treason would enter the Tower from the river. They would be imprisoned for a while and then, in all probability, they'd end up having their heads cut off.'

'Few societies go gently on traitors,' İkmen said.

'The Metropolitan Police have informed me that they are preparing themselves for some sort of attack tomorrow,' Commissioner Ardıç said to Süleyman. 'Obviously this information is not to be passed on to anyone.'

'No, sir.'

'The British are very grateful for the intelligence we have provided them.'

'But what will they do if nothing actually happens tomorrow?' Süleyman asked.

'I don't know. I am not privy to their every waking thought,' the older man said rather irritably. Ardıç was clearly nervous about this upcoming operation in a foreign country. Although quite why he should be so was a mystery to Süleyman.

'Officials at the British Consulate were sympathetic to the notion of our Pakistani gentleman visiting his old captain in England,' Süleyman said. 'But Mr Iqbal would like to stay permanently and I don't think they're very keen on that.'

'Can you blame them?'

'In principle, no. But he has helped us and by extension their own police force. Without Abdurrahman and his assistance, the police in London would not be mounting their operation tomorrow.'

'No . . .' In truth, Ardıç wasn't thinking about the old Pakistani man or the Metropolitan Police. He was thinking about Çetin İkmen. He was apparently going to be kept well away from the action should any occur in the vicinity of Mark Lane. But that didn't stop Ardıç from being concerned. İkmen had a bad habit of being in the wrong place at the wrong time.

'Five, so far, of the workers from Ülker's Tarlabaşı factory have tested positive for tuberculosis,' Süleyman continued. 'But the Afghans who lived with Abdurrahman and Tariq are still out there somewhere.'

'We need to find them,' Ardıç said. 'Did the factory workers prove positive for any other dreadful maladies?'

Süleyman's face dropped. What he was about to say was sadly fairly standard when it came to large groups of illegal immigrants. 'Most of the women are HIV positive as well as about a third of the men. All those people were escaping abuse of some sort.'

Ardıç did not reply. Not because he didn't care; strangely for such an explosive and often harsh individual, he did. But he was also a realist and he knew that if he thought too much about what would be done with the illegal immigrants now he would descend into a depression he would find hard to shift.

'And so we send them back,' Süleyman began. 'We send them—'

'The law must be upheld,' his superior cut in sharply. 'If we do not uphold the law then we get anarchy.'

'Yes, sir.' Süleyman lowered his head and then breathed out slowly in order to calm himself. He didn't want to send the stick-thin African women back to die of starvation in their drought-ridden villages. He didn't want to send the Cambodian youths with their dead, hostile eyes back to pimps and gangsters so cruel it was almost beyond belief. What was more, he didn't think that Ardıç wanted that either.

'There are now few hours before this anticipated incident in London and so I want you to go back to the illegals and to those foremen from the Tarlabaşı factory and question them again,' Ardıç said. 'They are not of course to know what may be about to happen. But we need to know if they have anything else to tell us. This Iranian cleric that Ülker has made some sort of pact with may yet be the key.'

'Tariq is the only one we have proof he radicalised, sir.'

'Mmm.' Ardıç looked unsure. 'Maybe that is what certain parties would like us to believe,' he said. 'But I'm not so sure that I do. Why that particular boy? Why go to all that trouble for just one lad? Why not radicalise all the young Muslim boys?'

'There weren't that many Muslim males in the workforce,' Süleyman said.

'Well, question closely those you have identified,' Ardıç said. 'Oh, and what about Tariq's diary? Did you get any more information from that?'

'The translator reckons that most of it consists of copied passages from the Koran,' Süleyman said. 'Tariq lost all but one member of his family back in Afghanistan and so the verses he copied were those which brought him comfort – intimations of the life to come. The only thing related to the supposed attack is the detail that Mark Lane is in the district of Tower Hill. But then I'm sure that the Metropolitan Police are well aware of that fact.'

Ardıç frowned. 'What does that bit actually say, do you know?'

'It just says, "Mark Lane, Tower Hill", as far as I am aware,' Süleyman said. 'Oh and the district code number too, EC3.'

'Why write both the district and the code? Presumably they are interchangeable.'

Süleyman shrugged. 'I don't know, sir. But Tariq was a foreigner, presumably he wrote down what he thought he needed to do the job. In this instance he clearly duplicated the information he was given.'

'Mmm.'

Süleyman left soon afterwards. Ardıç, still concerned about İkmen and still frowning deeply, rubbed his hands vigorously across his heavily stubbled chin.


'We'll use the underpass,' Ayşe said pointing to a flight of steps down beside the back of the church known as All Hallows. 'Byward Street is so busy it's impossible to cross.'

'The church looks as if parts of it have been rebuilt,' İkmen said as they began to descend.

'I believe it was bombed in the war,' Ayşe replied. Although a dedicated Mancunian, Ayşe had so far used her time in London well and had got around as much as she could. She'd learned a lot.

The walls of the subway were covered with pale blue tiles. Hardly the vibrant royal and aquamarine blues of Turkish İznik tiles, but they were at least functional. The underpass itself consisted of a rather dirty floor and walls and ceilings that seemed to be constructed from metal girders. Not long or even particularly dark, it was nevertheless unpleasant and İkmen wanted to be through it as quickly as possible. When he was about halfway across, from underneath his feet came a roaring, whooshing sound that was so very similar to what he remembered from the 1999 earthquake that he screamed.

'Çetin?'

'What the . . .' For just a second İkmen entirely lost his cool, and his ability not to use the English language. 'Ayşe what—'

'Çetin, Turkish!' she hissed. 'Even here, even now! Turkish!'

'Yes, but . . .' He reverted to his own language as requested and said, 'What?'

She put one of her hands on his back and said, 'It's just a tube train. The District and Circle lines run underneath here. I'm sorry it's upset you so, I would never have suggested—'

İkmen hurried past her for the stairs. 'For a moment there it sounded just like an earthquake.'

'Ah.'

'I was there in ninety-nine,' he said. 'One of my friends lost his legs.' Poor old Balthazar Cohen, the father of his daughter Hulya's husband, Berekiah.

'I'm sorry.' Ayşe followed him up the stairs and stood next to him as he slumped in front of the subway entrance, which was next door to a chain restaurant, and lit a cigarette. In front of them the traffic on Byward Street went past in one long, continuous parade.

'You know that having a cigarette actually increases anxiety rather than—'

'Oh please, spare me the Metropolitan Police guidelines on smoking!' İkmen said, suddenly really angry. 'I don't care! I am not one of you, I don't have to listen! Leave me to die before my time in peace!' He inhaled deeply. 'Now where is this Mark Lane?'

Ayşe, somewhat chastened, pointed towards the right. 'It's not far.'

They walked past some nineteenth-century buildings and a great block that looked as if it had probably been constructed in the 1960s. At ground level this block offered what İkmen was now coming to realise was a standard selection of coffee bars and sandwich shops. Thus was the City of London, thus was İstanbul

166

and almost everywhere that could be called urban across the globe. Then they turned right into what Ayşe said was Mark Lane. It was lined with office buildings both old and new, most of them unremarkable.

'At the top of Mark Lane on the right is Fenchurch Street main-line station,' Ayşe told İkmen. 'Trains run from there out to the east, to Essex and the commuter towns of Basildon and Southend-on-Sea. Thousands of people pass through there every day coming to and going out of the city. If a bomber chose that as his target, well, it would be carnage. Our people will be all over it tomorrow.'

'Mmm.' İkmen pointedly lit another cigarette and looked up at the huge building in front of him. 'What's that?'

'It's called Minster Court,' Ayşe said. 'It was built at the end of the nineteen eighties when confidence in the economy was still high. Just before it all collapsed in the early nineties. There are dozens of insurance companies, accountants, shops, bars and cafés in there.'

'It looks a bit like Dracula's castle,' İkmen said with a smile. 'The pointed rooftops and the strange angles.'

Ayşe nodded. 'One of the Met officers I know calls it the Fortress of Darkness.'

'But it is a significant structure.'

'Yes, it's quite a target,' Ayşe said.

'You're going to be here tomorrow?'

'I don't know,' Ayşe said. 'After I take you back to Stoke Newington I have to get myself to the Yard for a briefing.'

'And me?'

'Your role in all this is not what was envisaged at the beginning,' Ayşe said. 'We didn't know when you arrived that the threat from Ülker's organisation was so imminent. When I first

167

came down to London to infiltrate Ülker's fake handbag operation we believed it might be forming an alliance with other gangs. That is still a possibility of course but now we are in this other, rather more frightening world.'

'Yes.'

They walked along the street in silence. People came and went from buildings: singly, in couples, in groups. It was a nice day and some people were actually dispensing with their jackets as they walked out into the weak sunshine. The sight made İkmen shiver. Turks would never do such a thing so early in the year.

Ayşe, seeing where İkmen was looking, said, 'We grab whatever sunshine we can over here. There isn't much and so people just have to make the most of it.'

He smiled. 'It's all so normal,' he said as he watched two men light cigarettes and a young girl take a swig from a can of Coke.

'We don't know that tomorrow it won't just carry on like this,' Ayşe said. 'Hopefully all the effort we're putting in will be for nothing. But if it isn't . . .' She shrugged. 'Tonight, when you go to work, you must try to find out what you can, especially if Ülker and his henchmen are around. Get inside the factory.'

'They've caught me once already.'

'It's our last chance,' Ayşe said. 'You have to get in there and take note of anything and everything you can.'

İkmen would have been lying if he'd said that he wasn't scared. He was terrified. People like Ahmet Ülker pulled out other people's fingernails, burned them with red-hot irons. But he just smiled and said, 'Of course.'

A young businessman absorbed in eating a prawn sandwich barrelled into İkmen, spilling some tiny crustaceans down the front of his jacket, and then continued on his way without a word.

'Charming!' Ayşe called out after him as he went mindlessly about his business. She took a handkerchief out of her bag and gave it to İkmen and said in Turkish, 'Ever wondered why you bother?'

# Chapter 18

Ahmet Ülker returned home to his vast mansion on The Bishops Avenue just as his wife Maxine was putting their dinner in the oven.

'Pizza all right for you tonight, babe?' she said as he walked into the kitchen.

Lazy bitch! All she ever did was heat up pizzas and put ready meals into the microwave. But Ahmet smiled. 'Yes, that's fine,' he said.

'Take about ten minutes.'

'Oh.' He took his jacket off and put it on to the back of one of the kitchen chairs. 'Just enough time for a very quick quickie . . .'

She looked at him and smiled. 'You naughty boy!' She moved provocatively across the vast kitchen towards him, her arms outstretched. 'Upstairs or . . .'

'No, let's do it here,' Ahmet said. He moved to meet her and wrapped his arms round her waist.

'Amongst all the fitted units and extra virgin olive oil?' She smirked. 'How kinky!'

Even though she was common, Maxine was beautiful and Ahmet enjoyed running his hands across her breasts, putting his tongue into her thick-lipped mouth. But she had done this, and more besides, with that bloody awful Ali Reza. Nutcase! If only he wasn't such an athletic young man. That hurt.

Ahmet brought his hands up to Maxine's neck and said, 'You've always been a very good lay, Maxine. I'm just a little disappointed that you failed to keep your favours exclusively between us.'

His fingers started to press her throat a little and Maxine's eyes widened. 'What?'

'Ali Reza,' Ahmet said, and he began to squeeze in earnest. 'I suppose I should have expected it when I married you. You are a whore, after all.'

'But—'

'I saw you sucking him off!' Ahmet roared. 'In our bed! He was here today too, wasn't he? Saying goodbye!'

Maxine's eyes were wide and beginning to turn red as the blood supply to her head began to cease. She was bent backwards over the kitchen table, gagging but speechless.

'You shouldn't have done that,' Ahmet said as he tightened his grip still harder. 'You shouldn't have fucked other men and you should, my dear, have learned to cook. I could have forgiven at least part of it had you just occasionally provided me with a decent home-cooked meal.'

Maxine's head lolled back and her tongue stuck out of her mouth. Ahmet held her for a second, looked at her tenderly and then let her lifeless body drop to the floor. He showed no emotion whatsoever as he walked over to the oven to switch it off. Later, when he'd watched the news on the TV, he went back into the kitchen, took the pizza out of the oven and threw it into the garden. Then he made a telephone call. He didn't give his dead wife's body a second glance.

Ayşe didn't know many of the other officers in the room. There was Terry Springer of course and Inspector Riley to whom she had been 'loaned' by Greater Manchester Police. The others she knew only a little, like Inspector Carla Fratelli, a uniformed officer, who was standing beside Riley next to the board upon which photographs and details about the upcoming operation were displayed. Apart from Fratelli there was Superintendent Williams, their overall boss, and DC Ball. He was the one who called Minster Court the Fortress of Darkness. He was about Ayşe's own age and, she suspected, fancied her a little. As she sat down next to a uniformed officer she didn't know at all, DC Ball winked across the room at her. Ayşe lowered her head, but she smiled as she did so.

'OK,' Riley said as he rapped on the table in front of him to get everyone's attention. 'Tomorrow.'

Conversations straggled to an end and people coughed, cleared their throats and sat down. Once all the shuffling was over, Inspectors Riley and Fratelli stood at opposite sides of the board and Riley said, 'We are anticipating a terrorist attack, possibly of a suicidal nature, on a target or targets on Mark Lane, EC3.'

'As we all know,' Fratelli continued, 'this man,' she pointed at a photograph of Ahmet Ülker, 'is currently in league with a radical cleric known as Ayatollah Hadi Nourazar. Now we don't have any photographs of this person at the moment. He is sixty years old, was born in Isfahan, Iran. He is a known agitator across the Middle East and was deported from Egypt in nineteen ninety-seven but he has no history of involvement in terrorism. Not popular in his own country—'

'If I may interrupt,' Riley said with a smile at Fratelli. 'Intelligence just in today is that Nourazar is not just disliked in Iran, he is officially forbidden from going back there. Too radical and off message, they want nothing to do with him or his followers who call themselves the Brothers of the Light. There is a further dimension to this and that concerns this man.' He pointed at a picture of Ali Reza Hajizadeh. 'Radicalised at Birmingham University, and implicated in the making of a bomb that accidentally killed one of his revolutionary brothers, Ali Reza Hajizadeh is twenty-eight. Born just after the Islamic Revolution in nineteen seventy-nine, he too was born in Isfahan and, like Nourazar, he comes from a family that prospered under the Shah. Hajizadeh's family fled to the UK in nineteen eighty-nine and his parents remain very anti-Islamic Republic. Ali Reza currently lives in Stoke Newington and associates with various radical elements there, as well as with our favourite gangster, Mr Ahmet Ülker. For the last three years Ali Reza has lived in the Rize Guest House on Leswin Road, Stoke Newington, which is owned by a friend of Ülker's, a Mr Yigit. Now the man we currently have inside Ülker's Hackney Wick operations has told us that Ülker's right-hand man, Derek Harrison, has been given a room in the guest house, which he will be leaving tomorrow morning with Ali Reza Hajizadeh. What they're doing and where they're going we don't know. But what we do know is that Ayatollah Nourazar is in this country and has been seen at the Hackney Wick factory of Ahmet Ülker. We don't know whether Nourazar and Ali Reza know each other but because of their backgrounds it is possible.'

Fratelli cleared her throat and then took over. 'Evidence from our colleagues in İstanbul leads us to suspect that an attack upon a target or targets in Mark Lane will take place tomorrow,' she said. 'Nourazar until recently was in İstanbul and was radicalising a young Afghan boy who was to have made a suicide hit upon Mark Lane. İstanbul believes this was done with the agreement of Ahmet Ülker. But the Afghan boy died when the İstanbul police raided Ülker's factory over there and we believe that Ali

174

Reza Hajizadeh has taken his place. A suicide attack would be right up his ideological street. At the moment two of my officers are watching the Rize Guest House, particularly the movements of Harrison and Hajizadeh. Our mole, who is working as a security guard at Ülker's Hackney Wick place, has gone to work as usual. At present we are watching Ülker's factories, his Bishops Avenue place, his grotty flat in Dalston, the Leswin Road property and a flat on Evering Road, Hackney, which is the current abode of your friend and mine, Wesley Simpson.'

Everyone in the room except Ayşe groaned.

'Yes, I know Wes is a pain in the arse, screaming police brutality every time he is arrested,' Fratelli continued. 'But for all his faults Wesley isn't a violent person. He's everyone's favourite getaway driver, he never goes tooled up, whatever is happening. Violence isn't his thing. But according to our source at Hackney Wick, Wes has been driving vans full of counterfeit drugs for Ülker and so we can't discount the possibility of Mr Simpson being involved in some car-based capacity tomorrow. It is my firm belief, however, that Wesley is entirely ignorant of what may be happening on Mark Lane. In fact, if it does all kick off and Wes is in the vicinity, I can see him bolting.'

'We want Wesley Simpson watched because if he does twig that violence might be involved we may be able to use him,' Riley said. 'Where the ayatollah is at the moment, we don't know. We believe he and a group of his followers are actually living in the factories at Hackney Wick. These factories are, as we've said before, also under surveillance but we're having to keep our distance and rely upon our man on the inside. We don't want to spook anyone and blow the whole thing before it's even started. Our aim in all this is firstly to protect the public and secondly to catch this lot red-handed if we can.' He looked over at Ayşe and smiled. 'Now, as some of you may know, Sergeant Kudu from Greater Manchester has been embedded with the Turkish community in Stoke Newington for some months. Sergeant Kudu and our own Terry Springer have been liaising with our man undercover. Ayşe, I believe you have some input with regard to cultural issues.'

Ayşe told them how unusual it seemed for a Sunni Muslim, Ahmet Ülker, to be actively promoting the cause of a Shi'a cleric like Ayatollah Nourazar. 'Although we know that gangsters and terrorists are often in league with one another these days,' she said, 'this rarely happens across the Sunni/Shi'a divide. To give you a for instance, Iran as a nation is violently opposed to the Sunni forces of the Taliban in Afghanistan. It is well-known now that Iran at one time was even prepared to do a deal with the west in order to halt the spread of the Taliban and their ideology. Personally, I am very suspicious of this so-called ayatollah. It is my belief that there is some business reason behind Ülker's alliance with this cleric. The ayatollah may not be what he appears to be.'

'You think he might just be playing like a role? As a cleric?' DC Ball said.

'I think it's possible,' Ayşe said. She looked around the room. She was the only Muslim at the briefing. The only other 'ethnic' present, a DC Banerjee, was a Hindu. 'If this ayatollah is an inspiring speaker, he will be able to influence disaffected young people and get them to do things for him,' she said. 'Nourazar is educated and was once part of the elite that controlled Iran under the Shah. I doubt his motives are simply religious fervour.'

'Thank you, Ayşe,' said Riley. 'Our colleagues in İstanbul are of the opinion that the boy who blew himself up at Ülker's factory there was targeted by Nourazar because he was sick and

176

vulnerable and because of his anti-Taliban leanings. Nourazar would nevertheless have considered the Sunni boy one of the "enemy". The ayatollah "converted" him while at the same time marking him for death. Neat.'

'Sir, what about Ülker's Hackney Wick factories?' DC Banerjee asked. 'When can we close them down?'

A ripple of approval for what Banerjee had said went around the room. Riley looked first at Fratelli before he said, 'Look, I know you're all—'

'Sir, there are sick, dying people in those places,' Banerjee said. 'We can't—'

'I know you all want to get stuck in to the factories and, believe me, you will,' Riley said. 'But first we have to be sure that we avert any terrorist attack on our city and secondly we must get both Ülker and this ayatollah sewn up good and proper. We've got to catch these bastards and their henchmen at it. Ülker particularly is a clever bugger. Yacoubian Industries, his company, is officially "run" by his wife Maxine. Even a half-dead lawyer could get him out of that one. Only when we know we have Ülker, his people and any information we can get on the shady business partners our embedded man has heard him allude to will we be able to move in on Hackney Wick. But move in we shall, ladies and gents, believe me.'

'To that end,' Fratelli continued, 'we'd like you, Sergeant Kudu, to remain in situ in Stoke Newington in support of our undercover officer. Our team watching the factories will be ready to move in when authorisation is given by myself, Inspector Riley or Silver Commander who in this case will be the assistant commissioner.' She turned to Terry Springer. 'You've been on for too many double shifts lately, Terry. Get yourself home now. You have to rest.'

Terry Springer nodded gratefully.

'This is a big operation,' Riley said. 'Our activities will be coordinated centrally by Gold and Silver command which will operate from here at the Yard. Inspector Fratelli, Superintendent Williams and myself will be designated Bronze commanders. We will be based at the scene in Minster Court. We'll be supported by a CO19 unit and also counter-terrorism security advisers. At the end of this briefing you will all be allocated your various tasks, be they working undercover at the scene or staking out one or other of our suspects or suspect locations. What started out as an investigation into a slave master with some possible other operations overseas has become something much more threatening. I can't stress, ladies and gents, just how vital it is that we all take care of ourselves and our colleagues.'

Ayşe, who wasn't even designated to be at the scene, felt a shudder run down her spine.

Time was short now and İkmen knew that he had to find out as much as he could as soon as he was able. And so when he saw Derek Harrison arrive at Hackney Wick with Ali Reza Hajizadeh at nearly midnight, he made a decision to go inside the factory. They turned up in Harrison's BMW and were both carrying large sports bags. They didn't say anything to İkmen as they passed him, but he was very aware of the grim stare that Harrison gave him just before he entered. It told him the Englishman still didn't trust him at all. When they went inside, İkmen heard Ahmet Ülker greet them. Ülker didn't always turn up for the night shift or even during the day much, but tonight İkmen had seen his car enter the building. He had to get inside and soon. But how?

Mustafa generally checked on him once an hour and so İkmen waited until he had been and gone before he made his move.

The noise from the machines inside would easily cover the sound of the side door opening. The problem was whether anyone of any significance spotted him as he slid inside. A number of foremen oversaw the hell inside the factory, including Süleyman Elgiz who İkmen knew slightly from the Rize. If Elgiz saw him come inside, he could say he wanted a drink of water and Elgiz might believe him. If it was anyone else, there could be a problem. But İkmen couldn't wait outside doing nothing forever. He looked through the cracks in the splintered wooden walls and decided that everyone he might be afraid of was in the office or at the other end of the building. He pulled the door open just enough to slot his thin body inside and then pulled it quickly shut behind him. The scene that met his eyes was almost as bad as the smell. Thin people hunched over antiquated sewing machines, their backs bent, revealing spines that rarely if ever lay down straight to rest. Blood and excrement stained the floor and the smell was overpowering. But as far as he could tell, none of the foremen were close by and no one had seen him. As quickly as he could, İkmen ran over to the small cubicle that constituted Ülker's office and pressed himself hard against one of the side walls.

He stood very still, short of breath, trying not to breathe too hard lest someone hear him wheeze. Then he noticed that one of the machinists on the very last row of workers was looking at him. Black and probably somewhere in his middle age, the man stared at him with huge, wounded eyes. His face, which was emaciated and out of which teeth poked at strange and crazy angles, was one of the saddest things Çetin İkmen had ever seen. With trembling hands, İkmen put a finger up to his lips and shook his head. The man did not respond. All İkmen could hope was that he had seen and understood, and didn't summon a foreman. The man turned back to his work and İkmen pressed

179

his ear to the side of the little wooden office. The conversation in there was in English.

'Derek, it isn't about you!' he heard Ülker's raised voice say. 'You do what you have to do to help Ali, then you get out. End of story.'

'Ahmet, this is the chance I've been waiting for,' the Englishman countered. 'To get even!'

'With a tube station? Derek—'

'Moorgate, a tube station, robbed me of my future. Now another station can pay for that,' Harrison said.

Tube station? Why were they talking about tube stations? Not Mark Lane or even Fenchurch Street station. İkmen felt his body go cold. Oh Allah, they were going to hit the underground!

'I want to see—'

'Unless you want to die, you can't stay to watch Ali detonate his device!' Ülker said.

'And anyway,' Ali Reza said, 'when I do what I do, I am doing it for the greater glory of Islam. You people forget that! That is why I am doing this, *that* is the point!'

'Yes,' Ülker said. 'That is the point – or one of them.' He paused for a moment. 'That and what will follow on from Ali's martyrdom.'

'And you won't count me in on that either!' Derek Harrison roared. 'You and your holy man have picked—'

'Derek, your job is to get Ali in, help him with his equipment and then get out,' Ülker said. 'You must get away, Derek! I am giving you this opportunity because you are my friend. Once that station goes up, the police will be everywhere. I do not want you to get arrested, I do not want you to tell the police about me!'

'I wouldn't! Christ, you do know that, don't you, Ahmet?' Harrison said. 'What do you take me for?'

180

'What are you doing?' The voice came from directly behind İkmen. But the words were in English and so he couldn't react immediately.

'Oi!'

İkmen took his ear away from the side of the office and turned. The man behind him looked Turkish, though he spoke in English. The main thing İkmen noticed about him was that he was pointing a gun at him.

'What you doin', guy?' the man said again.

İkmen shrugged. 'Er . . .'

'Listening to what the boss is sayin' ain't healthy, man,' he said and reached forward and grabbed İkmen by the front of his shirt.

'Um, Mr! Sir!' İkmen stammered.

'You come with me,' the man said, 'and let's see what Mr Ülker has to say about all this!'

# Chapter 19

Wesley Simpson had told the Turkish bloke that he wasn't interested in dodgy driving any more.

'Listen, man,' he told him, 'I don't do none of that no more.'

'Don't do none of what?'

'That crazy fast getaway driving,' Wesley had said. 'I don't
do it! Happy to drive in your moody pills and take away your
less than authentic handbags, but driving people? No way, man.
Especially not at speed. I know what that means and I ain't
doin' it!'

But then the Turk had made him, as the Godfather said, an
offer he couldn't refuse, and Wesley had not just weakened but
totally collapsed. *That* was money! That was money that could
make you disappear completely, and in some luxury too. Wesley
had always fancied Rio de Janeiro. The scenery looked great,
the beaches were beautiful, and as for the women . . . Also, there
was that whole Ronnie Biggs connection. So even if the Old Bill
did track him down to Rio, they couldn't get him. Unless that
whole situation had changed. That was a worry. That bothered
Wesley almost as much as thinking about who or what he would
be carrying in the car the Turk had given him. Nice motor. Subaru.
Plain, though, not so much as a different-coloured fin on it.
Wesley looked down at it parked outside on the street. Had it
been his he would have pimped that thing till it shone. But this

job was all about discretion. Discretion but no violence. Ahmet Ülker had promised no violence. All he had to do was get himself to somewhere in London he would be told about the next day and then he'd have to drive somewhere outside the capital. Simple! Money for old rope – except that there was no such thing.

Wesley had bought himself a curry from the Indian on the corner by way of celebration, but now he found that even though the food looked and smelled great, he didn't feel like eating it. The truth was that although the Turk said he wasn't going to hurt anyone, he actually did hurt people all the time. Those pills for arthritis were a case in point. They didn't work and so those taking them stayed in pain. That wasn't good. That wasn't like driving off from a robbery. No one had ever got hurt at any of the jobs he'd been on and that was something that Wes was proud of. But this job for Mr Ülker was making him anxious because it was Mr Ülker who'd asked him to do it. Not even the money was making him feel better about it.

The phone on Riley's desk rang just as he was about to leave for what little sleep he could get that night. He answered it. It was the acting commissioner.

DC Ball, who was just finishing up some paperwork at his desk across the office, kept his head down and listened to the one-sided conversation. He was none the wiser when the call finished.

Riley looked over at Ball and smiled. 'Religion, eh?' he said as he put on his jacket and made ready to leave.

'Sir?'

'Don't know about you, Ball,' Riley said, 'but I was brought up a Catholic. Went to Mass every Sunday, went to Catholic schools. Did it all in good faith, as it were. Believed it all for a

184

long time too. I still respect those who do believe, whatever they may believe in. What I cannot abide are those who just pretend. Know what I mean?'

'What, those who pretend to believe in something that they don't?'

'Yes. Although really it goes further than that,' Riley said. 'Those who just pretend for the sake of appearances are one thing. My dad went to church just to please my mum, I know that. But there are also those who use religion cynically for their own ends.'

DC Ball frowned. 'Who we talking about here, sir?'

Riley smiled and changed the subject. 'Back in the old days I would have probably asked you down the pub for a pre-op pint,' he said. 'But I imagine you'll just be wanting either a good night's sleep or a half-hour jog on the treadmill.'

'I was, er, I was going to have a bit of swim and then get some shut-eye,' Ball replied. 'But if you fancy a pint . . .'

'No, no. It's all right,' Riley said. 'I should go home and get some kip.' He began to move off.

'Sir, about religion . . .'

'Do your best tomorrow, Ball,' Riley said. 'If we're good and lucky then everyone will get what's coming to him. Just keep on your toes. Miss nothing, see everything. Goodnight.'

He left.

Ball wondered about the phone call. He didn't know who had called but it was clearly one of Riley's superiors. The subject of religion had come up in the briefing. So what was new? Obviously something had to be or Riley wouldn't have brought up the subject again. This left Ball with the question that if these people they were watching weren't blowing themselves up for their religion, why were they doing it?

*   *   *

Holding what remained of his nerve while at the same time continuing to maintain his lack of English was making Çetin İkmen's heart pound and his whole body sweat. Everyone in that stuffy little office seemed to be speaking at once. Some, like Harrison, in English, Ülker and the man who had found İkmen in Turkish and English, and Ali Reza Hajizadeh and the ayatollah in what İkmen guessed was Farsi.

'I'll ask you again,' Ülker said menacingly in Turkish to İkmen, 'what were you doing listening to our conversation?'

İkmen took a breath to calm his nerves and then repeated his story yet again. 'I came in to use the toilet, effendi,' he said. 'I have a bad stomach. The food here I think. I needed water. I was leaving.'

'This man,' Ülker said as he pointed to the person who had found İkmen outside the office, 'says that you had your ear pressed to the side of this office. Listening.'

'No, effendi, I—'

'He was definitely listening, Mr Ülker,' the man said. Then turning to Harrison he added in English, 'He had his ear to the wall. His face was concentrated, you know?'

Derek Harrison scowled at him and said, 'Who the fuck are you, mate?' Then looking over at Ülker he said, 'Bloody Yigit! It's all his fault. He found him!'

'He's the uncle of the girl in the nail bar, Ayşe,' Ülker said in English.

'Yes, who comes from somewhere up bloody north!' Harrison said.

'Manchester.'

'Yes, where we know—'

'Derek, there is an Ertegrul family in Manchester. I checked,' Ülker said. 'You think I'd leave anything like this to chance? She is perfectly on the level, even if her uncle here isn't.'

186

İkmen breathed a little easier; the Met and Greater Manchester police forces had obviously built Ayşe's cover story well.

'Doesn't stop him being—'

Ülker cut across Harrison's words and said to İkmen, 'What were you doing, Çetin? Were you trying to get information to maybe use to blackmail me?'

'No. I came to the toilet.'

'So you keep saying. But Çetin,' Ülker raised the knife that he had been pointing at İkmen's chest up to his throat and said, 'I just can't believe you. As my friend Derek has just said, although I know your niece Ayşe, I don't know you. You could have an agenda that Ayşe doesn't know about, you could be working for one of my rivals—'

'I swear—'

'And secondly, I have something very important I have to do tomorrow which means I cannot afford any slips-ups, weak links or other problems.' He smiled and then said to the others in English. 'I don't think we have any choice but to kill him.'

'His niece will come looking for him,' Harrison said. 'You going to kill her too?'

Ülker shrugged. 'If necessary. But by that time some missing girl and her illegal uncle will be the least of the authorities' worries in this city.'

'True.'

'Unless of course this man is actually a police officer,' a very cultured voice said in English from behind Harrison's tall body. Ayatollah Nourazar moved into the middle of the room as if his feet were on casters. 'Killing a police officer attracts a serious prison sentence in this country.'

'It is not in my plan to get caught,' Ülker replied acidly, also in English.

'No, but should something go wrong, a police officer as hostage gives us some power. If we kill him, they will hunt us down relentlessly. The police do not like to lose one of their own.'

'Yes, but is he a copper?' Harrison asked.

They all looked at İkmen who just stood breathing heavily. Was this a trick on the ayatollah's part to get him to reveal himself to them or was the cleric making a genuine point about the virtues of having a police hostage? He couldn't make up his mind. His thoughts and his heart were racing far too fast for him to be able to come to any sort of rational conclusion. All he felt was that it was for the moment essential he didn't speak English. He clung to that one coherent thought.

After what seemed like forever, Ali Reza Hajizadeh spoke. 'I am inclined to go along with the ayatollah—'

'You bloody would!' Harrison cut in.

'Derek! Let him speak!' Ülker said.

'I will be beyond such things by then but if this man is a police officer then maybe you can use him to bargain if you need to. Dead, he will be useless to us. Alive . . .' He shrugged. 'I am sure, Ahmet, that he can be kept secure here for the time being.'

Frowning, Ahmet Ülker looked at İkmen and then pushed the knife a little harder against his throat. İkmen gulped and then gulped again as he felt his mouth go bone dry.

# Chapter 20

Based in an office loaned to the Met by a firm of accountants on the fifth floor of Minster Court, Patrick Riley and Carla Fratelli looked down into Mark Lane at the first commuters of the day coming into the city from Fenchurch Street station. It was 7 a.m. and he'd only had one hour's sleep and was feeling as grey and dismal as the weather. She, on the other hand, was as fresh as new-mown grass.

'Squash,' she said in answer to his unspoken question. 'That's the secret of my bright-eyed and bushy-tailed look.'

'Playing squash.'

'As soon as I finished last night I was on that court,' she said. 'Hammering away until I was knackered. Then bed for three hours and here I am.'

'Minus coffee and fags,' Riley said as he peered down mournfully into his paper cup of muddy coffee.

Fratelli didn't answer. She knew that he drank far too much coffee. She also knew that he still smoked occasionally. She didn't approve.

'The super's arrived at the station,' Fratelli said as she took a swig from her small bottle of water. 'The first shift is in place.'

The early shift, which consisted of ten officers in plain clothes, were positioned in and around Mark Lane and Fenchurch Street station. Superintendent Williams was already in an office above

189

the station with a small team of junior CID officers. Riley and Fratelli were in place and the acting and assistant commissioners were coordinating the operation from Scotland Yard. In addition, three counter-terrorism security advisers were in attendance, as was a CO19 armed response unit. Nothing was being left to chance.

'Do you think they'll go for the rush hour?' Fratelli asked Riley as she looked down into the grey street below.

'It's possible,' Riley replied. 'Although as far as we know Harrison and Hajizadeh are still at the factory in Hackney Wick. Went there last night.'

'And they've not moved out since?'

'According to the team on the ground, Ülker left at about three and drove back to his Bishops Avenue place,' Riley said. 'There was no one else with him as far as they could tell. He's still there.'

'So Ali Reza and Harrison remain at the factory?'

'Apparently.'

'No movement from Wesley Simpson?'

'No. He's at home, although there is a performance car outside his place which isn't his, but . . . You know Wes. In addition, we have no real idea where Nourazar or any of his acolytes might be either. Possibly at the factories. Ülker's Dalston flat is quiet, the Leswin Road place is quiet – all quiet on the western front, it would seem.'

Fratelli scanned the street below once again and said, 'Yes. As you say. All quiet.'

Ahmet Ülker left Cengiz, the man who had found İkmen listening at the office, and the burly Mustafa in charge when he left. İkmen himself was not in a good state either physically or mentally. He had never employed torture himself, not only because he objected

190

to it on humanitarian grounds but because in his opinion it didn't work. And he had just proved that point.

It had all started out very conventionally with a good old-fashioned beating. A couple of the ayatollah's men had obliged but luckily for İkmen they were not the brightest buttons in the box – they kicked his ribs and back mainly, so he had managed to protect his head quite effectively. But when that stopped and Nourazar began on him with a razor blade, things deteriorated rapidly. There was something about the slow and deliberate cutting of flesh that was utterly terrifying. The term 'mad with fear' took on new meaning. The actual cutting didn't hurt, but afterwards the pain was excruciating and any movement caused the wounds to widen and ensured they kept on bleeding. Cuts to the face and the scrotum were the most difficult to deal with, both physically and psychologically. Part of him wanted to cry out and declare who and what he was when Nourazar cut him just underneath his eye. But fear of a double bluff on the part of his tormentors kept him silent. If Ülker and his friends found out that he could speak English, they would know he was a plant and they would kill him, police officer or not. And so he maintained his Çetin Ertegrul persona and not one word of English escaped his lips.

Before they did anything they had stripped him naked and crushed both his mobile phones on the floor, and now that they had finished with him he was cold, in pain, bleeding and barely conscious. After some argument, they had chained him to one of the benches at the back of the factory and then gagged him with sticky tape. İkmen had never been naked in public before, not that any of the poor slaves working away at their sewing machines seemed to notice. But he was vaguely aware of Nourazar's eyes on him from time to time, of the occasional cuff

191

around the head from one of the Iranian's men. Not that any of this was really exercising İkmen's mind at the present moment. The only clear thought in his head now was how he was going to get the message out that Mark Lane was not these people's intended target. Ali Reza, with the help of Harrison, was planning to blow up a tube station.

Ahmet Ülker had finally left the factory at what İkmen estimated was two or three o'clock in the morning. First he had unloaded boxes from his car, some sort of people-carrier, then loaded more stuff into it. He did this in full view outside. Ülker and his people appeared to either know or suspect that they were being watched. But before the car left the factory, both Harrison and Ali Reza Hajizadeh had got into it and lain down in it out of sight.

At one point, as he lay naked and chained, İkmen saw his fellow guest house resident, Süleyman Elgiz, but he didn't seem to want to register İkmen's presence at all. Only the black man with the wounded eyes who had seen İkmen listening at the office so much as glanced at him. It was just the odd stolen look but it told İkmen that he had the man's sympathy. Maybe he'd been through something like this himself.

The constant noise from the machines as well as the sickening smell of himself and of others made İkmen want to vomit. Had he eaten anything much the previous evening, he probably would have done so. But perhaps fortunately his stomach was fairly empty. One thing he did really want, however, apart from his freedom, was a cigarette. But that wasn't possible.

He was still thinking of the cigarettes in his jacket pocket when he blacked out. When he came to some time later, to his amazement his jacket was right in front of his eyes. It was being worn, along with the rest of his clothes, by Ayatollah Nourazar.

192

When the Iranian saw İkmen open his eyes, he smiled, took the policeman's cigarettes out of his pocket and put them just where he couldn't reach them.

'Unpleasant habit,' he said in English. He smiled again and walked away. İkmen, suddenly infuriated beyond belief, had to use every ounce of his self-control not to swear at him very colourfully in English.

Ayşe had been expecting İkmen to get to the nail bar at about nine thirty. That was what had been agreed. Officers observing the site at Hackney Wick reckoned that İkmen had left the factory over an hour before. He'd walked out with Süleyman Elgiz and two other men who were known to come and go from the property. They had all, as was usual, made their way to the bus stop up on Homerton Road, and they had all boarded a bus bound for Stoke Newington. But it was well after ten now and still İkmen had not appeared.

'Are you married?' asked the small, thin girl whose tiny fingers Ayşe was holding.

'Eh?'

'Married,' the girl repeated as she took one hand away and adjusted her headscarf. 'Are you married?'

'No.' Ayşe forced a smile. The girl had said she was getting married the next day and wanted her nails to be painted dark green.

'I'm very lucky,' the girl continued. 'My parents have chosen a very pious man for me and so I know that my marriage will be everything it should be. Such things give one confidence.'

'Yes.' Ayşe looked at her watch again and frowned. Even if he'd gone to buy fags, İkmen should have been here by now.

The girl, seeing that Ayşe was clearly distracted, said, 'Are you OK?'

'Oh, I'm sorry,' Ayşe said. 'I'm just a little bit worried about my uncle. He's new in town and . . . I'm just a bit concerned.'

The girl looked suddenly concerned too. 'Would you like to take a minute to call him?'

'Oh, yes, if you don't mind!' Ayşe said, 'I . . .' She stood up and took her mobile phone out of her handbag. 'Thank you!'

To the astonishment of the other two girls who worked in the bar, Ayşe ran through the shop and out to the back next to the dustbins. There she called İkmen's mobile number. It rang but no one answered. Maybe İkmen hadn't heard it for some reason. Or maybe he couldn't answer his phone because of where he was or who he was with. But then perhaps the reason he wasn't answering was a little bit more serious than that. He had said that he would do his best to get closer to what was going on and being said in the Hackney Wick factory. The operation in Mark Lane was already under way, but she hadn't heard from İkmen at all since he went to work the previous night. It did not augur well. Quickly Ayşe called Riley who told her to hold her position for the time being. Nothing had happened as yet at his end and with Ülker at home and Harrison and Hajizadeh at Hackney Wick, all appeared quiet.

'But sir, I'm uneasy,' Ayşe said. 'He's usually on time and anyway I would have thought he would have called in by now if only to tell us he had learned no more.'

Riley was quiet for a moment, thinking, then he said, 'When do you usually take your morning break?'

'Ten thirty if I squeeze one in,' Ayşe said.

'If our friend hasn't materialised by ten thirty then get yourself over to Hackney Wick,' Riley said. 'Let the team there know you're coming. But go in alone. You're looking for your uncle.

It's really quite reasonable. The team are at your back if anything should go wrong.'

'Yes, sir.'

Ayşe took a deep breath and walked back into the shop. As she entered, her client said, 'Any luck?'

'I'm afraid not,' Ayşe said. Then she turned to her colleagues and said, 'If he's not here by my break is it OK if I go and look for him? You know what these old people are like. If I lose him, my dad will kill me!'

Hatice, who owned and ran the nail bar, looked at Ayşe with sympathy and said, 'Yeah, babe, that's OK. I dunno, old Turkish blokes, what are you gonna do, eh?'

Staring into the darkness of the tunnel made Derek remember. Travelling by tube had not often been an option for him, not since Moorgate. But here in this place the feelings he had were not as panicky and fearful as they usually were. Maybe it was because it was hidden away from the usual bustle and crowds of the tube, or maybe it was simply because of what he, or rather that bloody Iranian, was going to do.

'You know I know you shagged the boss's wife,' he said to Hajizadeh as he looked into his shadowed, impassive face.

'Did you tell him?' Hajizadeh said without emotion.

'No.'

'Why not?'

A distant rumble in the tunnels heralded the rapid passage of another train past their half-lit position and for just under a minute they were silent until it had passed.

'When I first found out I thought you'd give yourselves away, you were that obvious about it. Or she was,' Harrison said. 'But then when I knew that you were going to be doing this job I didn't want Ahmet to kill you before you'd done it.'

'You care about my martyrdom?' the Iranian said with a smile.

'No. But I want this done and if you're prepared to do it then that's all right by me.'

Another train was approaching from the opposite direction. It was just gone ten, getting to the end of the rush hour. But traffic was still heavy.

When the train had passed, Ali Reza Hajizadeh said, 'When this is over, will you tell Ahmet about Maxine and me?'

Derek shrugged. 'Yeah.'

'Why?'

'Ahmet is my mate. He's been good to me. If his wife's a slapper then he should know about it. He should have the choice as to whether to keep her or chuck her.'

'You see women as things.'

'Don't you?'

Ali Reza looked away.

'Not that I blame you,' Derek said. 'Her being a tart means that Maxine is good at it, I have no doubt.'

'Ahmet might hurt her.'

'Well, if he does, that's his business.'

There was a pause before Ali Reza said, 'What will you say about the fact that you knew for so long but said nothing?'

Derek smiled. 'Oh, I'll lie about that,' he said. 'No one to hurt if I say I only just found out.'

'You don't think so?'

'No.'

Another train passed, its lights illuminating the jaundiced faces of the people inside. Derek recalled his first childish investigations into the tube, of tracing its progress through the city on maps, of walking right up to the edge of the tunnel whenever he was on the platform of a deep line station. His mother would scream and holler for him to get back and behave himself. His sister's face would always be white with fear. But not Derek's. Not then.

Once the train had passed, Ali Reza, looking tense now, said that he needed to relieve himself.

# Chapter 21

There was no one outside the first factory Ayşe came to on Ahmet Ülker's property. Both sheds were covered with moss and patched with corrugated iron and lumps of wood that were probably old railway sleepers. In fact, if there hadn't been any noise coming from the buildings, she could have been forgiven for thinking that they were deserted.

There was a bell beside the large, tattered double doors that led into the building. Ayşe rang it. As she did so she looked around, knowing that she wouldn't be able to see any of her fellow officers who now ringed the operation, but doing it anyway as an act of reassurance. Just before she'd entered the site she had called DI Roman who was in charge of the team observing the factories and told him what she was about to do. He'd been concerned, for her and for the integrity of the whole operation, but he'd also agreed that İkmen's position had somehow to be established. His apparent disappearance could mean nothing or it could signal that Ülker had worked out who and what he was, which could put everything that had been done so far in jeopardy.

'Yeah?' One of the doors slid to one side and Ayşe recognised the face of the other security guard, Mustafa Kermani.

'My uncle hasn't come home,' Ayşe said. 'Çetin Ertegrul?'

Mustafa shrugged. 'So?'

'We'd arranged to meet this morning,' Ayşe said. 'I thought he might still be at work.'

Behind Mustafa she could just see into the factory. A row of people seated behind sewing machines.

'Well, he isn't,' Mustafa said. 'I don't know where he is.' One of the men at the machines, an African by the look of him, turned away from what he was doing and looked over. 'Maybe he's gone to the coffee house. Maybe he's gone back to his lodgings.'

'I called the Rize. He isn't there.'

The African was looking hard at Ayşe now and she saw him move his eyes, twice in rapid succession, to his left. It was as if he was trying to signal to her.

'What are you looking at?' Mustafa had noticed and was not happy.

'Oh, nothing, I—'

'Your uncle isn't here,' Mustafa said.

'Yes but—'

'As far as I know he left at the end of his shift here at eight,' Mustafa said. 'I've stayed on because we're short-handed.' He raised his arms and shrugged. 'Now I have to get back to my work.'

He pulled the door rudely across in front of her face and she heard him lock it. Ayşe walked back towards Homerton Road, taking her phone out of her bag as she did so.

'It would seem that our Turkish colleague has disappeared,' Riley told Fratelli as they watched one of their officers go into the sandwich booth to the right of Fenchurch Street station. The rush hour was over now and traffic through the terminus consisted mainly of day trippers and school parties.

'Do you think he may have gone native?' Fratelli said.

Riley shook his head. 'Not a chance. I've heard that our man is the gold standard when it comes to policing in İstanbul. Like Ayşe Kudu, I think he's in trouble. She's of the opinion that he's still at one of the Hackney Wick factories somewhere.'

Fratelli peered down into the street again. 'Which means he may have told Ülker about this operation.' She glanced up at Riley. 'Patrick, there's been no movement at Ülker's Bishops Avenue place.'

'He's been seen pottering in the garden and he's having his pool cleaned apparently. A chap arrived a few minutes ago.'

'So he's still there. And nothing's happening in Dalston. Wesley Simpson would appear to be sleeping the sleep of the just, and Harrison and Hajizadeh are still at the factory. Nothing's moving.'

'Doesn't mean that nothing will,' Riley said.

'Morning rush hour when everyone is half-asleep is the optimum time to cause chaos in the city,' Fratelli said. 'Seven/seven was based on that.'

'Which is why it would not be the most intelligent thing to do again,' Riley replied. 'They know we're always waiting for it. Carla, whatever they have in mind will be unexpected. Ülker is no fool, even if the rest of them are. And remember that Ayatollah Nourazar, or whatever he wants us to think he is, is out there somewhere.'

Fratelli frowned. 'Whatever he wants us to think he is?'

Riley looked around the small office just to make sure that no one had come in without his noticing and then said, 'The acting commissioner has had a telephone conversation with an Iranian of some note.'

'What, like a—'

'I don't know who he spoke to,' Riley said, 'but it sure as hell

201

wasn't some office boy or disaffected refugee. Anyway, it would seem that there's more to our so-called ayatollah than we thought. We know he comes from a well-off family and that he was not initially part of the Islamic Revolution. What we didn't know was that he used to work for the Shah's secret service, SAVAK.'

Carla Fratelli looked shocked. 'God, weren't they really vicious and brutal?'

'Yes, they were,' Riley said. 'And apparently, come the revolution, Nourazar shopped most of his old SAVAK mates in Isfahan to Khomeini and his people before he started his own intensive study of the Islamic religion. For some years, apparently, he was a very enthusiastic born-again believer. So much so, in fact, that he was allowed to keep much of the wealth he had accrued under the Shah. But as things began to loosen up in Iran in the late nineties a lot of people found his shrill baying for the blood of infidels unhelpful and distasteful and he was asked to leave. Spent his time, as we know, agitating and raising money for his cause all over the Middle East.'

'Did the Iranians let him take any of his own money out of the country?'

Riley smiled. 'Ah well, that is where we get to the crux of the matter,' he said. 'No, they didn't.'

'So he goes around raising cash for international jihad . . .'

'While pocketing the money himself,' Riley said. 'He also, according to the acting commissioner's contact, charges top dollar for indoctrination and for his and his followers' services. It's a business. Ülker, for whatever reason, has not allied himself to religious fanatics. He has allied himself to another businessman.'

'Which is what Ahmet Ülker would do,' Fratelli said. 'That makes sense.'

Riley looked at his watch. 'I don't want to order DI Roman

and his team into those factories but apparently Roman has some sort of idea that involves a pig farm . . .'

Of course DI Roman didn't use a real pig. He had enough sense not to do that. He also had enough sense to tell the real pig farmer who he was and what he was doing. Apparently Mr Trimble didn't like either the foreigners who wandered about the Wick these days or the prospect of the bloody Olympic stadium.

'Oi!' Roman banged on the door that Ayşe had knocked on earlier and then shouted again. 'You in there! You seen my animals, have you?'

'Who is it? What do you want?' The voice was heavily accented and sounded to Ayşe very much like Mustafa. She was off to one side, ready to squeeze into the building between a sheet of corrugated iron and a plank of wood.

'I come from the farm the other side of Waterden Road,' Roman said.

'Not the pig farm?' The voice was filled with disgust.

'Yeah,' Roman said. 'Some silly work experience kid let me piglets out. Only little, they are, but they can't half go! You seen—'

'There are no pigs here,' Mustafa said through the closed door. 'Please go!'

'Well, you say there are no pigs,' Roman persisted, 'but they can squeeze in anywhere. What people don't know about pigs is that when they're frightened they can be quite quiet. Hide theirselves away, they do. Place like this, wood, they could be in and hiding and you'd never even know.'

The sound of furious whispering came from inside and then slowly Mustafa opened the door. He didn't open it much, just enough for Roman to see that there were other men at his back.

203

He gave Ayşe a look and she began to work one leg into the gap between the corrugated iron and the wood.

'If you let me in,' Roman said, 'I can come and flush them out for you.'

'This is private property!' Mustafa said. 'My boss is not here but I know he would not like it.'

'Fair dos,' Roman said. 'But mate, my animals are worth quite a bit of money. Know what I mean? I can't afford to lose them and I'm sure you don't want pig shit all over the place.'

Ayşe breathed in deeply and pushed her body through the gap. She felt splinters from the wooden plank tear at her chest and waist. Since coming to Stoke Newington she had pigged out on Turkish treats far more than she had ever done back in Manchester. Now she was paying the price.

More whispering, which Ayşe could hear was in Turkish and along the lines of what on earth could they do, they couldn't have pigs in there with them.

As Ayşe brought her head through the gap, she felt the corrugated iron cut into her forehead. Warm blood trickled down her face.

'Fucking hell!' Roman said impatiently. 'I haven't got all day. If you won't let me in, you're going to have to catch the pigs yourselves. But be warned, they can bite, you know, if they feel threatened.'

'We are Muslims, we cannot handle pigs!' Mustafa said.

'Look, I tell you what,' Roman said. 'I won't come in there, but if you come out here, I'll show you how to get hold of a pig safely.'

There were several moments of silence before Mustafa said, 'OK. OK you tell us. Some of our workers are Christian, they can do it.'

Mustafa, Cengiz and the other foremen walked out of the building and pulled the door shut behind them.

Ayşe stood for a moment in the foetid air around her, looking at row upon row of people of every age, race and religion labouring in front of her. Outside, she heard Roman say, 'Right, you'll need some sort of cloth or towel or something if you don't want to actually touch the porkers yourselves . . .'

After wiping blood and sweat from her brow, Ayşe began to scour the rows of people for İkmen. Many of the heads that laboured over sewing machines were dark, like the leather that sat in great piles at the end of each row. Most of the people had dark skin too. The man she had seen through the crack in the door earlier had jet-black skin. For want of any other plan she ran towards him and put her hand on his shoulder. He swung round as if he had been burned. His terrified eyes opened wide in horror until he took in who she was, and then he said in perfect English, 'Young lady, your uncle is here. I fear these people may have hurt him quite badly.'

It was then that Ayşe turned her head and saw the lone white, naked figure slumped next to the black man, his skin covered in cuts and crusted blood. From the look of him, he was unconscious.

It was going to be many hours before Ali Reza Hajizadeh could make his ultimate sacrifice. Timing was everything, he knew that, and the ayatollah was going to text him with the go-ahead. In the meantime he had nothing to do except think and listen, or rather try to blank out the drivel that Derek Harrison came out with every so often. He was so full of self-pity! So what if he'd been in a train crash back in 1975, he'd survived, hadn't he? He hadn't been able to do the job he had always wanted to do, but why was that so bad? Back in Iran, under the Shah, people had lost their lives every day in prisons so awful they defied description. When he had first met Ayatollah Nourazar, Ali Reza had recognised him immediately. He had not known him personally back in Iran, but he knew him by reputation. Nourazar was a troublemaker and a firebrand and Ali Reza loved him. Since the early days of euphoria in Iran, back in 1979 and the 1980s, things had changed considerably and someone so uninhibited in his love of the Almighty was no longer welcome. Luckily a lot of people outside Iran understood where clerics like the ayatollah were coming from and so he was thankfully still able to make a difference. For Ali Reza to give his life for such a cause was an honour that he could barely articulate. Of course had some nameless Afghan done the deed, it would have been more perplexing for the authorities. They would have been mystified as to who he was and why he had done what he had. It would also have been easier to move Tariq around; he himself was a known face in the UK jihadi community. But so far everything was going well. All he had to think about now was his own personal legacy.

He'd put a letter in the post to his parents, telling them why he was doing what he was doing. They would be upset, of course, which was why he was telling them himself. He didn't hate them, as such. He just didn't see why he should spend his time with people who couldn't or wouldn't face the truth. Dying for God was a far more important thing than living, as his parents did, for holidays, parties and alcoholic drink. But there was another aspect to his legacy, and that concerned the man who sat up against the wall behind him now. Derek Harrison couldn't tell Ahmet about his affair with Maxine. That would make him seem like a base man, which Ali Reza knew he most certainly was not. Of course some people would just see what he had done as the quite justifiable use of a woman from a damned and hated race. He had not, after all, enjoyed having sex with the gypsy. He had simply cultivated her to gain an entrée into Ahmet's house and his world. The Turk was a businessman with no interest in religion of any sort and therefore he, too, was expendable and needed to be watched. But that said, Ali Reza did not want Ahmet Ülker or anyone else to think badly of him after his martyrdom. It was a pure and sincere act and should not be tainted by scandal of any sort.

He looked over at Harrison who had his eyes closed. Was he asleep? Ali Reza could not tell. He needed Harrison to help him get into the explosive vest he was going to have to wear to do the job. It was a two-man job. So he couldn't do anything now. Once he was kitted up and ready, however, he could take Derek Harrison out. He could do nothing now about Maxine and what she might say but he could, and indeed should, silence Derek and that in itself would be very satisfying. It was, after all, what Ahmet Ülker wanted him to do.

# Chapter 22

Ayşe Kudu looked down at the padlock that kept İkmen fastened to the bench and then reached into her pocket. She took out a Swiss Army knife from which she quickly unfolded a corkscrew. İkmen, now just about conscious, said, 'What?'

Ayşe inserted the end of the corkscrew into the padlock, turned it and was unsurprised when the thing came away with ease. 'Never disappoints,' she said. İkmen slowly pulled his hand away and then instantly placed it over his private parts.

'Ayşe,' he said, 'I apologise.'

'I've got to get you out of here,' she said, looking around wildly. Outside she could hear Roman still droning on about pigs. But she knew he couldn't hold the men's attention for much longer. 'Come on.'

She put her hands underneath İkmen's armpits and pulled. He wasn't a heavy person by any means but wounded and beaten he was a dead weight. Ayşe grunted with the strain.

'My friend, you must lift yourself,' said the same cultured voice Ayşe had heard before. She turned to look at the African.

'I can't take you as well,' she whispered to him in English. 'I'm sorry.'

İkmen roused himself and started to push himself on to his feet.

The African nodded. 'I understand.'

'What's your name?' Ayşe asked him as she pulled İkmen towards her and began to move away. The door into the factory was shaking now as if someone was trying to get back in.

'Fasika,' the man said. 'I am from Ethiopia.'

'Fasika, from Ethiopia.' Ayşe would not forget the name. When this place was finally taken down, she would make sure that Fasika the Ethiopian was well taken care of.

As she pulled İkmen towards the hole in the side of the building, İkmen said, 'Mark Lane isn't the target.'

'What?'

'Mark Lane isn't the target,' he repeated. 'I heard them: the Ayatollah, Ülker, Hajizadeh.'

'But they're—'

'Ülker, Hajizadeh and Harrison left last night. The ayatollah left this morning, in my clothes.'

The door was opening now. Ayşe heard Roman say, 'So it could be worse, couldn't it? I mean, you try to deal with a boar on heat and you've got some real problems. These are just babies . . .'

'Bastard!' Mustafa swore. 'How can he let his filthy animals loose like that!'

As one of the men pulled the large door shut again, Ayşe pushed a wounded and bleeding İkmen through the hole. Hoping against hope that Roman would be there to take him, she shoved and pushed as hard as she could. İkmen groaned in pain.

'Be quiet!' she hissed.

The men who had just come back in were looking around – for pigs presumably. It wouldn't take long before they realised that İkmen was missing. İkmen was out now and Ayşe put a leg through to follow.

'I don't see any pigs here,' Mustafa said ill-temperedly. Then just briefly he seemed to look into the pool of shadow that surrounded Ayşe. But as quickly as he had looked at her, he looked away. Seeing and yet not seeing as people sometimes do. With a surge of adrenaline Ayşe pushed herself through, once again scraping her head on the corrugated iron. Outside, she found Roman with İkmen slung unceremoniously across his shoulder. 'Come on!' he said, grabbing Ayşe's hand. 'Let's get out of here!'

Ahmet Ülker looked at his watch and wondered whether he ought to make a trip to Waitrose on Ballards Lane. It was only lunchtime, nothing was due to happen for hours, and he needed more cleaning materials. He'd killed Maxine cleanly enough but all that post-mortem stuff had happened after a while. Dribble, urine and faeces. He'd got rid of most of it. What remained he'd tossed into the pool with her body. Now the 'pool man' had taken her away, but the kitchen still had that miasma of body fluids about it which he didn't like. That said, he would have to be careful not to scrub away too much. Harrison and, more crucially, Hajizadeh had taken coffee in the kitchen in the early hours of the morning and he wanted to be sure that traces of those two still remained. Such details could be crucial if things went wrong. They could take the blame for Maxine.

When he had brought Derek Harrison and Ali Reza Hajizadeh back with him in his Mitsubishi Warrior, he'd driven straight into the integral garage. No one had followed him, as far as he could tell, but his organisation had been watched by the police some months back, Ahmet knew that. Not that anyone, police or otherwise, appeared to have followed them. Ahmet had taken precautions and still the men hadn't got out of his car until the garage doors had closed, just in case. They'd then had coffee in the kitchen – keeping their voices low in order not to 'wake' Maxine upstairs – and Ahmet had given them the workmen's overalls he had got for them, and told them to put them on. He'd then disabled his alarm to allow the two men to get out of his back garden and into the lane behind the property. This eventually came out three houses along at the junction with Canons Close. There the two of them continued on foot, two workmen going about their business in the early hours of the morning.

They had apparently successfully entered their target, so all was well on that front. Now for him it was just a waiting game. And so why not do some cleaning? Waitrose also did a very nice line in cupcakes, Ahmet recalled. He could wipe some of the residual stains off the floor, make himself a nice cup of coffee and have a lovely lemon or maybe pecan cupcake with it. Mmm.

'Where is he?' Mustafa screamed at Fasika the Ethiopian. 'The white Turkish man, where did he go?'

Fasika, his mouth already bloodied from one blow Mustafa had landed on him, uttered not a word. Behind him, some of the other foremen were opening the factory door to go out and search.

Cengiz was sweating. 'He doesn't speak English!' he said to Mustafa.

'Well, what does he—'

'I don't fucking know!' Cengiz yelled at him. 'Are you sure you turned the key in the padlock when you chained him up?'

'Yes!' And then something occurred to Mustafa. 'Allah, the man from the farm! The pig farm man!'

The pig farm man?' Cengiz looked at Mustafa blankly.

'The man from the pig farm who came here to tell us about the escaped—'

One of the men who had been searching outside came back in again. 'I guess the pigs must have run off because—'

'Shut up about the fucking pigs!' Mustafa screamed. 'Don't you see, you stupid fools, all that was just to distract us! How many pigs do you see around here, eh? None! Because there never were any pigs. That man turned up to give Çetin Ertegrul or whoever he really is time to escape! Although how he got the padlock off after the beating I gave him, I don't know.' He drew his arm back and hit Fasika hard across the mouth yet again. 'Mr Ülker is going to break my balls for this!'

'They're going to bomb a tube station,' İkmen said as he slumped into the back of the unmarked car Roman's men kept up at Hackney Sports Centre. 'I have no idea which one. Ali Reza Hajizadeh is going to blow himself up.'

DI Frank Roman and Ayşe got into the car with him. Ayşe draped a blanket across İkmen's lap.

'The only station that anyone mentioned was Moorgate,' İkmen continued. 'Harrison—'

'Derek Harrison was injured in the Moorgate tube disaster of nineteen seventy-five,' Roman said. And then he added for İkmen's information, 'It was an accident. No one knows what really happened to this day. A tube train just ploughed into a wall at Moorgate station. A lot of people were killed and injured.'

'Harrison said he was taking revenge for Moorgate,' İkmen said. 'Not that Moorgate was the target.'

Roman opened his mobile to call this information in to Superintendent Williams at Fenchurch Street.

'What on earth did they do to you?' Ayşe asked İkmen, looking at his weeping wounds.

'A simple razor blade was all they used after they'd kicked

me around the floor a few times,' İkmen said. 'Their version of the famous death of a thousand cuts.'

'We'll get you to a hospital.'

İkmen shook his head. 'No. Just get me some clothes. If we can go back to the Rize . . .'

'You need to go to hospital'

'Ayşe, you too are bleeding. Your head . . .'

'That's nothing,' Ayse said as she very briefly put a hand up to the cuts in her forehead. 'You were tortured . . .'

'Yes, sir,' they heard Roman say. 'I think the most likely candidate, given what we already know, is Tower Hill.But the acting commissioner . . .'

'There's no way we can safely go back to the Rize now,' Ayşe said. 'DI Roman's men reported to him just before we reached the car. Mustafa and some of the other men at the factory went out and began scouring the area for you about a minute after we got away. They know you've gone and they will be telling everyone to look out for you. I'm assuming they don't know that you're job?'

'Job?' It wasn't often that İkmen didn't understand an English expression, but this was one of them.

'A police officer,' Ayşe said. 'You didn't—'

'I did not talk,' İkmen said. 'No. They spoke about the possibility of my being a police officer, but they didn't know for sure. That was one of the reasons I was allowed to live. Because they didn't know what I was they didn't know whether or not I might be valuable to them.'

'But we must get you to a hospital.'

'No.' İkmen shook his head. 'No, Ayşe, please just get me some clothes! I want to know, I need to find out what is happening now. I can't—'

'The super's diverting some bodies to Tower Hill underground station,' Roman said as he clicked his mobile shut and turned to face Ayşe and İkmen in the back of the car. 'There isn't a tube station on Mark Lane, the nearest one is Tower Hill, so we have to assume that's the most likely target.'

'Harrison and Hajizadeh got into Ülker's car and then lay down on the floor,' İkmen said. 'Then the ayatollah left wearing my clothes this morning. I don't know where he went.'

'Ülker drove back to East Finchley in the early hours of the morning,' Roman said. 'He's still there but apparently alone. Either Harrison and Hajizadeh are still with him or they slipped away at some point. According to the super, Ülker hasn't moved, his flat in Dalston is empty and some dodgy ex-getaway driver who sometimes works for him hasn't left his place either. But we have to assume that it's going to go off sometime today.' He looked at Ayşe. 'The super wants both of us over to Fenchurch Street now. The obbo will carry on with Carter in charge.'

'And me?' İkmen asked.

'You, Inspector, need a hospital,' Roman said.

'No.'

'Sir, if you don't mind my saying so, you look like a fucking Dragon fruit. Lesions all over. Christ, you could have any sort of infection!'

'Inspector Roman, I have come so far with this now I really want to finish it.'

'Superintendent Williams will be horrified if he sees you like this! If I let you—'

'If any of your superiors become agitated with you on my account then just tell them that I refused to go to hospital, which I do,' İkmen said. 'If you and Sergeant Kudu are going to Fenchurch Street then that is where I want to go too.'

Roman shrugged and turned to the front to start the car. Then he turned back again. 'Inspector İkmen,' he said, 'you're stark naked.'

'Yes, I know, I—'

'There's a Matalan at Dalston,' Ayşe said impatiently. 'We can stop off and get him something there. We need to get moving. The super is expecting us.'

# Chapter 23

'Mustafa,' Ahmet Ülker said as calmly as he could, 'if the pig farmer says that his pigs got out and that he sent a man over to tell you about it, then that is what happened.'

'But Ertegrul escaped while the pig man was talking to us!' Mustafa screamed hysterically down the phone. 'It has to have been a plot! The same man wasn't there when I went to speak to the farmer. He said he'd gone home.'

'Then maybe he had,' Ülker said. What Mustafa was saying was worrying but there could be other reasons why Ertegrul got away when he did. 'You padlocked that man to the bench, Mustafa. Maybe you failed to do so properly.'

'No, I swear, Mr Ülker—'

'Mustafa, everything proceeds as planned,' Ülker said. 'Do you see policemen at the factory door?' There was a silence. 'No. Everything is arranged and we have one chance and one chance only at this. It is a shame that the Ertegrul man got away but soon no one, including the police, will have any time to deal with some foreigner who has been beaten up in some factory somewhere. The man came into this country via a known trafficker. He speaks no English!'

'He was naked!'

'Then he is probably hiding in a bush somewhere, covering his shame with an old Coke can! Mustafa, forget Ertegrul and the pig man and get on with running my business for me.' Ahmet Ülker ended the call by snapping his mobile phone shut. He didn't need Mustafa losing his nerve now! He was having enough trouble holding on to himself to bother about the grunts down at his factories. As for the pig man, the chances of his being a friend of Ertegrul or his niece, given his profession, had to be slight. He didn't need this. Neither did his partners. Ülker held his nerve and went to Waitrose.

It was one thirty by the time DI Roman got İkmen and Ayşe to the office that Superintendent Wyre Williams was using as his base at Fenchurch Street station.

'A detailed capital-wide investigation of every single tube station is just not possible,' he said as Roman and his colleagues walked through the door. 'Gold Commander has allocated manpower resources to Tower Hill and is keeping those officers on the ground here where they are for the time being. If we knew which line was at risk, we could close it. But closing the whole system . . .' He shrugged. 'Not possible.' And then he looked at the small, dark man wearing a very baggy and cheap-looking suit standing next to Roman and he said with a smile, 'Inspector İkmen?'

İkmen nodded. 'Sir.'

Then Williams frowned. 'Your face . . .'

'Our friends had a little fun with me,' İkmen said.

'Our "friends" need taking down ASAP,' the superintendent replied. 'Are you sure you're all right?'

'Yes.'

Superintendent Williams, who had an accent İkmen recognised as being from Wales, was a man of about his own age. Slim and tall, he wore his Metropolitan Police uniform well although his face was heavily lined and careworn.

218

Williams sighed. 'Well, at least we now know that it's a tube station these people plan to hit,' Williams said. 'Thanks to you.'

'What is the situation at Tower Hill?' İkmen asked.

'We've officers in the booking hall and down on the platforms,' Williams said. 'So far no one resembling either Harrison or Hajizadeh has been seen. Officers back at the Yard are reviewing CCTV footage from this morning in case they arrived earlier and are hiding just behind the entrances to the tunnels. We are starting, as discreetly as we can, to look at where the platforms end and the tunnels begin.'

'Can you not just close Tower Hill?'

'The acting commissioner, Gold Commander, is against it,' Williams said. 'Whether he will be of the same opinion when we get to the evening rush hour, I don't know. What we need to do is find Harrison and Hajizadeh.'

'And Ayatollah Nourazar,' İkmen said.

'Not that he really is a man of God,' Williams said. 'More radicaliser for hire.' He looked at İkmen and frowned. 'Nourazar peddles his own violent version of your religion for money, Inspector İkmen. Sniffs out the vulnerable and then unleashes them for the highest bidder. We don't know why Ahmet Ülker is buying his services. Ülker blowing up a tube station doesn't make sense.'

'And yet he is clearly involved,' İkmen said. 'I heard him with the ayatollah and Hajizadeh. He definitely wants this done.'

The room went quiet for a moment as everyone in it looked down into the station below.

'Is Ahmet Ülker still in his house on Bishops Avenue?' Ayşe asked.

'Yes,' Williams said gloomily. 'Apparently just before you arrived here, Sergeant Kudu, Ahmet Ülker took a jog around the

219

tennis court at the back of his house. The minutiae of that man's life continues to deaden and frustrate my day.'

Someone, no one yet knew who, had opened fire on a jeep carrying Turkish army officers. The incident had happened in the south-east of Turkey, just outside the city of Hakkâri. All the officers, plus one civilian, had been killed. At Police Headquarters in İstanbul no one who had any knowledge of where Çetin İkmen might be spoke of it. According to Commissioner Ardıç, the names of the dead would be released as soon as the authorities down in Hakkâri could do so. But there was an air of gloom about, particularly in Süleyman's office. At lunchtime he went out into Sultanahmet Square to buy cigarettes and possibly clear his head with some air and sunshine. But he found as he walked that he was still knotted up inside, still distracted. In fact, so preoccupied was he that he bumped into a small, plump, headscarfed lady just in front of the cigarette kiosk.

'Oh, I'm so sorry.'

'Oh!'

He looked down into the tear-stained face of Fatma İkmen. Since the death of her son Bekir, he had hardly spoken to her. He had, after all, been present when the boy had been shot by the local Jandarmes. Süleyman felt his face flush hot. 'Ah.'

'Inspector Süleyman,' she said.

'Fatma Hanım.'

She attempted a smile and then said, 'It's a beautiful day, isn't it?'

'Yes.'

He looked down at the large bag of shopping she held in her hands. Even with most of her family now gone, Fatma İkmen still shopped for many. Süleyman put his hand out towards her and said, 'Would you like me to help you to—'

'No!' She drew back from him quickly as if scalded. He retreated from her with an understanding smile.

'Of course I—'

'And Dr Halman, is she well?' Fatma said quickly, nervously changing the subject.

'Yes, my wife is very well. Very kind of you to ask.'

The man who ran the cigarette kiosk and who knew Süleyman as a regular customer gave up waiting for his attention and served a woman with long red hair.

'Little Yusuf must continue to bring you joy,' Fatma said, referring to Süleyman's young son.

'Yes.' But as he said it, Süleyman's face darkened. He did not want to get into any kind of conversation about children with Fatma İkmen, particularly not sons, particularly not when Çetin İkmen could possibly be lying dead in Hakkâri mortuary. 'Fatma Hanım, I need to get cigarettes and then return to work.'

'Oh, of course. Of course!' She hefted her bag and Süleyman watched her walk away. She looked so dejected, her shoulders hunched, her head down; on impulse he ran over to her.

'Fatma!' They had been such good friends in the past. She had been like an indulgent older sister to him.

'Oh, Mehmet!' she cried. 'Do you think it might be Çetin? On the television? In that jeep in Hakkâri? With those soldiers? Do you . . .' She let her shopping bag drop to the ground, put her head in her hands and howled.

Without any thought for how she might take it or what passers-by might think, he put his arms round her and said, 'Oh Fatma, I don't know. If I did I would tell you. But I honestly do not.'

She raised her wet face from her hands and said, 'Do you know one of the last things that I said to Çetin before he left?'

'I . . .'

'An evil, terrible thing for a wife to say to any husband!' She lowered her voice. 'I told him I didn't care what happened to him when he went away. I told him he was nothing to me. Oh, Mehmet, I wished him dead! For what he did to Bekir I wished him . . .' She broke down completely, sobbing her heart out with the misery of it.

'But you didn't really mean it, did you?' Süleyman said as he rocked her gently from side to side underneath one of the blossoming magnolia trees. 'You were just hurt. He knew that. He *knows* that,' he corrected himself.

'What time is it?'

Derek Harrison switched his small torch on and pointed it at his watch. 'Nearly half past two.'

Ali Reza Hajizadeh sighed. The waiting didn't breed fear in him, rather it made him impatient. But that was hardly surprising given his philosophy. Once the explosives in the jacket he was going to wear had detonated, he was going straight to Paradise. No more struggling to make who and what he was understood by people who in no way could understand. No more occasional disappointed calls from his parents. This would show them! What he was going to do would make London and the whole country sit up and take notice. And it would bring such joy to the life of Ayatollah Nourazar. That saintly man his fellow Iranians had discarded for being an 'extremist' would be listened to after this. There was nothing, the old man had told him, so good at getting people's attention as a grand and violent action.

'Keen to get to heaven, are you?' Derek Harrison asked out of the darkness.

Ali Reza looked over to the darker patch of shadow that was Derek and said, 'What would you know about it?'

'Nothing.' He cleared his throat. It's just that I can hear you shuffling about being all impatient, that's all.'

A tube train on its way ultimately out to Essex thundered past and briefly illuminated their faces. Ali Reza tried to see if the train was full but it was going too fast for him to make out anything other than a blur. Not that it mattered much anyway. Two thirty was not a particularly busy time for the tube. Ayatollah Nourazar would text him to let him know when exactly to detonate his device, but it was going to be sometime during the rush hour, that was for certain. Harrison had been instructed to help him get into the jacket at four thirty. Then it would be real.

As the train disappeared down the track and Ali Reza's world slipped into darkness once again, he wondered how he would feel once he was truly a soldier. Because that was what he was doing – going into battle. Taking the fight to those who, by their advocacy of the state of Israel, their past colonial crimes and their rejection of religion in any form, were bringing this holy wrath down upon themselves. Just thinking about it made Ali Reza smile.

# Chapter 24

Subaru Imprezas were not Wesley Simpson's favourite type of getaway car. Back in the day he'd driven all sorts: big black Mercs, nippy sports cars, bog standard saloons. His favourite, for speed as well as looks and general street cred, had to be the Mitsubishi Evo. He'd only driven one once and that was for one of the south London gangs. They'd done this post office down in Norwood and he'd driven the three of them plus the ten grand from the hit down to Brighton. Not until much later had he discovered that one of the guys had been packing a pistol. When he and all the rest of them were finally caught, Wes had gone down for three years. It had been after that that he'd decided to make the career change from driving people to jobs to driving dodgy gear to people. With dodgy gear, people only got hurt indirectly, and if the coppers found you with it you could always plead ignorance about what it was. Dodgy gear was someone else's problem.

Now as he made his way out of his flat and over to the Impreza, he was back in the old routine. He was going to pick up some blokes from a car park in Stratford, take them where they wanted to go and then wait for them to come back – with his engine running. He didn't know who they were, what they were doing or where he would ultimately have to take them. But Ahmet Ülker had promised him a lot of money to do this and so for better or worse that was what he was going to do. When it was all done and dusted, he could bugger off somewhere hot for a while, somewhere far away from London and the Old Bill. But before that he had to do the job.

Wes pressed the remote control to unlock the car and climbed inside. Just like the old days, he felt a combination of excitement and nausea. There was no two ways about it, driving was a drug and Wes was an addict. Whatever was going down with these blokes Ahmet Ülker was involved with, Wes wasn't interested. Provided there was no violence, and Ahmet had assured him that there wouldn't be, he was cool. But half a million quid in cash said otherwise. It was more money than a lot of hitmen got. It was way too much for a getaway driver. Wes was no fool, but as he put the key into the ignition and pulled away from the kerb, he closed his mind to questions that had sticky answers.

Wesley Simpson was halfway down the road when the innocuous Ford Fiesta that had been parked outside his house all night drove off after him.

At four o'clock, after consulting his superiors, Superintendent Williams moved his temporary headquarters from Fenchurch Street Station to Cooper's Row, the road that leads down from Crutched Friars to Tower Hill tube. An office above a small wine bar was quickly cleared and taken over and at just after four Inspector Riley arrived to join Williams' team.

'I'm expecting the acting commissioner to order the closure of Tower Hill any minute,' Williams said to Riley. 'It's a Friday, people will be leaving their offices early. The second rush hour of the day is about to begin. We can't take risks.'

'Still no sight of Harrison and Hajizadeh?' Riley asked.

'They haven't been seen since Inspector İkmen saw them leave

226

the Hackney Wick factory with Ülker last night,' Williams said. 'But we know the hit is going to be today. After all, Ülker and company didn't know they were being overheard last night. They didn't say what they said for our benefit.'

Ayşe Kudu left İkmen by the window and came over to her superiors. 'But Harrison and Hajizadeh aren't in the station, are they?'

Williams sighed. 'No.'

'And sir, I assume that trains will still run through Tower Hill.'

'Yes, they will.'

İkmen, who had been listening, said, 'But they are definitely going to target a tube station. Not a train or a tunnel. I heard them. I think that to get a station is essential for Harrison's sense of revenge.'

'Sir!' A detective constable who had been on the phone called over to Williams.

'Yes?'

'The CCTV footage we've been able to get hold of has come up negative,' the young man said. 'Harrison and Hajizadeh are not on any of the media we've managed to look at so far.'

'Sir,' Ayşe said, 'maybe they're coming into the City from one of the tube line terminus points. From Harrow on the Bakerloo line, for instance.'

'That is a possibility,' Williams said.

'In which case,' she continued, 'if they're already on their way, closing Tower Hill as they approach it will alert them to the possibility that we're on to them. Under those circumstances, they could do anything.'

'The impression I got from the Iranian,' İkmen said, 'was of a man who will not be easily diverted from his mission. He has chosen martyrdom and that is it.'

The superintendent's phone rang and he walked away from the group to answer it.

DI Roman threw his hands up in the air and said, 'And anyway we don't *know* it's going to be Tower Hill, do we? We're basing all of this on some entry in a diary of a refugee in İstanbul.'

'Who we know was being groomed to come here and commit a suicide bombing,' Riley cut in sharply. 'That much has been established by Inspector İkmen's colleagues in İstanbul. We know that. The reference to Mark Lane found in his diary was written against this date and it is the only real indication about where the attack might take place that we have.'

'Why don't we bring Ülker in?'

Riley put a hand on Roman's shoulder. 'Frank,' he said, 'I can understand your impatience—'

'Can you?' Frank Roman twitched away from him. 'That obbo out at Hackney Wick has been going on for weeks. On the few occasions Ülker's men let his workers out for some air and a piss, those of us looking on can hardly stand it. They're working people to death in there! And look at what they did to Inspector İkmen! I want it closed down. We all want it closed down!'

'I know you're sick of waiting, Frank—'

'OK, I've just received instructions from Gold Commander to shut Tower Hill.' Williams came back to his colleagues. 'The acting commissioner is fully aware of what the implications of doing this might be but he feels he doesn't have a choice.'

Everyone looked anxiously either down at the floor or out of the window.

'I'm now going to call the mayor to inform him and I'd like you, Inspector Riley, to lead a team to go and close the station.'

'Sir.'

'Uniform officers are on their way over from Fenchurch Street now.' He looked at Ayşe and Roman. 'I'd like you to accompany Inspector Riley.'

'Right.'

'The official reason we are using to close the station is that a suspicious package has been found on one of the platforms,' Williams said. 'Let's get to it.' He picked up his phone again and called Haluk Üner, mayor of London, on his direct line.

'Ah, Superintendent . . .'

He looked up. 'Inspector İkmen?'

'Sir, would it be acceptable if I accompany Inspector Riley to the station? I am anxious to see this through.'

Williams listened as the phone began to ring and said, 'Yes, Inspector, go ahead. But please follow all instructions you are given. We are very grateful to you and your superiors and I would hate to end our relationship with further damage to your person.' Then he turned away and said into the phone, 'Mr Üner, yes . . .'

İkmen followed Ayşe Kudu and the others out of the office and down the stairs.


'Süleyman!'

Unusually, the commissioner's door was open. Either by chance or design he saw Süleyman pass by and called him into his office.

'Sir?'

'Close the door and sit down,' Ardıç said, motioning Süleyman in with his cigar. Süleyman did as he was asked.

'I'm happy to be able to let your know that the civilian killed in an attack on a military vehicle in Hakkâri was no one connected to this station.' Ardıç cleared his throat. 'I know that speculation has been rife about that person possibly being our own

Inspector İkmen, but I can assure you that it is not. I would be grateful if you could convey this information to Mrs İkmen. You know her better than I do and I am sure she is aware of the news story in question.'

'I know she is, sir,' Süleyman said. As he spoke he let out a small sigh of relief. When Ardıç had called him in he had experienced a moment of terrible panic. The prospect of İkmen's death was almost too awful to contemplate.

'With regard to İkmen,' the commissioner continued, 'it would seem that his sojourn elsewhere is not to be as protracted as we thought. I have not yet been informed when he will return to us, but I understand we will not have too long to wait.'

'That's excellent,' Süleyman said. 'Sir, I—'

'Ask me no questions about where he is and what he's doing,' Ardıç said and then added brusquely, 'Now get back to your duties and close my door behind you when you leave.'

Summarily dismissed, Süleyman stood up and left, carefully closing the door behind him.

Alone in his office, Ardıç leaned back in his chair and looked up at the ceiling. According to his opposite number in London, events there appeared to be entering some sort of final stage. Apparently with İkmen's help they had discovered that the terrorist attack on the British capital was going to take place in a metro, or what they called a tube station. They were closing the station they felt was the most likely target. Ardıç wondered what part İkmen was playing in that operation. Apparently he had been wounded in the course of his undercover work for the Metropolitan Police. But he had as yet refused any treatment for his wounds. That was typical. It was difficult enough to get İkmen to have a routine medical. To say he had a phobia about hospital treatment was probably understating the case.

230

Ardıç just hoped that İkmen, in his enthusiasm for his exciting foreign posting, didn't get himself killed.

The vest was heavy and unwieldy. Unlike suicide vests worn in populous areas it didn't need to be concealed underneath clothing and so could be as large as was required. Usually weighing a maximum of 20kg, this one weighed in at 30 and was packed with large cylinders of top quality Composition 4 plastic explosive. Around the explosive was another, outer vest which contained the nails, metal bolts and plates that would constitute the shrapnel element of the bomb.

Derek Simpson hefted it out of the large sports bag he had used to transport it and looked it over by the light of his torch. Once on Hajizadeh's body, he'd have to check that all of the wiring was correct and then fit the detonator. It was he who had the skill and knowledge in this area, not the Iranian. All he had to do, as far as Derek was concerned, was die.

'Come here,' he said when he saw that Hajizadeh had taken his T-shirt off.

The Iranian walked over and, with a smile, slipped his arms into the vest.

'You'll have to keep very still while I check the wiring,' Harrison said.

Ali Reza felt various tuggings on the vest as he stood looking out into the darkness. It was very heavy and cut into the tops of his shoulders deeply. But he was proud to wear it and was relieved that at last the time had come to kit up and get ready for his mission.

'You don't touch the detonator until you're absolutely in position,' Harrison said to him. 'Understand?'

'Yes. I'm not stupid.'

'I know,' Harrison said. 'I just don't want you running away with yourself before you get the text. I know what you lot are like. I've been around you long enough.'

Ali Reza put his hand into the pocket of his trousers and said, 'You lot? What do you mean you lot?'

'Jihadi types,' Harrison said. 'You're so keen to get to the other side you often forget the details you have to go through to get there.' He looked into the Iranian's eyes and said, 'I'll be honest with you, Ali, I don't like the fact that Ahmet has taken to working with you lot lately. All this religion stuff, it don't sit well with me. Don't sit with Ahmet either, much as you might like to think it does. He drinks, does all sorts of things Muslims ain't supposed to do. He ain't doing this for God.'

'I know what Ahmet is,' Ali Reza said. 'He's a means to an end.'

'Well, for myself, I can't say I'll miss you, but I am grateful that you're taking revenge for me,' Harrison said.

'It's a strange sort of revenge, blowing up something inanimate. After all, Derek, it wasn't the tube itself that hurt you, was it?'

'My life ended down here,' Harrison replied. 'Moorgate weren't no one's fault. What else but an inanimate object can I take it out on? Anyway, you're not perfect, whatever you might think.'

'Shagging the boss's wife?'

'Bloody Maxine. Why Ahmet married a fucking lap dancer I—' Suddenly something hurt – a lot.

More slowly than he had shoved it in, Ali Reza pulled out the short knife he had just thrust into Harrison's abdomen.

'Fortunately for my reputation, no one will ever know,' Ali Reza said. He threw the knife to one side and then held Harrison as he began to sink slowly to the floor. 'I'm doing this for myself but you should also know that Ahmet asked me to kill you. He didn't want any loose ends.

'You bastard!' Wet bulging eyes looked at Ali Reza through the gloom and Harrison repeated, 'Bastard!'

Although he could hardly see what he was doing and he was weighed down by the cumbersome suicide vest, Ali Reza managed to lower Harrison to the ground. Halfway through, a train went by and briefly illuminated Harrison's grey, dying face. It also showed Ali Reza that there was a lot of sticky blood everywhere. He moved away from it before he got too much on his hands. Then he just listened to the sound of Harrison's demise as he wiped his bloodied hands on the sides of his trousers.

# Chapter 25

Tower Hill station, İkmen learned, had one entrance, which doubled as an exit, and one dedicated exit. Apparently the single exit on Cooper's Row had once been the only entrance and exit to the station. But an increase in passenger numbers had meant that another, bigger entrance had been built, with a ticket office.

İkmen was standing in Trinity Square Gardens with a small group of London Underground workers, one of whom, an elderly man called Alf, had tried to pump him for information about what exactly the police were doing. In line with his instructions, İkmen had assisted his colleagues in clearing out the station but now, along with Ayşe Kudu, he was to keep well out of the way. As he understood it, Inspector Riley and DI Roman were now coordinating a minute search of the station while trains had been instructed not to stop at Tower Hill. Neither Harrison nor Hajizadeh had been picked up on CCTV and so the chances of their being down on the Tower Hill platforms were slight. But apart from anything else, the police had to maintain their story about a suspect package and so they needed to be down there, and there was always a chance the men were in fact down there. It was possible to walk from station to station along the track. There were little alcoves in the wall where those working on the line could stand when trains passed. These could also be used by terrorists. There were three possible routes in: from the east on the Circle line from Aldgate, from the west on the District line from Monument, and from the east also on the District line from Aldgate East.

'Suspect packages don't normally take the coppers that long to deal with,' Alf said as he offered İkmen a cigarette. 'Even back in the old days when the IRA were at it all the time, suspect packages never took that long. Do you know if they're calling out the army? To take it away and blow it up?'

İkmen took the proffered cigarette with a smile. 'No,' he said. 'I don't.'

'If the officers down there think they need bomb disposal, they'll call for it,' Ayşe said. 'They'll make a judgement about that.'

Alf lit his own and İkmen's cigarettes and then said gloomily, 'Better not blow up my station.'

'I'm sure that won't happen, sir,' Ayşe replied. 'You've obviously been around these things many times before, you know how often they turn out to be hoaxes.'

'Yeah.' Alf sucked hard on his cigarette and then said, 'Mind you, this al Qaeda mob we've got now, they don't muck about, do they? Back in the old days with the IRA you generally got the warning phone call. But not this lot. Just blow people up. For God, they say, although I can't see that myself.'

'Al Qaeda believe they're working for God,' Ayşe said, 'but their view of God is not the same as everyone else's.'

'You can say that again!'

İkmen and Alf smoked in silence for a while, watching as the uniformed officers outside the station turned people away. A couple of people, angered at having to use an alternative station, argued uselessly with them, but in general people took the inconvenience well. In that the Londoners were very similar to

İstanbullus, İkmen thought. Things cancelled or shut were inconvenient but what else could a person do but shrug his or her shoulders and just carry on?

'Mind you, if they blow this place up, we could always go back to using the old station,' Alf said as he looked up into the pale grey early evening sky.

'The old station?'

'Old Tower Hill station,' Alf said. 'Not many people remember it now. Shut in the late sixties, I think it did.' He nudged his colleague. 'When did old Tower Hill station close, Reg?'

Reg was older than Alf. 'Gawd,' he said. 'I don't know. Sixty-eight? Sixty-nine?'

'About then,' Alf said. 'When this place was built they shut the old station, locked it up and turned off the lights.' He smiled. 'Like something out of the war, it was, old Tower Hill, or rather to give it its proper name, Mark Lane.'

'Mark Lane?' İkmen began to feel his heart increase its beat.

'Mark Lane is what old Tower Hill was originally called,' Alf said. 'It's like a proper time capsule down there. Posters on the wall for Marmite and Ovaltine. Course you can't go down there now, not since the bombs in two thousand and five.'

Ayşe looked at İkmen who looked at her with the very same thought in his head.

'Is this station on Mark Lane?'

'No,' Alf said. 'You actually get into it, or you used to be able to get into it, by going down the Byward Street underpass. From the back of All Hallows underneath the road, to an opening next to some bar on this other side.'

İkmen turned to Ayşe. 'That subway you took me down,' he said. 'The one where the trains running underneath reminded me of the earthquake. That's where Mark Lane is!'

237

Ayşe took her phone out of her jacket pocket and began to scroll through numbers as she grabbed İkmen's arm and started to run towards the west. 'Come on!' she said.

Ever since four o'clock the number of trains running in both directions had increased significantly. So timing – getting down on to the lines, detonating the device – was going to be crucial. Ali Reza switched the torch on again and pointed it at his watch. It was now one minute to five but still he hadn't received anything from the ayatollah. Slightly anxiously he wondered what he would do if the text never came but then decided that that was just not possible. What he was doing was all part of Nourazar's great work and so nothing would get in its way. And besides, even if the text didn't reach him, he was committed to his course and would detonate eventually come what may.

Ali Reza smiled. Soon he would be in Paradise with all the pettiness and horror of the world very far away. For a second he trained his torch towards the back of the old platform and saw Derek Harrison's slack body. One thing was for sure, he wouldn't be meeting *him* in Paradise. What a ridiculous person he had been! To want to take revenge upon a means of transport on which you'd had an accident was insane.

Ali turned his mind back to thoughts of Paradise. Then, as if by some noble sacred magic, his phone beeped to tell him he had a text.

Both Ayşe and İkmen panted as they looked at the plain metal-faced door at the bottom of the staircase leading to the underpass. There were stickers all over it saying 'No Entry', 'Keep Clear', 'Eye protection must be worn' and 'These doors are alarmed'.

238

There was a numerical keypad halfway up the wall on the left-hand side of the door.

'There must be some sort of entry code,' Ayşe said as she panted to catch her breath.

İkmen, who felt as if he was about to pass out from lack of oxygen, said nothing. This door, when he had first seen it, had barely entered his consciousness. Now he read, 'Keep clear. Exit from emergency escape route'. It was known about – as an escape route.

The clatter of heavy boots on concrete stairs heralded the arrival of Riley, Roman and a team of uniformed officers, one of whom was carrying a metal battering ram. As they approached, Riley terminated the call he had been engaged in on his mobile and turned to the uniforms. 'Break it down,' he said.

'Sir, there's a code,' Ayşe said.

'Yes, I know,' Riley replied. 'But we don't have time for that now.' He stood out of the way of the ram as a particularly burly officer began smashing it into the door. 'I want you and İkmen out of here,' he said to Ayşe. 'If Harrison and Hajizadeh have set a bomb down there, I want you two a long way away from here. Now!'

For a moment İkmen stood rooted to the spot, mesmerised by the sight of the metal on the door buckling under the force of the battering ram. But then Ayşe took hold of his arm and said, 'Come on, Çetin!'

They began to run towards the All Hallows exit.

Ali Reza had just jumped down on to the track when he heard the commotion up above. Either the man who had given Harrison the code had grassed them up to the police or someone had finally worked it all out. Not that it mattered. He could already see tiny pinpoints of light in front of him, meaning that a train was coming. It was the train he was going to destroy.

Up above, the hammering continued. In front of him the lights from the train grew closer at speed. Ali Reza put his hand inside the explosive vest and twisted his fingers round the cord that was connected to the detonator. If he pulled the cord too soon he would damage the old station without actually blowing up the train. But if he left it too late, the train might mow him down before he could pull the cord and then who knew what would happen? He assumed the device would still blow up but he couldn't be certain.

Strange the way that everything suddenly felt really slow. The lights that had been coming toward him at such a fast rate now seemed as if they were only edging forward, centimetre by centimetre. It was odd. The sensation in his head felt very like his one and only experience with cannabis: floaty and without a care for anything much. There was something he wanted to say before he died but suddenly be couldn't recall what it was. The only thing he could remember as the lights in front of him suddenly became massive in his eyes was that he had to pull the cord. This Ali Reza Hajizadeh did just before the front of the train barrelled into his chest.

The blast from the explosion in the tunnel beneath them picked İkmen and Ayşe up off their feet and slammed their bodies up against the tiled walls of the underpass. As the bomb detonated, the officers who had just broken through the door into the old station were also knocked off their feet. Dust and debris from the explosion blew out through the open door.

'Christ!' Riley pulled Roman and another officer down on to the ground with him as the vast compressed dust cloud engulfed them. The officer who had been breaking down the door lay motionless beside his battering ram, half in and half out of the doorway. Down below, the sound of crashing, twisting metal screamed as what remained of the tube train smashed both into itself and into the walls of the tunnel. Later, the blasted driver's cab at the front of the train would appear at the end of the east-bound platform of Tower Hill station, slowly and horrifically coming into view to the officers still searching the platforms.

İkmen only blacked out for a second. Unlike Ayşe, he didn't actually crack his head when he was thrown up against the wall. But he was disorientated and for a few moments he couldn't catch his breath. The air was filled with dust and what tasted like metal and if he tried to breathe in he felt as if his chest would burst. Then there was the noise. It was like the earthquake of 1999, crashing and shuddering below him as if some monster of the deep had awakened in a fury, hell bent upon rising to the surface on some terrifying mission of revenge. Everything in him recoiled from the sound and for a moment he just curled himself up into a foetal shape and howled. But as he unravelled himself, he saw that Ayşe was lying quite still beside him. Instinctively he called out in Turkish, 'Help! Help me!'

But not a soul responded. He pulled himself across the concrete towards her and put his head down to her mouth. She wasn't breathing. With a superhuman effort of will he made himself remember some English and he yelled, 'Ayşe isn't breathing! Help me!'

He could hear screaming. Whether it was from down below or in the underpass, İkmen couldn't tell. Desperate, he tried to rise to his feet but his legs seemed to be made of jelly and his attempt left him stranded on the ground like a beached fish. 'Help me!'

He looked at Ayşe. She still wasn't breathing. But then suddenly, out of the dust and filth that surrounded him, the figure of a man appeared. He came from the All Hallows end of the underpass and he had some sort of mask over the lower half of his face. He was in Metropolitan Police uniform.

'Help her!'

In one rapid movement the officer picked Ayşe up and then turned to run with her back down the underpass. Another man, also in uniform, bent down and pulled İkmen to his feet. His legs were still shaking but as he leaned against the man he found that he could just about manage to put one foot in front of the other. When they got to the stairs, the officer picked İkmen up in his arms and carried him out into the open air. It felt so cool and sweet, he almost cried.

'There are other officers in the subway,' İkmen said as the officer placed him on a bench beside the church. On the pavement just to the side of him, a man was breathing into Ayşe Kudu's mouth. The noise all around, although not as terrifying as the sounds he had heard from the tunnel, was tremendous. Sirens wailing, people shouting, emergency vehicles pulling up and paramedics, firemen and police officers getting out of them.

A woman in a green jumpsuit put a blanket round İkmen's shoulders and looked deep into his eyes and said, 'Are you all right, my love?'

'There are other officers down there,' İkmen said and pointed to the smoke-swathed entrance to the underpass. 'They're hurt.'

'We'll get you to hospital soon,' the woman said with a smile.

'I'm fine,' İkmen said. In a way it was true, he felt a little sore and his lungs hurt but he wasn't bleeding and he didn't feel sick. 'You must get the others. The others are hurt.'

She smiled again. 'Don't worry, sweetheart.' She straightened and began to move away. 'We'll get to them.'

He turned to see how Ayşe was doing but she was no longer in sight. İkmen began to feel cold. He also began to feel as if he wanted to lie down and sleep. He knew he didn't want to go to hospital. There was no need. They'd only treat him for shock and he knew how to deal with that without a doctor telling him. A chocolate bar and a cigarette usually fixed most things. Not that he had any chocolate on him. But he did have cigarettes and so as soon as his hands stopped shaking he lit one.

İkmen threw everything in his stomach up on to the pavement in one huge, glittering arc. When he had finished, he felt much better. He lit another cigarette and began to walk towards the Tower of London and the river.

The officer who had battered in the door that led down to the old station was dead. Flung backwards by the blast from the explosion down below, he had landed on the concrete floor on his head. Everyone else in Riley's team had survived so far, although all of them were now on their way to various local hospitals.

Superintendent Williams was speaking on his mobile phone to his superiors, the acting and the assistant commissioners.

'Yes . . . Yes . . .' he said as he ascended the stairs behind All Hallows with Inspector Carla Fratelli. 'Yes, one officer dead and one just about clinging on . . . No . . . We're going down now. Yes, I will let you know.'

Voices, some screaming, ripped up at them from the earth below. Fratelli shuddered.

When they reached the mangled doorway leading down into the old station they were met by a group of fire officers. A particularly

243

grimy individual stepped forward and said, 'I'm ACFO Harwood from Dowgate Station.'

Williams knew that Dowgate was the closest station to the site. They'd got to the scene very quickly.

'Superintendent Williams,' he said and held out his hand to the acting chief fire officer.

Harwood shook his hand. 'What looks like an eight-carriage train has suffered an explosion as it was travelling east through the old station. Vehicle was full and so we've got multiple casualties down there. The station itself appears to be undamaged and we've managed to get some lights put up. The old platform, such as it was, is quite a state.'

'Are there any medics down there?'

'Yes,' Harwood said. 'From Barts. There was also one on the train. At the back. He's shaken up but he's unhurt and he's helping others. We've no idea as yet as to numbers of casualties. But we're taking them out here and through Tower Hill.'

'Can we look?'

Harwood passed them both mouth masks and said, 'Stand at the top of the stairs. As I said, we've got lights up.'

Williams and Fratelli stepped through the door and found themselves at the top of a mottled, rickety staircase. Large arc lamps had been strung above the tortured train carriages and smashed platform. The air was filled with smoke and dust which lent a sinister diffuseness to the scene. Williams was aware of groans of pain as well as the screams he had heard from the subway. The carriage at the far eastern end of the platform, near the front of the train, was trapped, concertinaed down to maybe half its size between the platform and the tunnel wall. No sound or movement came from it. The one directly behind it moved a little as two fire officers used cutting tools to remove its windows. There was no sound coming from it either. But further along the train towards the west, fire officers were helping bloodied men and women stagger on to what remained of the platform. One man, sobbing uncontrollably, was carried from a carriage further back. As the fire officer carrying him walked past Williams and Fratelli, they could both see that he had only one hand. Where the other had been there was just a large blood-soaked piece of cloth.

Williams took his mouth mask off and said, 'God help us!'

# Chapter 26

Çetin İkmen knew that he wasn't himself. But he also knew that
he wasn't ill. In fact he felt rather lighter and airier than he had
for a long time – in a sense. He was worried about Ayşe. He
assumed she'd been taken to hospital and knew that if he
consented to go to hospital too he may well find out more. But
İkmen and hospitals had never mixed easily and so when he left
the back of All Hallows and staggered down towards the Tower
of London, he knew what he was doing – getting away. Williams
and the others wouldn't let him help with the horror down in
the old station and in a way that was a good thing. Although he
had never balked at staring the reality of man's inhumanity to
man straight in the eye, he had attended his fill of hideous
explosions. If they had let him help with rescuing the victims
or counselling the shocked and wounded, he would have done
that gladly. But İkmen knew that they wanted their foreign guest
kept secure and safe. That meant hospital and that was just where
he wasn't going.

He went where Ayşe had taken him, down Thames Path, by
the river. A light breeze was blowing down the river and the
coolness of it on his face felt good. Behind him, up on Tower
Hill, all hell had broken loose. But he couldn't look at that.
Someone should have known about old Mark Lane station. If
the sounds he had heard coming from the tube tunnel were

247

anything to go by, a lot of people had been killed and injured. Ayşe Kudu among them. He should have protected her. He had no idea how, but he knew he should have done so. Had she been his own Ayşe, Ayşe Farsakoğlu, he would have made sure she got out of the underpass even if he'd had to die in the attempt. That, as her immediate superior, was part of his job.

More sirens sounded and he heard some people who passed him say, 'Bloody Islamic nutters!' He felt both angry and ashamed. That someone like Ali Reza Hajizadeh should distort the religion so beloved by his wife and many of his friends and family made İkmen furious. The essentials of Islam revolved around love and respect. But in this particular case, a secular person like himself was involved too. Ahmet Ülker had at the least facilitated the bombing. He had allowed or even encouraged Ayatollah Nourazar to recruit in his factories, Hajizadeh and Harrison had hidden in his car and maybe in his house. Ülker, in fact, had been key to the whole operation. But how on earth could the deaths of Londoners he didn't know help him?

İkmen leaned against the wall that separated Thames Path from the river and lit a cigarette. He looked at the oddly shaped glass building that Ayşe had told him was City Hall. That was where the London Assembly, those who made policy for the capital, met. Mr Üner, the slick young mayor whose parents were Turkish immigrants, was in overall control. How wonderful, İkmen felt, that someone from such humble beginnings should end up as mayor of London. Working in a weird but fantastic building set in such a prestigious and lovely location. Now he looked at it, City Hall was situated in a small park. In that it was like his own place of work, behind Sultanahmet Park. But Mr Üner made rather more use of his park than İkmen did of his. He went out jogging. But then Ayşe had told him that Üner sometimes had to have a cigarette too. How weird modern life was! Thinking about this made İkmen laugh at first but then very quickly what had been funny was suddenly overtaken by the tragedy he could hear unfolding behind him. Tears ran down his cheeks. They blurred his sight, making the strange building on the south bank appear even more distorted than it really was. He went to dig into his pocket for a handkerchief when his attention was caught by the sound of screaming.

At first he thought that maybe it came from behind him but the sound that he heard did not come from that direction. He looked first left and then right, but he was entirely alone. Only one direction remained and so he looked back across the water again. What he saw was a car pulling up to the side of the building and some people milling around at the front. He couldn't make out individuals but there was a general impression of suitedness which made him assume that they were probably all men. At least one of them was shouting now but he couldn't hear what was being said. İkmen narrowed his eyes. Then suddenly he understood what was happening and it made him go white with fear. Now, at last, everything was clear to him.

'That was DI Roman from Barts,' Superintendent Williams said as he watched yet another dead body being stretchered out of the old station and into the underpass. 'I'm afraid that Sergeant Ayşe Kudu, our colleague from Manchester, has just died.'

Inspector Fratelli shook her head. 'Oh, my God.'

'She was bleeding into her brain. They tried to relieve the pressure . . .' He shrugged. 'She died on the operating table. Carla, I'm going to have Ülker brought in and I'm going to tell DI Roman's men to move in on his factories. We can't wait any longer.'

'Sir—'

'Sir, this place is filling up,' another, rougher voice cut in, one of the firemen. 'We need to get a makeshift morgue erected up on the surface.'

Williams looked at the roughly covered line of bodies that lay on the concrete, an ever lengthening line from the northern end of the underpass to the southern end at All Hallows Church.

'A marquee – anything,' the fire officer said.

'Yes,' Williams said. 'Yes.' He took his phone out of his pocket. 'Of course. I'm sorry, we've just discovered that one of our colleagues has died, I—'

'Sorry about that, sir,' the fire officer said, 'but—'

'Superintendent Williams!' Another, foreign voice called down the underpass from the All Hallows end. This was followed by the sight of a small, shabby man hurriedly picking his way through the blanket-covered se bodies.

Williams peered at him. 'Inspector İkmen?'

İkmen was breathing hard. He had run all the way.

'Superintendent,' he gasped as he came to a halt in front of Williams and Fratelli. 'Sir . . . you must get over to City Hall. Now!'

'City Hall? Inspector İkmen, the emergency is here.'

İkmen shook his head. 'No, or yes it is, but they are taking the mayor. Over at City Hall, men with guns!'

Williams's eyes widened.

'Sir, we must get there now!' İkmen said. For a couple of seconds Williams said nothing, he seemed quite stunned. 'Sir!' İkmen shouted. 'Sir, Mr Üner will die!'

And then the spell of inaction broke and Williams said, 'Carla, stay here and get a makeshift morgue organised. I'll square it with the acting commissioner to have Ülker brought in and his

250

businesses shut down.' He began to step over the corpses. 'Come on,' he said to İkmen, 'you and I will get over there. Armed, you say?'

'Yes,' İkmen said as he picked up speed in front of him.

Williams dialled a number, put his phone up to his ear and then requested the services of the armed response unit CO19 at City Hall. After that he called his boss, the acting commissioner.

Wesley Simpson had duly picked four blokes up from Stratford – an old Arab man he'd seen before, two Asians and one other Arab by the look of him. Then there had been a bit of stuff about losing first the Ford Fiesta that had picked him up and then the Mini that had taken its place. But Wes was used to losing tails. He'd told the blokes that they had tails and that in his experience they were probably the police. He thought that maybe the knowledge might make them cancel what they were intending to do. But the old Arab said that whatever happened they had to continue on their way.

'We must go on to Potters Fields,' he said. 'We have business there.'

Wes shrugged. If the coppers were following them they probably wouldn't give up just because he lost them twice. They would be back and he would have been lying had he said he wasn't worried. But these blokes were clearly in charge and there was also that load of money at stake for him. 'All right, mate,' he said as he turned off London Bridge and down on to Duke Street. Potters Fields, where these characters wanted to go, was a turning off Tooley Street, around the back of City Hall. There was a lot of noise, sirens and klaxons, as Wesley pulled into the small side street that was Potters Fields. But he didn't take too much notice of that. He began to pull over to the side of the road when the old bloke said, 'We need you to drive across the park and up to City Hall.'

'I don't think you're meant to drive on the grass,' Wes said but by that time he'd seen in his rear-view mirror that two of his passengers were carrying guns. 'But I suppose I can make an exception . . .'

Wesley drove across the grass and came to a halt at the side of the building. The men got out, the old one telling Wes to 'Wait here!' as he did so. As he watched the men race across the grass, Wesley did wonder whether he should just cut his losses and leave. After all, there didn't seem to be anybody about to see what he'd just done or who he was with. He could dump the car somewhere and then go home on the tube. Or he could leave the car where it was and let the blokes do the driving themselves. Ahmet the Turk he'd known for some years and Wesley liked him. This lot with guns were quite another matter. To Wes's way of thinking, there was a touch of the al Qaeda about them.

But he carried on waiting in spite of his misgivings. It was the thought of the money he was going to get that made him. But when he heard shots being fired about ten minutes later it wasn't cash but fear that ensured Wesley could not move from the spot.

Tower Bridge had been closed to traffic after the explosion on the tube. Now it was opened for one police car. In that car, Superintendent Wyre Williams and Inspector Çetin İkmen sped towards what could now be seen was a very violent affray outside City Hall.

'I could not understand why someone like Ahmet Ülker would get himself involved with terrorists,' İkmen said as Williams' car whizzed across the bridge towards the motorcyclists guarding the entrance on to Tower Bridge Road. 'Then I saw that incident.

I heard gunfire. I remembered that the mayor sometimes needs a cigarette to calm his nerves. He goes outside.'

The motorcyclists moved out of the way quickly, allowing Williams to pass without hindrance.

'Mr Üner wants to put people like Ülker out of business,' İkmen went on. 'He has a campaign against such people. Ahmet Ülker cannot allow him to do that and so he makes this terrible alliance with Nourazar, the man who hires himself out as a one-person jihadi training and suicide operation. Superintendent Williams, the explosion in the underground was merely a diversion.'

Williams was driving like a demon. 'CO19 are on their way,' he said. He was completely focused on the task in hand and did not express any sort of opinion about what İkmen had said.

Williams turned right, and right again up a tiny side road, which brought them to the back of City Hall. A group of shouting, hostile men with guns held out in front of them were pushing a very pale Mayor Haluk Üner towards a bright blue Subaru Impreza. İkmen instantly recognised his own clothes on one of the men, and the person wearing them was Ayatollah Hadi Nourazar. He went to get out of the car, but Williams stopped him. Up on Tower Bridge he could see another police car, sirens wailing, blue lights flashing, headed in their direction. 'That's CO19,' Williams said, 'the armed response unit. You stay here.' Then to İkmen's horror the unarmed Williams got out of the car.

'You had better get back in your police car,' Nourazar said and pointed his gun at Williams. 'We need to take Mr Üner for a ride.'

'You're not going to get out of here,' Williams said.

The Iranian shrugged. 'You think?' he said, then he smiled. 'You let me out or I will kill your mayor.' While two of his men

253

trained their guns on Williams, Nourazar put the muzzle of his gun up to Üner's head.

'The roads—'

'The roads are closed to the north of here,' Nourazar said. 'The explosion took place on the other side of the river, didn't it?' He smiled. 'Of course it did. I helped plan it myself. We will go south.'

The driver's door of the Subaru opened and a familiar figure to Williams got out. 'Explosion? What explosion?' asked Wesley Simpson.

'Nothing of any consequence,' Nourazar said. Then pushing Haluk Üner in front of him he said, 'Get in the car.'

'Is that the mayor?' Wesley persisted. Then he looked at the ayatollah and his men and said, 'Fucking hell, man, are you kidnapping the mayor?'

'What I am doing is of no concern to you,' Nourazar said. 'Get back in the car and when I tell you, drive.'

'Oh, I don't like—'

Nourazar briefly turned his gun on Wesley. 'Get in the car!'

Wesley Simpson did as he was told. Just before he got in, Williams looked into his eyes and said, 'Wes, be careful.'

The other police car had crossed the bridge now. Nourazar hustled his men and Üner into the Subaru, and got in himself. 'You had better think carefully about what you do now,' he said to Williams. 'I will not hesitate to kill Mr Üner.' And then he pulled the door shut and shouted at Wesley to get going.

Just before the car took off back down Potters Fields, the ayatollah looked in to the police car where he spotted Çetin İkmen. There was a moment when surprise and maybe even a little anxiety registered on his face.

# Chapter 27

The residents of one of London's most exclusive addresses, The Bishops Avenue, East Finchley, were not accustomed to visits from the police. Apparently there had been some awful terrorist outrage down in the City, people had died, but that had nothing to do with them. Strange then that such a lot of police officers should fetch up and surround Mr Ülker's house. At such a time of emergency, the residents of The Bishops Avenue would have imagined that the police, especially the local force, would have better things to do. What they didn't know was that the police officers who came for Ülker were not local and they were very much concerned with what had happened in the City.

Ahmet Ülker had just got off the phone when armed police smashed in his front door and someone who introduced himself as DI Hogarth arrested him in connection with terrorist offences. He was, they told him, going to accompany them to Scotland Yard. Ahmet, grey-faced, said nothing. Then one of the armed men accompanied him to his bedroom to retrieve his jacket and wallet.

Just before they left Ahmet's sixteen-million-pound house, DI Hogarth said, 'I understand you're married, Mr Ülker. Would you like us to inform your wife about where you're going?'

'I would if I thought she might care,' Ahmet replied with a sudden smile. Then he added, 'My wife and I had an argument two days ago. She walked out.'

DI Hogarth looked as if he didn't quite believe that. 'OK,' he said. 'You don't want me to contact her at her new address or—'

'I don't know where she is,' Ahmet said. 'Things have been bad between us for some time.'

'Fair enough.'

And then they left. Down the long, curving drive, out through the great big expensive but cheap-looking iron gates and on to the avenue. Because it was Bishops Avenue and people there just did not do such things, no curtains twitched at any of the windows as the police car made its way down the road. But that didn't mean that no one noticed. Everyone who was not at his or her country cottage or second home in Marbella took very careful note of the fact that the rather smart Turkish businessman who had a stripper for a wife had been taken away by the police.

'Fucking hell!' The car carrying the CO19 officers was blocking the exit from Potters Fields. Wesley looked quickly at the pavement on either side of the road but decided that it was far too narrow for him to drive his car on to.

'Go back! Go back!' Nourazar said, waving his gun wildly about in the back of the Subaru. 'Go back towards the river!'

As two huge and heavily armed men got out of the police car, Wesley Simpson did the fastest three-point turn he had ever done in his life. As he did so he said, 'OK, OK, there's a path down there, I can drive along it, get back to Tooley Street.'

'Good man!'

Then suddenly realising that what he was doing was in fact something he had vowed never to do again, Wesley said, 'But you better not hurt the mayor! I ain't doing time for assisting in no killing. I do not do that stuff!'

256

'Just drive,' the man sitting next to Wesley said, handling his gun in a sinister fashion.

Wesley drove the car up into the park and around the other police car. Superintendent Williams, a man he had some past experience with, and some guy he thought he'd seen at Ahmet's factory stood beside it. As he passed them, they got in their car, no doubt to pursue him. If he got caught this time, they'd throw away the key. Wes looked at Haluk Üner's white face in his rear-view mirror, and he decided then and there that if there was any way he could stop these characters from hurting him, he would. Half a million quid was a lot of money but it was bloody useless if you were doing big time in the Scrubs for accessory to murder. Not that prison was his immediate concern right now. First he had to somehow get away from these nutters with guns. He had to do that while still driving and without putting the mayor in danger.

'What do you want?' he heard Haluk Ülker say to the men in the back of the car with him.

None of them answered him. He looked pleadingly into the rear-view mirror at Wesley who said, 'I have no idea what this is about. I'm just the driver.'

Now on the Queen's Walk in front of City Hall and right beside the river, Wesley stole a glance in the direction of the Tower and saw what looked like a cloud of smoke in the area. 'What's that?' he asked.

'It's—'

'Someone has blown up a tube train,' the mayor said. 'These guys—'

Nourazar slapped Haluk Üner across the mouth with his pistol. Wesley heard something break and said, 'Fuck!' He looked in the rear-view mirror and saw blood pouring out of the mayor's mouth.

257

'Be quiet, sodomite!' Nourazar hissed at the mayor. Then seeing the look of alarm on his driver's face, the Iranian said, 'This man performs unnatural acts with other men. Your mayor, Mr Simpson! London should be ashamed!'

Wes didn't much care what Haluk Üner got up to in the sack. As far as he was concerned, Üner was a bit of a knob when it came to counterfeit goods, but otherwise he was a decent guy. He certainly didn't wish him any harm. But if this old bloke and his posse of creepy men were terrorists then that meant that he himself was probably in danger too. He wondered if Ahmet Ülker knew. The mayor was probably his enemy in a sense but to get back at him using people like this was mad. Behind him now was Williams and that other man in their car, blue lights flashing, sirens going. Wes hoped in a way that he was wrong about this path eventually joining up with Tooley Street. But he knew deep down that he wasn't. They were going to make it and then he was going to have to think about how he might get the mayor and himself away from these people. What he hadn't counted on was the fact that CO19 had anticipated what Wes was about to do and were now positioned at the end of the pathway, guns drawn, in front of their car.

Wesley slammed his foot on the brake and said, yet again, 'Fucking hell!'

Only a couple of seconds passed, but because they passed in silence, they seemed to go on forever.

'What are they doing?' İkmen asked Williams.

They were out of the car, crouched down behind the boot. The CO19 unit was in front of the Subaru and another armed unit had joined Williams and İkmen behind.

'Probably trying to think their way out of it,' the superintendent

258

said. 'They've got armed men in front and behind now. They're boxed in.'

'Superintendent, the men with Nourazar are I think prepared to die for what they believe,' İkmen said. 'They could just shoot everyone in that car, blow it up . . .'

'I know, I—' Williams' phone began to ring. For a second he listened intently to what was said and then he put the instrument on to speaker. 'It's Nourazar,' he whispered to İkmen.

'This man here tells me your name is Williams,' Nourazar said.

'Wesley and I go back a long way,' Superintendent Williams replied. 'Is he OK?'

'I think so.' It was said without concern. 'Mr Williams, we find ourselves in something of a situation, yourselves and us.'

'I think it is only you who is in a situation, Mr Nourazar,' Williams said. 'But it isn't one that cannot be negotiated.'

'What do you mean?'

'I mean that you need to talk to me about what you want so that I can do what I can to accommodate that.'

There was a pause and then Nourazar said, 'Well then. What I would want, superintendent, is to complete my mission and dispose of this sodomite.'

'Sodomite?'

'Mr Üner,' Nourazar replied. 'My colleagues and I wish to cleanse the world of such people. That is all we want.'

Williams exchanged a look with İkmen. The Turk knew this kind of mentality of old. But this situation was not following the usual path taken by religious fanatics.

'Mr Nourazar,' Williams said, 'may I speak to Mr Üner, please?'

'Speak to him?'

'I'd like to know that he is all right.'

A slight shuffling into a pause ended with the voice of Haluk Üner on the line. 'Superintendent,' he said. 'I'm all right.'

'Sir—'

'But this man, the driver . . .' Haluk Üner's voice wavered. 'Can you please get him out? He's terrified—'

'That's enough!' Nourazar was back in charge of the phone again. 'The driver goes nowhere!' Then suddenly screaming his fury he shouted, 'Williams, you have thirty minutes to move your cars! In thirty minutes we will blow our vehicle up! All your buildings here will be destroyed!' Then he cut the connection.

Williams sighed.

'Well, that makes sense,' İkmen said.

'In what way?'

'If Nourazar were a real suicide bomber he would have blown up the car by now,' İkmen said. 'But then we know that he isn't and so he will not do that. Nourazar wants to get away from all of this to collect his money from Ülker. But he has to kill the mayor to get it. That is what I think.'

'Ahmet Ülker has been brought in for questioning,' Williams said.

'Then Nourazar must not know that,' İkmen replied. 'While he has some hope, he is not as dangerous as he could be. What he would do without that hope, I cannot tell. We know he and his people have guns but we don't know if they have explosives, do we?'

'No.'

The sky, which had been clouding over for some time, now gave up its moisture in the form of a thin drizzle. One of the armed officers from the car behind the superintendent's ran over and squatted down beside Williams.

'Sir,' he said, 'the unit at the front can line up the character in the front passenger seat. We've got three heads at the rear but we can't get a proper view. Do you know where the mayor is sitting?'

Williams looked into the back window of the Subaru and saw three dark-haired heads.

'I imagine Mr Üner must be between his captors, so he is probably in the middle,' Williams said. 'But if you're thinking of taking shots—'

'Only if we have to.'

'You must wait for my command,' Williams said.

'Yes, sir.'

The officer went back to his own car and Williams turned to İkmen and said, 'I must speak to the acting commissioner.'

Ahmet Ülker smiled. 'How the people who work for my wife recruit their machinists, I really don't know,' he said. 'Maxine's company makes handbags . . .'

'Fake handbags,' DI Hogarth corrected. 'My colleagues found dodgy Prada, Gucci and Versace labels when they raided the place. What other treasures, apart from a load of dying Gambian illegals, await us, Ahmet?'

'I am sure I don't know,' Ülker replied. 'You will have to ask Maxine.'

'When we find her.'

'Maxine is the managing director and owner of Yacoubian Industries.' He smiled again. 'If you have entered the factories at Hackney Wick then she needs to know.'

'You have no idea where your wife might be?'

'No. I told you. We argued. She left.'

Ülker was very relaxed. So much so that he had refused to

261

engage legal representation. Everything was in Maxine's name, after all, and even if the police questioned his foremen, they would only implicate her. The only slight fly in the ointment was the apparent escape of the new security guard Çetin Ertegrul. He had listened in to things that he shouldn't. Çetin Ertegrul should have been taken care of. But he'd got away and had either gone back to his niece in Stoke Newington or, more worryingly, he had gone to the police. But then he was an illegal. He'd come across the Channel in a lorry courtesy of Wolfgang in Berlin. Unless he was a police informant . . .

'Then there are the fake drugs,' Hogarth continued.

Ahmet Ülker looked confused.

Hogarth looked down at his notes and said, 'Percodan. Pain control, or not, for arthritis.'

Ülker shook his head.

'No bells ringing?' Hogarth smiled. 'Never mind. I'm sure that our informant will fill in the gaps. He saw you, Mr Ülker, take delivery of a truckload of Percodan driven to Hackney Wick by a scrote called Wesley Simpson.'

Ahmet Ülker continued to look confused.

'Mr Simpson has numerous convictions for taking and driving, for being an accessory to armed robbery and for being in receipt of stolen goods,' Hogarth said.

'Who my wife employs . . .' Ahmet Ülker shrugged.

Acting Commissioner Dee, who was observing the proceedings from behind the two-way mirror to the left of Hogarth and Ülker, spoke via a microphone into Hogarth's earpiece. 'We haven't got time to indulge in these games,' he said. 'Nourazar and his people have the mayor at gunpoint. Tell him about Inspector İkmen. Tell him what the situation is now. Threaten him.'

DI Hogarth, who was by nature really rather a gentle soul, cleared his throat. 'All right, Mr Ülker,' he said, 'let's cut the crap, shall we? We've had an informant in your factory, a Turkish police officer. We know from him as well as from the police in İstanbul that you have a business relationship with an Iranian called Hadi Nourazar. Likes to call himself an ayatollah but we know he's as fake as your handbags. In short, we know that you aided another Iranian, Ali Reza Hajizadeh, to blow up the disused tube station in Mark Lane, taking a train out of commission in the process. We've twenty dead so far and over a hundred injured.'

'I'm sorry about that.' Still calm, Ülker's face was nevertheless very pale now.

'No. You're not. You're no more sorry about that than you are sorry about what Nourazar is doing right this minute,' Hogarth continued. 'We know that Mark Lane was only a diversion. Luckily for us, our informant, our Turkish colleague, worked it out. Unfortunately he didn't manage to do this until Mr Üner the mayor had been kidnapped by the ayatollah and his people. However, we have them trapped.'

Ahmet Ülker frowned.

'Two CO19 teams have a blue Subaru Impreza sandwiched between them on the Queen's Walk, on the south bank,' Hogarth said. 'Mr Üner, Wesley Simpson, your ayatollah and three of his goons are surrounded.'

Ülker maintained a tense silence.

DI Hogarth leaned forward across the table and smiled. 'We believe,' he said, 'that unlike Ali Reza Hajizadeh, Ayatollah Nourazar is not in the business of committing suicide for God or anyone else. He's in this for money, your money.'

'I—'

'It's our belief that he still wants to try to get to you to collect

263

his cash. What we need to know is whether he has explosives in that car. He says he does. We think he probably doesn't. You will know.' He looked Ülker deep in the eyes and said, 'So tell me, Mr Ülker, does the ayatollah have explosives with him or not?'

# Chapter 28

Inside the Subaru all was quiet until Haluk Üner said, 'Did you kidnap me with the intention of killing me?'

Hadi Nourazar looked at him with an expression of complete contempt on his face.

The mayor read this as an affirmative response and he said, 'I thought so. But you should let this driver here go.'

Wesley Simpson didn't say a word.

'He obviously didn't know what you were doing and he's obviously scared,' Üner said.

Neither Nourazar nor any of his three man so much as registered that Üner had spoken. Infuriated by their silence, he said, 'Oh, for God's sake, let the driver go! Keep me if you must—'

'You are a sodomite!'

'Let the driver go!' So angry he was almost beyond fear, Haluk Üner spat his words into the ayatollah's now red and furious face. 'You keep on saying you'll kill me! Get on with it!'

The man on the other side of the mayor jabbed his pistol into the back of Mr Üner's head. 'If that is what you want.'

Haluk Üner froze in terror.

'The time is not yet right!' the ayatollah warned and motioned for his man to lower his weapon.

'Not—'

'We can still play with the police for a while longer.'

'Yes, but we're going to kill the sodomite anyway,' the man sitting next to Wesley at the front said.

'Of course.' Nourazar looked at his watch. Fifteen minutes had passed and Williams and company had still not done anything. But then moving their cars away would require them to get all sorts of permission from all sorts of people. Besides, Nourazar knew that they wouldn't do that. Not that this glitch in his plans was actually flooring him. It wasn't. The police turning up was unfortunate but not necessarily disastrous. If he could get away with the mayor he could still either film himself killing the sodomite and get that evidence to Ahmet Ülker or deliver the man to the Turk in person. He could still collect his money. But some sort of diversion would have to distract the police while he attempted to do that.

'We need to die,' he said to his men. They all smiled.

'Oh Christ!' Wesley Simpson muttered under his breath.

'We also need to use the element of surprise,' Nourazar continued. 'It is important that they don't expect what we are about to do.' He smiled. 'This is how we do it . . .'


Superintendent Williams put his mobile phone back in his pocket and said, 'That was DI Hogarth. Ülker won't be drawn. According to him everything is down to his absent wife – the knock-off handbags, the ayatollah, the works. Says he doesn't know whether Nourazar has explosives on him because he says he doesn't know the man.'

İkmen frowned. 'Presumably Inspector Hogarth has now told him about me.'

'Yes,' Williams replied. 'But he's still sticking to his story about his being a mere pawn in his wife's hands.'

'So where is she?'

Williams shrugged. 'We don't know.'

'She was having an affair with Hajizadeh,' İkmen said.

'Who is now dead.'

'Do you think Ülker had found out about his wife? Or maybe—'

Williams' phone began to ring. He took it out of his pocket and answered. Then he briefly put his hand over the mouthpiece and said to İkmen, 'It's Nourazar.'

For upwards of two minutes Superintendent Williams listened to the words of Hadi Nourazar in silence. Then he said gravely, 'I have to check this out before I can—'

What, to İkmen, sounded like a scream of fury from the other end of the line resulted in Williams saying, 'All right! All right! Five minutes. OK.' He folded the phone up and looked at İkmen. 'They want to get out of the car,' he said. 'A couple of them want to relieve themselves. I had to agree to it. He was threatening the mayor's life.'

İkmen looked dubious. Williams quickly called to the CO19 team behind them and then radioed the team in front so that everyone was aware of what was about to happen. Finally he called Acting Commissioner Dee who said that another armed response unit was on its way to take up position in and around City Hall itself. He accepted that Williams had had little choice but to accede to Nourazar's demand. For a few minutes everyone just sat or stood and waited.

Eventually, at exactly five minutes after the end of his call to the superintendent, Hadi Nourazar got out of the left-hand side of the Subaru. The mayor, pulled out roughly and used to cover the Iranian's body, had a gun pushed very firmly against the side of his head. The two armed men who had been sitting next to Üner in the back of the car got out of the right side and aimed their guns at Williams' car. Wesley Simpson, too, got out on the right where he was quickly joined by the man who had been sitting next to him in the passenger seat. All of them stood in silence.

'Ahmet, we know that Nourazar was recruiting in your factories both here and abroad with your knowledge,' DI Hogarth said wearily. 'We have evidence from the police in Turkey and we had a man in your factories here.'

'Who? Who did you plant in my factory?'

'As I said, a Turkish police officer. Trust me, you would know him,' Hogarth said.

'Tell me his name!'

Behind the two-way mirror, Dee spoke into Hogarth's earpiece. 'Tell him.'

'Çetin Ertegrul,' Hogarth said. 'The man you chained to a bench, beat and cut, whose life you threatened.'

Ülker, for whom this was not entirely news, sighed. 'As you know, Mr Hogarth, I am an immigrant here,' he said. 'I don't always understand the rules. My wife, she suggests I do things, act in a certain way. I must be guided by her.'

Hidden as he was, Dee nevertheless rolled his eyes.

'Nourazar is holding Wesley Simpson and the mayor of London, Mr Üner, hostage,' Hogarth said. 'We know that someone with a business like yours is by definition an enemy of Mr Üner. It is our belief that you, maybe with others, contracted Nourazar to kill him. The ayatollah has many misguided followers who don't seem to understand that he is not so much a cleric as a businessman.'

'I don't know what you're talking about,' Ülker said and turned his face away from Hogarth.

'Don't you?'

'No.'

'Well, we shall see, won't we,' Hogarth said. 'If Mr Üner is killed we will have to find out why. If a plot was involved then we'll have to root out who was involved and why. We'll have to speak to your wife, Mr Ülker, that will be essential. If Mr Üner is not harmed then those involved in any plot will not be punished as severely as they could have been.' Ahmet Ülker said nothing. Hogarth sighed. 'But the bottom line is that Çetin Ertegrul gathered a lot of information against you, things he saw and experienced directly. We know that you unleashed Hajizadeh to blow up Mark Lane. We know that you allowed Nourazar to recruit and we very strongly suspect you did all of this in order to kill a man who would have brought your business down.'

Still Ülker said nothing.

'Ahmet, if you help us to capture Nourazar and free the mayor—'

'I think now that your stories about me are getting so crazy, I need a lawyer,' Ahmet Ülker said. 'Get me a lawyer now, will you, please.'

Behind the two-way mirror, Acting Commissioner Dee sat down and put his head in his hands.

All over the city, sirens blared as ambulances took the wounded and the dead to various hospitals. The whole of London seemed alive with the practicalities, the fury, the grief and the horror of the event that had taken place at the old Mark Lane tube station. Everywhere people talked, helped where they could and sometimes just looked on helplessly when there was nothing else to do. The only exception to this was the area around City Hall. This cordoned-off portion of the city was as still and silent as the dead.

Superintendent Williams knew the term 'Mexican stand-off'. It was the situation where two gunmen had their weapons aimed at each other, creating a kind of stalemate. Why it was called a *Mexican* stand-off, he didn't know. But what he and his men were facing now appeared to be much the same. For almost five minutes Nourazar and his three men had faced the armed police officers – two of them looking towards Williams, their weapons out in front of them, and a third facing the CO19 team, his gun aimed at Wesley Simpson's head. Nourazar, one arm round the mayor's neck, his weapon pointed at his head, stood to one side. No one had as yet made any attempt to relieve himself. Williams, though tense, was very calm and very patient, waiting to hear what might be asked, what might be done.

İkmen was fascinated by the tableau before him and intrigued as to how these apparently pious men were going to relieve themselves in front of a group of infidel policeman, but his attention was fixed on Nourazar and the mayor. The latter was breathing hard and his face was white as if he'd just powdered it in order to take part in a Japanese Noh play. When Mr Üner had decided to take on the counterfeit gangs, he had never, İkmen felt, envisaged this. The mayor had security but not of a very obvious type, and what there was had obviously let him down. How Nourazar and his men had got to Üner, İkmen didn't know exactly but he was pretty certain Üner had been grabbed when he'd left City Hall to have a smoke. Everyone knew that he did that. He certainly wouldn't be doing it again. If the mayor survived, no one would ever be allowed to get close to him again. Nourazar, İkmen saw, was smiling. He was wearing İkmen's clothes and the sight was freakish. İkmen knew that even if he got them back he would never be able to wear them after that. Now that he really looked at Nourazar,

İkmen could see that his eyes were a very pale and arresting shade of blue. He'd never noticed that before.

The ayatollah cleared his throat and immediately all hell broke loose.

At first Superintendent Williams thought that the men were firing at them. Instinctively he ducked down low to the ground as the officers around him shouldered their weapons and shouted. The terrible sounds of fired weapons and screams, the smell of cordite and blood and just the sheer hideous, ugly mess of it all . . .

No one saw the three men actually move their weapons and take aim. But suddenly they were all dead on the ground with parts of their skulls blown out, their faces distorted by the actions of bullets on brains, their features knocked into expressions of shock and fear. Wesley Simpson, who had thought his last moment had come, was also on the ground. Unhurt, he was lying in a puddle of his own piss, mouthing something over and over to himself. But Çetin İkmen didn't see any of this. All he saw was Nourazar running, dragging his hostage after him, heading across the park and towards the main road, Tooley Street. If he got there, armed as he was, what would he do? Would he get hold of another car somehow? Would he maybe start shooting indiscriminately to induce fear and thereby clear the path ahead? İkmen didn't even think about it. His lungs were shot anyway, what more harm was a little bit of exercise going to do? As the officers around him began to realise what was happening, İkmen threw himself across the grass and towards Nourazar and the mayor at full pelt.

'Get after them but keep your distance!' Williams shouted to the men who now ran off in pursuit after İkmen, Nourazar and the mayor. 'God knows what Nourazar might do!'

The superintendent also ran. It was not that much easier for him than it had been for İkmen. He was impressed by how quick off the blocks the Turk had been. Çetin İkmen was apparently a heavy smoker who also liked a drink. He was very far from being any sort of athlete. But he was tearing towards Tooley Street and gaining on the mayor and his captor.

About halfway across the grass, Williams looked back towards the two police cars and the Subaru. Three CO19 officers had taken charge of the scene, its dead bodies and its weapons. God, to just kill themselves like that! Not that he had actually seen the moment of death himself; like his officers, like everyone involved, he suspected, he had been unable to believe and therefore process what he had seen. The moment was a thin wash of colours punctuated by one simultaneous lethal roaring sound. He couldn't imagine what it had been like to have been in the middle of all that but Wesley Simpson would know. Wesley Simpson, who had for some reason just been left to tell the tale. But then Nourazar's men had died for their cause, which had probably been more important to them than the death of some getaway driver. If Nourazar had indeed taken the mayor at Ülker's behest with the intention of killing him for money, where and when would he do it?

Williams ran behind his men all the way up to Tooley Street. When he got there he saw İkmen getting into a black cab and heading east. Nourazar must have somehow got hold of a car, which the Turk was now following.

# Chapter 29

Ahmet Ülker's mobile phone had 'The Flight of the Bumblebee' as its ringtone. It was irritating but not nearly as annoying as the rap tune that DI Hogarth's young daughter used on her phone. Ülker ignored it. Acting Commissioner Dee, still in the observation room and just done with a call from Superintendent Williams, had other ideas.

'Get him to answer that phone!' he shouted into Hogarth's earpiece. 'Nourazar has gone on the run with Mr Üner. That could be him.'

Hogarth looked at Ülker and smiled. 'Why don't you answer your phone?' he said. 'Your wife is missing. It could be her.'

Ahmet Ülker just sat. His solicitor, a thin man in his fifties, frowned. 'The Flight of the Bumblebee' continued. Ülker had either switched his voicemail facility off or he did not have one.

DI Hogarth rose from his seat and began to walk round to Ülker's side of the table. 'If that is your wife then we need to talk to her,' he said. 'Answer your phone, Mr Ülker.'

'It's not her.' Ahmet Ülker put his head down and continued to ignore the phone.

'Oh, is it the wrong ringtone?' Hogarth asked. My kids have personalised ringtones for all their mates. Who's "The Flight of the Bumblebee" for, Mr Ülker? Is it one of your dodgy suppliers? Is it maybe some pole dancer who is younger and prettier than your missus?' The 'Flight' went on relentlessly in the background. 'Answer it,' Hogarth said.

Ahmet Ülker didn't speak or move.

'If you don't answer it, then I'll have to take it off you,' Hogarth continued.

Ahmet Ülker looked over at his solicitor who just shrugged. Slowly he put his hand into his jacket pocket.

'And don't think about switching it off,' Hogarth said. 'I, for one, am just too fascinated about who might want to speak to you so urgently.'

Ahmet Ülker took the phone out of his pocket and then clicked the answer button. He held it very tightly to his ear.

'I've never done this before, you know,' the man driving the cab said to İkmen. 'I've had "follow that cab" before. That was some sort of prank on this girl's birthday. She worked in some broking office in the city. But then you know what them lot up there were like back in the day.' He smiled. 'Then again, I suppose you don't, do you?'

'What?'

At first it had been a bit of a problem for İkmen getting this man to 'follow that Ford Escort'. He'd told him he was a police officer, but of course he had no badge to prove this. He'd then probably made matters worse for a bit by telling him he was a Turkish policeman. His bloodstained, scruffy appearance hadn't helped either. But the way the Ford Escort in question had pulled out into the traffic with the apparent hijacker waving a pistol around had eventually persuaded the cabbie to help. Once on the road, İkmen had explained that the hijacker of the Escort was holding the mayor of London hostage. If he hadn't seen that gun the driver, Sidney, would have thought that maybe İkmen was

274

mad. It would not have been the first time he'd had a nutter in his cab. But that gun, plus the sight of the Escort's real owner screaming in fear by the side of the road, had shaken Sid, that and all the chaos around and about Tower Hill. People were saying that al Qaeda had bombed London again and so if the bloke who'd kidnapped the mayor was one of them then Sidney was only too pleased to go after him.

'You being foreign, you wouldn't know about all the nonsense in the City with the bankers and their big bonuses and before them the yuppies and all their rubbish.' Then suddenly changing the subject he said, 'You got a gun, have you?'

'No,' İkmen said. 'I am a Turk, Mr . . .'

'Sidney,' Sidney said. 'Just call me Sid.'

'Sid, I have been working with your police. I am not one of them.' He looked behind to see if he could spot any police pursuit vehicles. He couldn't, but he could hear them. Three cars in front of the cab, the blue Ford Escort tore down Jamaica Road, Nourazar or someone almost permanently on the horn.

'You got any idea where this character might be taking the mayor?' Sidney asked as he negotiated his way around the side of a large delivery lorry.

'No, I don't,' İkmen said. 'I think he just wants to get away.'

'Looks like a bit of a snarl-up up ahead,' the driver said.

'Snarl-up?'

'Traffic jam, an obstruction. Just beyond the roundabout.' He pointed ahead and then said, 'What's he doing now?'

İkmen, rattling about in the back without a seat belt, strained to see what was coming up in front. He was exhausted, running only on adrenaline and, if he were honest, quite frightened. Without a mobile phone or any other way of contacting the police he felt exposed and vulnerable. He was in a foreign city, he'd

275

been battered and cut with a razor blade, and he no longer had Ayşe to guide him. He wondered about her. What had happened after she had been taken to the hospital? He hoped she was going to be all right.

'Oh, turning right on to James's Road, are you?' Sidney said, pulling his cab round to the right. 'You sure you ain't got a clue where this bloke's going, mate?'

'No.' Then suddenly a voice from nowhere crackled out of something at the front of the cab and İkmen said, 'Is that a radio?'

'Yeah.'

'Can you tell your office where we are and what we are doing and tell them to call Scotland Yard.'

'I can but—'

'Sid, you must ask your people to call Superintendent Williams,' İkmen said. Then he looked at the road behind and added, 'He can't be far.'

'Oh, turning into Clements Road. Where the fuck is he going?' Sidney said.

'Sidney!'

'All right, all right, I'll call me controller,' Sidney said.

'You must,' İkmen replied. 'I cannot take on a man with a gun alone and neither can you.'

Hadi Nourazar switched off the phone that nestled between his legs and smiled. As far as he knew he'd left the police behind at City Hall. That Turk had attempted to follow, but the last he'd seen of him was some mad flapping dance he'd done in the middle of Tooley Street to try and flag down a cab. He couldn't be sure but he felt fairly confident he had lost him. That said, he was he knew far from at the end of this adventure. The original plan had been to take the mayor out into the countryside and kill him in a wood in Kent somewhere; one of the boys, Rashid, had known where. Now Rashid was dead and, besides, everything had changed when the police turned up at City Hall. That was not meant to have happened. How it had done so, he couldn't imagine. And yet there had been that man with the police at City Hall, that Turk he'd taken his clothes from, the one who was following . . .

'What happens now?' asked the mayor who was still bleeding heavily beside him. When Nourazar had hit him he had also knocked out his top front teeth.

Nourazar waved his gun at him. 'Why are you still bleeding like that? What's wrong with you?'

'I bleed heavily,' Haluk Üner said. 'I always have. Why? Do you think I have AIDS?'

'Do you?' He looked over his shoulder and saw that the car directly behind was a red Chevrolet.

'Do you?' the mayor countered.

Hadi Nourazar gave him a disgusted look. 'Hamdi had an apartment in this area,' he said, naming another of his dead acolytes. 'You heard Mr Ülker, he will meet us there.'

Haluk Üner had indeed heard the voice of Ahmet Ülker when Nourazar put his phone on speaker. Ülker had taken an age to answer and Nourazar had got quite rattled before he answered. Apparently Ülker had been in his jacuzzi. They had arranged to meet at Hamdi's flat in Rotherhithe Street. It was a first-floor council flat.

Ülker had told Nourazar to head for the Rotherhithe tunnel and, from there, Rotherhithe station. Rotherhithe Street from then on was easy. But now they were on Lower Road, a one-way street, going south, absolutely not where Nourazar needed to be heading. There was a lot of traffic, people wanting to get out of a city they saw as a terrorist target yet again. Nourazar pushed the gun with the side of the mayor's head and told him to turn off left down a road called Chilton Grove. Nourazar could control that. What he couldn't control was Ahmet Ülker. The Turk had promised Nourazar a million dollars for Haluk Üner and all the chaos the Iranian had created around the mayor's abduction. He had, after all, supplied all the weapons needed, all the explosive required for Harrison and Hajizadeh to blow up the station. A million dollars for jihad – or not. The million dollars would in fact be spent on comforts for himself and his family. If the Iranians wouldn't let him live in his own country, what else was he supposed to do? And yet Ülker had been strange on the phone. He had sounded reticent and nervous and Nourazar was worried. What if the police had somehow worked it all out? What if that little Turk whose clothes he had taken had been able to speak some English? On top of that there was the driver of the Subaru. But he knew nothing.

Remembering those who had died made Nourazar frown. Had Rashid, Hamdi and Omar known what they were really involved with, they would never have sacrificed themselves as they had. But then that was why this operation had been so perfect, because he inspired that sort of dedication. He was a holy man, a warrior for Islam. People followed him without question. People believed they would end up in Paradise if they did as he asked. Hadi Nourazar wondered where exactly Rashid, Hamdi and Omar were at this moment. He doubted very much that they would be receiving their reward in Paradise. Personally he didn't believe in any of that stuff. His god was what it had always been – power.

*   *   *

278

Now that he had contact with İkmen, Superintendent Williams felt relieved. The cab the Turk was travelling in still had sight of the blue Ford Escort Nourazar had taken, though the route he was following was somewhat eccentric. It was clear that Nourazar didn't know his way to Rotherhithe Street. Williams and three CO19 officers were due to rendezvous with DI Hogarth and his team, who were bringing Ahmet Ülker, at a two-bedroomed flat on Rotherhithe Street. They would get to the home of the late Mr Hamdi Khan before the others and would therefore have to conceal themselves in the garages underneath Trinity Wharf opposite until Hogarth arrived with Ülker. Thank God the man had finally crumbled under questioning. There was not going to be any way they could warn Khan's wife, should she be at home, which was going to be terrible for her. Williams had no doubt that the first thing Nourazar would do when he saw her was tell her about her husband's glorious death. The Khans had only been married for a year. Williams did not think that Mrs Khan would approve, however pious she might be.

They pulled on to Rotherhithe Street just after the YMCA on Salter Road and headed for Trinity Wharf. The caretaker of the building had been told to open up the garages for the police and when they arrived the gates were wide open. As the police car swept down the ramp and into the bowels of the building, one resident, a middle-aged bespectacled man in a suit, gaped at them. 'Fucking hell!' he said. But apart from that, no one seemed to notice or care about their sudden appearance. An eerie silence settled across Rotherhithe Street.

# Chapter 30

The cab pulled up just before the low block of flats that Nourazar had taken his hostage into. İkmen got out and said to the driver, 'Wait here. Call Superintendent Williams. Don't get out.'

'You haven't paid me yet, I'm not going anywhere,' Sidney said. 'What are you going to do?'

But İkmen wasn't listening. He was looking up at a block of old council flats where long, concrete balconies provided access to apartments characterised by scuffed and time-worn doors. He could see Nourazar and the mayor standing in front of the one at the far end of the balcony, nearest the stairs. Via the cabbie, İkmen had learned that Williams and a CO19 unit were on their way, as well as DI Hogarth from Scotland Yard with Ahmet Ülker. A phone call from Nourazar to Ülker at Scotland Yard had apparently put the factory owner into a position where he had no choice but to cooperate with the police. But İkmen knew that Nourazar would not necessarily wait until Ülker arrived before he killed Mr Üner. All he was interested in was the money and all Ülker wanted as far as Nourazar was concerned was the mayor of London's death. İkmen wasn't sure what he could do about this on his own and unarmed, but he felt he had to be where Nourazar and the mayor were.

Up on the balcony, the door to the apartment the Iranian and his hostage stood outside opened and İkmen caught a glimpse of a young headscarfed woman. He jogged wearily over to the concrete stairwell and began to make his way up. The walls, covered in graffiti tags, were grimy and splashed with what smelt like rancid cheese, underneath which was the unmistakable smell of piss. İkmen kicked a pizza box out of his way and reached the first floor. He listened to Nourazar and the woman talk.

'It will only be for a few moments, Fatima,' he heard Nourazar say. 'Nothing bad will happen, I promise.'

'Yes, but Ayatollah Hadi,' a distinctly Cockney voice replied, 'I can't have any trouble, not in my condition. Where's Hamdi?'

'If you let us inside, I'll tell you,' Nourazar said.

There was a pause and then the woman said, 'Ayatollah Hadi, that man is the mayor of London, what—'

There was a metallic click, which sounded like the safety catch being taken off a pistol. The woman gasped audibly.

'Fatima, go inside and let's talk,' Nourazar said. 'You will not be hurt, I promise.'

İkmen heard them go inside and after several seconds he moved out of the stairwell and on to the balcony. The door to the apartment had been left ajar, possibly for Ahmet Ülker. Inside he heard, at first, the sound of a television. This was switched off and replaced by the low rumble of Nourazar's voice. Out in the street, a large silver BMW car pulled up in front of the block. At the same time the door to the underground garages of the executive apartments opposite began to move upwards.

From inside the flat he heard the woman shout. 'No! *No!*'

İkmen could not see what was happening inside, the gap between the door and the door frame was too small.

'I thought you were a good man! I thought—'

'Fatima, Hamdi is a martyr, a saint, he has gone straight to Paradise!'

'Hamdi never wanted that!' the woman screamed. 'We talked about it. He wanted to serve Allah in this life, with me and with our baby!'

He heard her get up, heard her feet slap down on the wooden floor.

'That on the news, was that you?' she said. 'Killing people on a train and . . . What do you think they will do to Muslim people if you do these things? And now here with Mr Üner—'

'He is a homosexual!'

'So? He wants to build more play parks for the kids,' she said. 'Wants to make the roads safer.' İkmen heard her footsteps on the wood again.

Opposite the block, Williams and the CO19 officers were emerging and quietly cordoning off the street. Two men had got out of the BMW; one of them was Ahmet Ülker.

'I wasn't happy about Hamdi getting involved with you,' Fatima continued. 'I told him! I said we should stick to our own, not go getting involved with people from Iran. We, he didn't understand your country! We—'

'Shut up! Shut up!' There was silence for several seconds. İkmen pushed the door open a little more and looked inside. The woman was at the door of the room at the end of the corridor, her hands braced against the posts, blocking İkmen's view of anyone else.

'A woman shouldn't talk to a man like that!' Nourazar said. 'Sit down, disgusting bitch! Hamdi—'

'Hamdi was flattered by you, but I never was,' she said. 'Mr Ülker gave him a job, which was good, but you – you're not even wanted in your own country! Hamdi told me! I was suspicious of that, I—'

'Whore!'

He must, İkmen reckoned, have been standing already when he hit her. Fatima fell to the ground and suddenly İkmen found himself looking into the eyes of Hadi Nourazar.

DI Hogarth handed Ahmet Ülker a large briefcase. The factory owner was shaking.

'You get up there, Ahmet,' he said. 'You give him this and you ask him to hand over the mayor, alive.'

The briefcase contained hastily assembled stacks of paper topped off with a thin layer of £50 notes.

'He'll know it's not—'

'We'll be right behind you,' Hogarth said.

'Will you kill him?'

Superintendent Williams joined them. 'If necessary,' he said.

'Allah,' Ülker muttered and gritted his teeth to help control his shaking jaw.

'We can't leave it any longer,' Hogarth said and began to push Ülker towards the stairwell. 'One of our men is up there already. But you just go past him.'

Ülker looked up but he couldn't see anybody. He mounted the stairs nervously, feeling as if his bladder was going to give way at any moment.

'Who *are* you?' Nourazar asked, trying to keep his gun trained on both the mayor seated on the sofa by the TV set and Fatima lying on the floor.

'My name is Çetin İkmen and I am a police officer from İstanbul,' İkmen said. 'You caused some misery in my city, Mr Nourazar.'

'Ayatollah . . .'

'*Mr*,' İkmen repeated. 'You are no more a man of religion

than I am. You use religious people to make money for you. You trick them. This lady's husband—'

'Hadi!'

Nourazar looked up. 'Ahmet,' he said with some relief.

Ahmet Ülker pushed past İkmen, frowning at him as he went. 'What's this man doing here?'

'He says he's a policeman, from İstanbul,' Nourazar said. 'You know Derek Harrison always had a bad feeling about him.'

But Ahmet Ülker didn't respond to that. 'Things went wrong,' he said.

'Yes, I—'

'Here's your money.' He put the briefcase down on the floor in front of Nourazar and then reached out a hand. 'Give me the gun.'

Nourazar frowned. 'Why?'

'Because I will have to take the mayor away from here and do what I have to where we originally planned, in the country-side.' The Iranian looked unconvinced. 'Hadi, no one knows we're here. I wasn't followed, you—'

'This man followed me,' he said and tipped his head towards Çetin İkmen.

'So we'll get rid of him and the woman!' Ülker said.

From down on the floor, Fatima muttered, 'Bastards!'

'Come on, Hadi!' Ülker began to feel sweat breaking out on his brow. 'Give me the gun. I'll do it. You take the money and get out of here.'

For just a fraction of a second Ahmet Ülker and Çetin İkmen exchanged a glance. It was fleeting, meant little and was really no more than an acknowledgement of each other, but Nourazar saw it and he said, 'No, I think I'll keep the gun for the moment, thank you, Ahmet.'

'But Hadi, to open the case—'

'I can do that very well with one hand,' he said and proceeded to open first one catch on the case, then the other.

Now almost fainting with tension, Ülker said, 'Hadi—'

The aiming of the pistol and the subsequent shot happened in less than half a second. But Nourazar was not a good shot. He aimed for Ülker but hit Fatima, wounding her in the top of her arm. Çetin İkmen threw himself on her, putting his body between hers and any further shots. But none came.

'Put the gun down, Nourazar!' A heavily armoured CO19 officer was now where İkmen had just been. He was staring down the barrel of an HK MP5 submachine gun.

Nourazar instantly pointed his pistol at the mayor's head. 'No, I think that it is you who should—'

'This place is surrounded,' the officer said. 'Go outside and you'll get your head blown off. Surrender.'

Nourazar jabbed his pistol hard into the side of Haluk Üner's head. 'No.'

'Then bloody kill me!' the mayor's voice suddenly echoed around the room. 'You've kidnapped and beaten me, you've killed people in my city, you've called into question my—'

'Shut up!'

'No, I will not!' Haluk Üner said. 'Kill me! You are as fake as Ülker's handbags, Mr Nourazar! Let's have an end to it, shall we? You kill me and then this officer will kill you. Then you can go to Paradise! That is, after all, what you want, isn't it?'

But Nourazar didn't shoot. He didn't shoot even though everyone could see that he wanted to. The CO19 officer walked slowly forward, reaching out a hand as he did so.

'Put the gun down,' İkmen said from beside Fatima. He was

covered in her blood but she would be all right. Whether her baby would survive the experience was another matter.

'Put it down!' Another officer had entered behind the first one. The small room was filling up. Nourazar's face was now white.

'Put it down!'

Whether he lost his grip on the pistol or whether he consciously let it clatter to the floor, no one knew. But suddenly Nourazar's pistol was on the floor, one officer picking it up almost before it had landed, the other officer twisting Nourazar's arms behind his back and kicking him to the floor.

'Get down and spread your legs, you fucking cunt!' the officer screamed.

İkmen saw the mayor wince at the brutality of it but then he shakily came over to İkmen and looked at Fatima. 'Madam, I am so, so sorry,' he said. And then he turned to the ever increasing number of officers in the room and said, 'Can we please get an ambulance for this lady?'

DI Hogarth, who was now cuffing Ahmet Ülker, called through to Superintendent Williams outside. 'Sir, could we have an ambulance here?'

Williams was already on it.

İkmen helped Fatima to sit up. 'You'll be fine,' he said.

She smiled and then looked up into Haluk Üner's concerned face and said, 'You were very brave, Mr Üner.'

'He hijacked our religion,' Haluk Üner said. 'He made me very angry.' And then tears slowly began to roll down his face. Fatima, crying too now, put a hand up to his face and began to gently wipe the tears away.

# Chapter 31

Çetin İkmen hadn't really wanted to go to hospital on his own account.

'They have far too many injured people to deal with to be bothered with me,' he told Superintendent Williams as the latter nevertheless made him get into a bed at Guy's Hospital. In reality İkmen knew that Williams had no choice. He couldn't send him back to İstanbul until he had rewarded İkmen's work for the Met by making sure that he was OK. İkmen was exhausted, dehydrated and his pulse was very high. The doctor recommended a sedative and a night of observation in hospital. As İkmen drifted off to sleep, more trolleys carrying the injured from Mark Lane were brought into Guy's. At that point there had been thirty-two confirmed deaths and a hundred and twelve seriously injured.

Sunshine beating down on the window outside his room was not something İkmen had been expecting. Not just because he was in the UK but because somehow he had not imagined that such a thing could happen amidst such horror. Something else he hadn't reckoned on was the sight of his son.

'Sınan?'

At first he thought he had to be dreaming. But then he remembered, of course his son worked in England now.

'Dad.' He leaned down, put his arms round his father's neck

and kissed his cheeks. 'Dad, the police came and got me. You're something of a hero. What have you been doing?'

It took İkmen a few moments to really come into full consciousness, but when he did he told his son that he had been working with the Metropolitan Police.

'I don't know how much I can tell you,' he said as he took a glass of water gratefully from his son's hands.

'Mum, everyone in fact, thought that you were out east,' Sınan said.

'Does your mother know I'm here?'

'Once you were safe, the Met called Commissioner Ardıç who went personally to the apartment and told Mum,' Sınan said. 'We're all really proud, you know, Dad. Even Mum.'

Sınan no longer lived in İstanbul but he was well aware of the tension that had scarred his parents' marriage in the wake of his brother Bekir's death.

'You know you can call home now,' Sınan said.

İkmen shook his head. 'Later. As long as they know.'

'They do.' And then Sınan watched as his father's eyes closed. 'I'll leave you to rest for a while, Dad.'

But İkmen didn't hear him and as Sınan left he began snoring heavily once again.


In spite of the very serious charges being made against him, Ahmet Ülker looked really quite relaxed.

'Hadi Nourazar approached me,' he told Superintendent Williams. 'It was his idea to kill the mayor. I knew nothing about that. I was paying him to frighten Mr Üner.'

'Mr Ülker, you were instrumental in recruiting men to blow up a disused tube station,' Williams responded. 'Thirty-four people have died so far.'

One of those was Derek Harrison. It appeared, the police told him, that Derek had been stabbed.

'Superintendent, Ali Reza Hajizadeh was a fanatic,' Ülker said. 'Even Nourazar, a fanatic himself, was wary of him. He wanted to die. What can I say? He was to create a diversion by blowing himself up on Mark Lane station. He was there to create a noise! An old railwayman that Derek knew gave us the code. Do you think that such a person would have given us the code if he had known that people were going to be killed?'

'Give me his name and I'll ask him,' Williams said.

'He's called John Richards and he lives in Barking,' Ülker replied. 'I think you'll find he is a member of the British National Party. Not someone who would help jihadis. He didn't know that Hajizadeh was going to climb down onto the rail track. None of us did!'

'But by your own admission you knew that Hajizadeh was a fanatic,' Williams said. 'You must have realised there was a possibility he would blow up a train.'

Ülker looked at his lawyer and sighed. 'I meant no harm.'

'You meant no harm?' Williams laughed. 'Mr Ülker, we put a police officer inside your organisation. The illegal workers we knew about anyway but from him we got your dodgy arthritis drug scam as well as much about your plans for Mark Lane and our mayor, Mr Üner. That officer—'

'He is a Turk.'

'Yes, he's a Turk,' Williams said.

'You cannot trust the Turkish police.'

'No?' Williams laughed again. 'Ülker, this officer and his colleagues were on the team who closed you down in İstanbul. Inspector Çetin İkmen has yet to be fully debriefed, but when he is, we'll get even more on you. Not to mention poor old Wesley Simpson.'

Ülker looked up and frowned.

'Beyond a bit of dodgy goods moving, Wes had retired,' Williams said. 'He is not best pleased about what Nourazar and you put him through.'

'The man is a thief,' Ülker said.

'Oh, so I can't take İkmen's word for anything because he's a Turkish policeman and I shouldn't be listening to Wesley because he's a thief?'

Ahmet Ülker didn't answer.

'And then of course there is the issue of your wife, Mr Ülker,' Williams said. 'Her family haven't heard from her. They're worried.'

'I don't know where she is,' Ülker said. 'She left me, Mr Williams. How should I know where she is if she doesn't tell me?'

'Maybe the search we're going to make of all your properties as well as those registered to Yacoubian Industries will help to solve the mystery,' Williams replied.

'I don't see how.'

'Then you're obviously not worried about what we might find,' Williams said. 'So maybe you didn't kill her.'

Again, Ülker didn't answer.

'But then again, it's not just Maxine we're looking for, is it?' He smiled. 'A lot of money won't look good for you. Neither will a stack of blank British passports.'

Ülker frowned. 'Passports?'

'Like the ones our Turkish colleagues found at your factory in İstanbul,' Williams said.

Ülker, grave, did not answer.

'Something else we'd like to know, Mr Ülker. Movie Star Pools turned up at your place yesterday, I imagine to clean your

292

pool. Trouble is, there's no such company and so I was wondering who Movie Star Pools might really be. Think you can help me with that, do you?'

Ülker turned to his lawyer and, for a moment, the two of them whispered between themselves. When they had finished, the lawyer said, 'Superintendent, may I please have a word with my client in private?'

The Iranian official sat down beside the acting commissioner and said, 'That's him.'

They were observing an interview between a still visibly scarred Patrick Riley and Hadi Nourazar. The ayatollah had refused any legal representation and was currently saying nothing.

'Hadi, when we found you,' Riley said, 'you were aiming a gun at the mayor of London, having just shot an entirely innocent woman.'

Nourazar looked up at the ceiling and then down again at his hands.

'You were instrumental in the torture of a man you knew as Çetin Ertegrul, actually an undercover police officer,' Riley continued. 'Together with others who were encouraged by you to end their own lives, you kidnapped Mr Haluk Ülker and held him against his will.'

The Iranian official asked, 'The men who committed suicide, how do you know that Nourazar encouraged that?'

'The driver of the car, a civilian, hired simply to drive hard and fast, told us,' Dee replied.

'Can you trust him?'

'In this instance I think we can,' Dee said. 'And besides, Hüseyin, why else would those men do such a thing? Two of them had families, they were all decent blokes. Nourazar got his hooks into them . . .'

'That is his skill,' Hüseyin the Iranian official said. 'People follow him. Even we were taken in.'

'When he returned to his religion?'

'He was a model.' Hüseyin smiled. 'A SAVAK agent, burdened with remorse, finding solace in speaking against other royalists and, of course, in the mercy of Islam. Only later did we realise that his conception of Islam was not in accord with our own.'

'That must have been worrying for you,' Dee said.

Hüseyin didn't reply.

In the interview room, Riley spoke again.

'Mr Nourazar—'

'Ayatollah,' Nourazar interrupted.

Riley smiled. 'You can drop the holy man routine with me,' he said. 'We know all of this jihadi thing is only for money.'

Nourazar turned away.

'Mr Ülker has already told us that he was going to give you money. Although he says that he only wanted the mayor "frightened". He says that killing the mayor was your idea.'

There was no response at all.

'You want to know what I think happened?' Riley asked. 'I think that at the beginning you were so afraid of the Islamic Revolution you shopped all your old mates in SAVAK in order to save your own skin.'

This time, at the word SAVAK, Nourazar did respond. His face went white and he emitted a tiny gasp.

'Oh, we know all about SAVAK and your role in it,' Riley said. 'We know about how you took to Islam and then how it just wasn't really for you.'

Nourazar looked at Riley with disgust.

'If only he would talk!' Dee said to his Iranian guest.

'He won't do that,' Hüseyin responded calmly. 'Silence is all that remains to him. If you would give him to us, David . . .'

'Hüseyin, if I could give him to you, I would,' Dee said. 'I know he's caused trouble in Iran, but here he's committed crimes that include incitement to murder. Between ourselves and the Turks . . .'

'I understand,' Hüseyin smiled. 'You have lost people. That is hard to forgive.'

Dee leaned back in his seat. 'He's not done much for Anglo-Iranian relations,' he said. 'We have to try and control that.'

Hüseyin lowered his head a little.

'Know what I think?' Riley said to Nourazar as he leaned over the table towards him. 'I think that what you really are just couldn't help breaking through. You were a bully and a torturer with SAVAK and so you naturally gravitated towards the most extreme examples of religion. The Taliban are Sunni, right?'

Nourazar neither moved nor spoke.

'You're Shi'a, but you liked their style. You wanted some of that. What you also wanted was some money too, wasn't it, Hadi? Because money was what you'd had before, wasn't it? From the state, from people you'd tortured, from their families, willing to pay anything to get them out of your clutches.'

'You have no idea what you are talking about,' Nourazar responded quietly.

'Oh, don't I?' Riley said. And then suddenly his face clouded. 'When your mate Hajizadeh exploded himself at Mark Lane, a young policewoman got killed. She was a Muslim, Hadi. She was a good copper, a nice woman and she was a Muslim. And you know what?'

David Dee saw something familiar and ugly in Riley's eyes.

295

He looked at his Iranian guest and said, 'I think that maybe I should stop this interview now.'

Hüseyin nodded his assent. Dee left the room. Not that Hüseyin cared about Nourazar at all. But he knew how things worked in the UK, he knew how the guilty could sometimes get free by claiming they had been led or brutalised by the police. Sometimes, of course, it was true.

'There were Muslims on that train!' Riley shouted. 'Mr Üner is a Muslim! The men you told to kill themselves, they were Muslim! What are you trying to do, you stupid old bastard? Kill all your own people?'

The door of the interview room opened. 'Inspector Riley,' Dee said. 'Could I have a word?'

Back in the observation room, Hüseyin the Iranian watched as Riley left with Dee and Hadi Nourazar began to smile.


'I wanted to frighten Mr Üner,' Ahmet Ülker said. 'My wife's company produces counterfeit goods. I knew that, I admit. I wanted to protect her.'

'Oh, come on, Ahmet!' Williams said impatiently. 'You run those factories!'

'My wife runs and owns Yacoubian Industries,' Ülker corrected. 'I may have given her the money to start the business and given her my support. But it is Maxine's name and not my own that is on every piece of documentation that is concerned with the company.'

Williams, aware that he wasn't going to get anywhere if he kept on denying that what Ülker said was true, even if it wasn't, kept quiet.

'Everything I did, including assaulting the officer you had working undercover, was because I wanted to protect my wife.

I needed to frighten the mayor so he would leave us alone. Think what you like of my wife's business, but people like fake goods. There is a market. Üner was threatening to put Maxine out of business.'

'So you engaged the services of the Brothers of the Light,' Williams said.

'I met Hadi Nourazar in İstanbul,' Ülker said. 'As I told you, he approached me. The people he recruited were fanatics. He already had some disciples in London. But Nourazar himself is a man of money. He convinced me that he and his people could frighten Mr Üner. I would not have to dirty my hands. He began to prepare a boy who was working in my wife's factory in İstanbul.' He smiled. 'Of course my wife can only have a business in Turkey in my name, but it was hers, you understand. This boy was a fanatic, he wanted to come to England to see his brother. The idea, Mr Williams, was to have the boy set an explosion on the old station. To bring the tube to a halt, you understand.'

'Why?'

'Firstly an explosion would cause chaos and fear and would, we knew, bring Mr Üner out of his safe office and into the open to smoke a cigarette. He does that when he's nervous or something bad occurs.'

Unfortunately Haluk Üner's habits were too well-known.

'There, Nourazar and his men could find and take the mayor with little risk to themselves,' Ülker said. 'Secondly, I wanted to create fear – in Mr Üner and in the people of London. Mr Üner had to know that we were serious, that he had to stop his campaign against business people like my wife.'

'You didn't mean to kill him?'

'Not at all! Superintendent, Nourazar was to deliver Mr Üner to me and I was going to do a deal with that man, believe me.'

'You were going to pay Nourazar?'

'Yes. Then he and his men would go. That was the deal.'

There was a pause.

'My client knows nothing about passports of any type,' Ülker's lawyer interjected.

'I see.' Williams put his head down in a posture that seemed to suggest that he was thinking. 'And what about your right-hand man, Harrison, and Ali Reza, your one-time driver. Tell me about them.'

Ahmet Ülker took a deep breath. 'Well, as you know, the young boy we were going to bring from İstanbul died,' he said. 'Blew himself up.' He shook his head sadly. 'Then my driver put himself forward. Derek Harrison had always been involved. As I imagine you know, his experiences in the Moorgate disaster during his youth had made Derek very strange. He loved and he hated the tube. He had this friend who still worked for the organisation, who knew the security code into Mark Lane station. This man—'

'John Richards of Barking,' Williams repeated the name that Ülker had given to him earlier.

'Yes. Well, he is poor and so Derek gave him money. Once the door had blown off, no one would know how we got in. We told him that.'

'Well, you either lied to him or you and your people really are as amateurish as you'd have us believe,' Williams said. 'Blown door or not, our forensics people would know whether whoever had got in had activated the code or not.'

'But—'

'And then there are all the contradictions,' Williams said. 'If you only meant to set a small explosion at Mark Lane, why did you send Hajizadeh and Harrison down there with so much explosive?'

298

'I didn't,' Ülker said. 'Nourazar prepared the explosive and Ali Reza killed himself. Threw himself under the train. That was not meant to happen and was not my doing.'

'But if that is the case, Ahmet, and you really did mean only to set a small explosion, how on earth was that going to blow out the door leading to the underpass?'

For a moment Ülker looked confused.

'It wasn't, was it?' Williams said. 'The explosion was going to be big. Hajizadeh was always going to die, he wanted to. I don't know about Harrison. It seems to me your Ali Reza might have fought and killed him. Who knows why, unless of course Harrison was pissed off at Hajizadeh for sleeping with your wife.'

A dead, frozen silence ensued. The lawyer looked at his client slightly askance.

'Is that why you killed her?' Williams asked.

Now the lawyer looked stunned. Ülker remained apparently impassive.

'We found blood in your swimming pool, Mr Ülker,' Williams said. 'Same group as Maxine's. Further tests should confirm that it is hers. Now, are you going to tell me who your pool guy was or what?'

Still Ülker said nothing.

'I think the story you've just told me is largely fiction,' Williams continued. 'You wanted to kill the mayor. To "frighten" him, as you put it, would be a waste of time. He could still basic-ally do what he wanted once he'd got away from you. Anyway, if you'd wanted to frighten him why not threaten his family or blackmail the man? Everyone has a skeleton in their closet some-where. No, you wanted to kill Mr Üner. And you know what, Ahmet, that isn't going to be at all hard for me to prove.'

# Chapter 32

Mrs Fatima Khan, widow of the late Hamdi Khan, had expressed a desire to see Çetin İkmen and, if possible, Mayor Haluk Üner. Mrs Khan believed that between them they had saved her life and that of her baby. Although still weak after the operation to remove the bullet in her arm, Mrs Khan was determined to see her saviours.

'They're going to keep me in for a bit just to make sure I'm OK,' she said to Çetin İkmen as he sat beside her bed. 'But the baby's fine. If only Hamdi were here . . .'

When she spoke of her husband it was with dry eyes. But then, however much she had loved him, by doing what he had done, he had in a sense betrayed her. As with İkmen and his son, Bekir, she would cry later and she would regret deeply all and any cross words she had ever said to her husband.

'Mrs Khan?' Haluk Üner joined them.

Strangely for him, the mayor of London looked tired and a little dishevelled and of course he'd lost his upper front teeth.

'Oh, Mr Üner . . .' She went to raise herself up on her pillows but he motioned for her to stop.

'Please, you don't have to sit up on my account,' Haluk Üner said with a smile. And then he looked across at İkmen and said, 'Inspector.'

'Sir.' Up close the mayor seemed smaller than he did on the

TV and in fact smaller than he had appeared to be in the Khans' flat. Maybe his anger had made him big. Mr Üner had, after all, been very angry indeed.

They both sat with Mrs Khan for about twenty minutes. The press pack was outside the hospital waiting for Üner to emerge but he was in no hurry to go out and meet them. He also had things he wanted to say to Çetin İkmen.

'You know,' he said as he motioned for İkmen to sit down next to him out in the corridor, 'it is down to you, Çetin, that I am still alive. My acting commissioner told me what you did.'

'I was in the right place at the right time, Mr Üner,' İkmen said.

Haluk Üner smiled. 'You are still my hero, Çetin. My parents, too, are immensely grateful.'

İkmen, who was never easy with praise, looked away.

'That'll teach me to smoke!' Üner said, making a joke of it. 'It really is bad for me, isn't it?'

'Sir, with respect, your security—'

'You think the answer is to increase my security? Security is a barrier. Sometimes it is necessary but most of the time it is not. I expect this will make you cringe as a policeman, but I am in no way going to increase my security. In no way am I going to stop going out for the odd cigarette. I'm the mayor of London, I need to be out and about amongst Londoners. I have to know what they're thinking. Gives the police a headache but . . .'

'Your prime minister doesn't do that,' İkmen said.

'Nobody's prime minister does,' Üner replied. 'And that is what is wrong with this world, if you ask me. Nobody talks to the people any more, nobody cares about what they think. I tried to stop them getting ripped off by slave masters. I nearly lost my life because of it, but I see that as something to be proud of.' He got up and went over to the window. Down below a loud throng of shouting press and jostling photographers were only just being held back by the police officers stationed at the hospital entrance. Haluk Üner looked at them with blank eyes. 'This city has gone mad.'

'That happens when people are threatened,' İkmen said. 'You've seen this before.'

'Of course. They want to make me a celebrity,' he said bitterly. 'Even the broadsheets are calling me a hero.'

'When you stood up to Nourazar in Mrs Khan's apartment, you were a hero,' İkmen said.

The mayor turned away from the window, looked at İkmen and smiled. 'Was I?' he said. 'You know that when those men abducted me, I took the least line of resistance? I went with them, I cringed in fear beside them and even when Nourazar was on his own with me I didn't have the guts to tackle him. Only at the end did I truly react. On and on he went about how I was a poof and a sodomite and not once did I have the guts to say, "You know what? Yes, I am gay but I'm also a good man, a man of faith!" How can I ever look gay Londoners in the face again?'

İkmen did not respond. He didn't know.

'If that lot had their way,' Üner said and flicked a thumb in the direction of the window, 'I'd be on some ghastly reality show by the end of the week. I can see it now, *Celebrity Big Brother* with some has-been footballer, a vacuous WAG, a disgraced government minister and me!'

'It doesn't have to be like that, I am sure,' İkmen said, although he knew that celebrity culture was now a universal phenomenon that Üner would have to work very hard to counteract.

The mayor sighed. 'Whatever.' He put a hand on İkmen's

shoulder. 'I'm so glad we've been able to meet so that I can thank you, Çetin. I owe you my life and, believe me, everyone knows it.'

Embarrassed, İkmen looked away again. He'd already seen a couple of photographs of himself on the front of several national newspapers. İkmen alongside Mr Üner, two Turks who, according to some, had almost single-handedly saved the city. Ridiculous! Already the stories were starting about good Muslims, İkmen and the mayor, and bad Muslims, Nourazar, Hajizadeh and Ahmet Ülker. When it all finally came out about how Nourazar had actually only been interested in money, how Hajizadeh was deluded, how Ülker was just a slave master with no concept of religion, would people see the Mark Lane bombing for what it was? A distraction that could allow a murder to take place, a way for Ülker to frighten those opposed to his trade into submission. Probably not. But at least his own part in London's latest drama was almost at an end. In due course he would have to return to the city to give evidence at the trial of Ülker and Nourazar, but for the moment he could just look forward to going home.

The two men took leave of each other at a back door of the hospital, Mr Üner to be whisked away in an unmarked Mercedes and İkmen by his son Sınan in a taxi. Before they parted, Haluk Üner put his arms round İkmen in true Turkish fashion and then kissed the older man's hand.

'Çetin Bey,' he said in Turkish, 'know that you are always welcome in London. My city is your city just as my home is always yours.' And then he left.

İkmen, moved to tears, allowed his son to take him by the arm and guide him to the taxi without word. What the mayor had said had affected him profoundly. But he had also only just

304

that morning learned of the death of Ayşe Kudu and was still very raw about that. He had tried to save her, and he was sure that the doctors who had treated her in hospital had done their best, but that didn't bring her back. A young woman, a good officer and someone's beloved daughter had died. What was more, there were no pictures of her in any of the newspapers he had seen.

John Richards of Barking had been a silly if rather sly old sod. Yes, he'd given his old mate Derek Harrison the code to get into Mark Lane station, but he hadn't asked him why he wanted it. Money had changed hands, considerable money; John had jumped at the chance to have enough cash to move off the estate. As for any connection to terrorism, John claimed that he'd not known about any such thing. As Ahmet Ülker had told Williams, John Richards was very much against that sort of thing.

'That Turk old Derek worked for wasn't a bad sort,' John told Williams when he interviewed him. 'I mean, I knew that poor old Del never really got over that Moorgate business, but I never thought he'd blow up a station! I never knew that Turk was involved with terrorists. I mean, I know he's in bed with the Gentlemen of Honour and you'd think they'd have done any business he needed doing . . .'

But Williams didn't hear anything more. Without a word, his blood cold with fear, he left John Richards with a constable and went immediately to get Ahmet Ülker back from the cells for another interview. As soon as Ülker was in the room, Williams said, 'Since when were you hooked up with the Gentlemen of Honour?'

Ülker went white and then green in the face.

'Ring a bell with you, Ahmet?' Williams said. He knew his

voice was trembling and he sat down just before Ülker. His legs
didn't feel too strong. 'No? Well, let me fill you in,' he continued.
'The Gentlemen of Honour are probably this city's biggest
criminal gang. They do it all: drugs, counterfeit goods, dodgy
passports, prostitution, identity theft, contract killing. They're
run by two charming characters, one Bermondsey bastard called
Dane Chitty, some sort of self-styled Cockney anti-hero, and an
Albanian called Enver Shkrelli.'

'I don't know anything about—'

'Oh, come on, Ahmet!' Williams said. 'You and the Gentlemen
are in the same business! How does it work, eh? Do they get
the dodgy passports for you to distribute to your workforce or
is it you with the contact up at Peterborough?'

Ahmet Ülker did not respond.

'What's the deal?' Williams said harshly. 'Was it passports?
Or was it maybe something to do with Maxine's disappearance?
I'm sure that the Gentlemen can arrange a very efficient pool-
cleaning service. Did you and the Gents cook this whole thing
up between you? A blame-it-on-the-terrorist kind of arrangement? Bloody hell, Ahmet, I thought for a bit there that old
Nourazar was pulling your plonker, but it turns out you—'

'I want my lawyer,' Ahmet Ülker cut in sharply. 'Now.'

'Oh.' Williams sat back in his chair and smiled. 'Rattled,
are we?'

'Get me my—'

'All right, all right. Keep your hair on. But you know that if
you were killing the mayor for the Gentlemen, you're on your
own now, don't you? An alliance with the Gentlemen? How
could you be so stupid?'

Williams got up and left, leaving a grey-faced Ahmet Ülker
with a constable. If Ülker was indeed in bed with the capital's

306

biggest and most feared gang, then that could be very interesting as well as a great coup for the police. Not that Ülker would talk about the Gentlemen of Honour. No one ever did. Not even those faced with a life sentence. The Gentlemen had a very particular way of dealing with those who grassed on them. It wasn't pretty.

Ahmet Ülker's heart raced. Derek Harrison must have told that silly old man John Richards about the Gentlemen. Probably trying to impress him. He knew Williams had been interrogating Richards. Stupid Derek! It must have come from him because only he had known. Dane Chitty himself had advised Ahmet to 'off' Derek as soon as the Mark Lane event was over. He knew he was gobby. But then Derek's death hadn't been a big deal for Ahmet, not once he realised he'd known about Maxine and Ali Reza Hajizadeh and not mentioned it to him. As soon as the English police had told him about how the Turkish police had found the UK passports in İstanbul, he knew he was on shaky ground. He'd taken all the risks! Glamoured by the trips the Gentlemen had arranged to their factories in China and Cambodia, Ahmet had happily allied himself with them. Right up until Williams had talked about the passports, everything had been all right. The Gentlemen had disposed of Maxine's body, he'd helped the police catch Nourazar and rescue the mayor. He would do time because his plan had failed and of course his business was now in ruins. But if he so much as whispered about the Gentlemen, it could be much, much worse.

Like most gangs, the Gentlemen of Honour had their own mythologies. One of the stories that went around about them concerned how they dealt with traitors. Chitty and Shkrelli, it was said, held the miscreant's head in a fire until he expired. It wasn't a myth. Ahmet Ülker had seen them do it with his own

307

eyes. Just the thought of it made him sweat. Even in prison he wouldn't be safe if he talked. But Ahmet was not about to do that. He wasn't about to tell anyone how he had ingratiated himself with the Gentlemen when they tried to take him over by offering them the mayor. He'd been a bit desperate. Even he had considered his own plan ill thought out. Nourazar had been far too greedy and volatile, Ali Reza stupid and theatrical. If only the Afghan boy had set the bomb. A kid like that would just have blown himself up without taking some random fucking train with him!

Ahmet was, he felt, going to go to prison forever. He imagined Dane Chitty and Enver Shkrelli rubbing their hands with glee and he felt sick. How, indeed, could he have been so stupid?

# Chapter 33

Abdurrahman Iqbal arrived at Heathrow airport where he found his old employer, Captain Rodney Jackson, waiting for him. The years had not been particularly kind to Jackson; he was confined to a wheelchair, pushed on this occasion by his daughter, Rosemary. But as Abdurrahman went to greet him, a tiny, thin stick of a man shuffling painfully towards the waiting crowds at arrivals, it was all too apparent whose life had been the hardest.

'Abdurrahman, my dear man!' the captain said as he held a gnarled hand out to his old driver.

'Captain!' Abdurrahman took the captain's hand like a drowning man clutching the side of a lifeboat. 'Oh, Captain!' He began to cry.

'Good God, Abdurrahman, what has happened to you?' Jackson asked.

But the old man was crying so much he couldn't answer. Jackson put a hand on his shoulder and said, 'Well, let's get you home. Then we can talk. The chap at the consulate in İstanbul told me you'd had some adventures.' He turned to his daughter. 'You ready, Rosie?'

Rosemary Dean, a disappointed woman in her mid-fifties, took the brake off her father's wheelchair, put a smile on her face and said to Abdurrahman, 'Come on then.'

She'd felt this meeting was ill-advised, but the appearance of this old man did seem to make her father happy. He'd actually smiled for the first time in years when he'd been told that Abdurrahman was coming. And anyway, even if it did all go wrong and the old man wanted to stay on, he couldn't. Abdurrahman, in spite of his desire to live in England forever, had only been given a tourist visa.

As Abdurrahman arrived, Fasika the Ethiopian, who had helped to save Çetin İkmen's life and whose name the dead Ayşe Kudu had committed to memory so she might help him later, was being put on to a plane back to Addis Ababa. Still sore from the beating he had taken in Ahmet Ülker's terrible factory, he was going home with no money, bad memories and a complete lack of hope.

As soon as İkmen cleared immigration and customs at Atatürk airport, İstanbul, he found himself surrounded by the press.

'How does it feel to be a hero, Inspector?'

'What's the first thing you're going to do when you get home?'

'What was it like working with the Metropolitan Police?'

'Do you prefer tea or coffee when you first get up in the morning?'

Tea or coffee? What kind of question was that? But then Haluk Üner had told him that at least three-quarters of the questions the media would pose would be either pathetic or trivial.

With the aid of two of his uniformed colleagues, he pushed through the gaggle of newshounds and looked to see whether any members of his family had turned up to meet him. At first, with flashbulbs going off in his eyes and microphones thrust towards his mouth, he couldn't see anything. Allah, but the press were a terrible fate for someone who was supposed to be a hero!

But then he felt a tug on the sleeve of his jacket and, looking down at the hand that tugged, he saw that it belonged to his son, Bülent.

'Dad!'

He took hold of the slim, brown hand and hung on tightly. 'Bülent!'

The two uniformed officers at İkmen's side pushed the press pack hard and then shoved their man out towards what looked like another vast pack of vultures on the other side of the arrivals area. Except that it wasn't.

'Dad!' It wasn't one voice, it was many. Six young people flung themselves towards him.

İkmen felt the tears fill his eyes as, still clinging to Bülent's hand, he flung himself into the arms of Çiçek, Gül, Hulya, Orhan, Kemal and Berekiah.

Cameras flashed and people shouted. But neither İkmen nor his children cared. All crying and laughing at the same time, they just clung to each other as relief at having their father safe home once again washed over them. It was several minutes before a more calm and measured voice intervened.

'Çetin?'

He looked up into the smiling eyes of Mehmet Süleyman. 'Oh . . .'

'Welcome home, my friend.'

Once he had managed to extricate himself from his children, İkmen and Süleyman embraced.

'I've brought another couple of people to see you,' Süleyman said. 'Very keen they were to be here.'

As if on cue, the children moved to one side and İkmen saw two figures at the far end of the arrivals hall. One was his oldest and greatest friend, Arto Sarkissian, the other was his wife, Fatma. Both of them were smiling and Fatma, to Çetin İkmen's delight, had her arms open to him in welcome. She was also, he saw as he fell into her embrace, wearing her wedding ring once again.